TEARS OF A THOUSAND YEARS

PRAISE FOR
TEARS OF A THOUSAND YEARS

"Part *Stargate*, part *Children of Men*—but without the relentless violence—*Tears of a Thousand Years* is a moving and thought-provoking exploration of civilization's cost. Glen Olson doesn't just ask what happens when an intelligent species is held accountable for its actions—he dares to imagine that they might respond with grace, empathy, and transformation.

"As I turned each page, I couldn't help but wonder: Would we rise to the challenge like Olson's beautifully crafted characters or falter under the weight of our history? The answer isn't simple, but the hope is real. We may not have a thousand years to fix what we've broken—but maybe, just maybe, we don't need that long.

"Olson's richly imagined worlds and unforgettable alien species offer more than escapism—they offer a vision. A future not rooted in despair but in possibility. *Tears of a Thousand Years* is essential reading for sci-fi fans hungry for something beyond dystopia—a future worth believing in and fighting for."

—Lauren Cipollo, co-author of the *Parallax* series

"A triumph of far-future storytelling, *Tears of a Thousand Years* by Glen Olson is space opera at its most resonant. With the grandeur and intricacy of Asimov's *Foundation* and the ethical clarity of *Star Trek* at its peak, Olson crafts a sweeping interstellar epic that never loses sight of its human core—even though there's not a human to be found. The narrative rushes forward with the tension of the best noir mysteries yet leaves room for keen character work, political nuance, and haunting ecological insight. The characters are layered and memorable—I found myself mourning their absences as much as cheering their triumphs. For lovers of cerebral sci-fi that still knows how to entertain, this is not to be missed."

—Matt Conant, co-author of the *Parallax* series

"Glen Olson delivers a tour-de-force novel. *Tears of a Thousand Years* is a heartfelt tale of memory, empathy, and transformation wrapped in an epic science fiction adventure. Spanning a millennium, the story weaves the tales of two Remembers, nearly a thousand years apart in time, charged with preserving their culture amid apathy, waste, and carelessness. The task feels disheartening and tragic for the Remembers. But when a seer from a dying race creates a miracle, the soul of an entire civilization awakens. What happens when a race becomes enlightened and desires atonement and healing? If you want a thrilling page-turner with deep characters, and unique, yet accessible sci-fi, *Tears of a Thousand Years* is for you."

—Brian Fitzpatrick, author of the *Mechcraft* series

TEARS OF A THOUSAND YEARS

G. W. OLSON

ISBN (Paperback): 978-1-966369-38-7
ISBN (eBook): 978-1-966369-39-4
ISBN (Audiobook): 978-1-966369-92-9
Library of Congress Control Number: 2025920767

Designed by Sami Langston
Project managed by L. Merredith

Published by
Belle Isle Books (an imprint of Brandylane Publishers, Inc.)
5 S. 1st Street
Richmond, Virginia 23219

BELLE ISLE BOOKS
www.belleislebooks.com

belleislebooks.com | brandylanepublishers.com

This book is dedicated to

The child in all of us;
The adult in all of us;
The adventurer in all of us—
This one's for you!
I hope you don't mind if I come along

ACKNOWLEDGMENTS

"No man is an *Iland*, intire of it selfe . . . ."

Golly, John Donne is correct.

Dorothy Parker and Robert Benchley had the Algonquin Round Table, J. R. R. Tolkien and C.S. Lewis were Inklings, Virgina Wolfe and E. M. Forrester hung out with the Bloomsbury crowd—I have been blessed to have met so many friends and fellow travelers on the road to creating my short stories and novels. Among other associations I have been privileged to be a long-time member of Los Angeles Science Fantasy Society, and also Jay Wiseman's writing group, modeled on the "Shut Up and Write" format.

I have met and been influenced by many wonderful people, including Steven Barnes, an accomplished author and filmmaker who also mentors other authors. Thank you, Steven. Your inspiration and prodding got more stories into the world than I knew I was going to write. Many other people were vitally important to the creation of this book. To each of you, even if I failed to mention you, I offer my deepest thanks.

My project manager and editor, L. Merredith, who is a powerhouse and challenged me every step of the way to turn a rough manuscript into this (much more wonderful) story.

My wife and soulmate, Susan, has a busy career with insane hours; but when I needed to bounce ideas off her, she made the time and supported them or discouraged them and gave me better ones. Thank you for everything!

Terry Brussel-Rogers, my best friend since high school, has read every story, claimed she loved them all, and encouraged me to write more. Paul Gibbons, Athena Roberts, David Beal, thank you for pre-reading my novel and asking important questions. My son, Johnathan, who has become an amazing man. I love you, son. Thank you all!

CONTENTS

A VISIT TO SMALL HOME

"You said he was a god."

The words struck the back of Vega's ears, and the fury ignited, flowing down her brown, furred arms and sending her pickax deep into the face of the scarp. Mercy, how she hated it when Wren misquoted her.

"I did not say he was a god! I didn't say that!" She paused and breathed deeply. *I am not going to push him off the mountain. Mercy, help me not push Wren off the mountain.* "I *said* the natives report he has enormous unexplained powers, and our gods of old would have laughed and welcomed him as one of their own." *It's a cultural reference, you naapo.* Vega glared at her brother.

Wren looked comically unconvinced. Smiling up at her while clutching the guide rope, a small furrow in his brow formed, and his eyes twinkled merrily. "He performs miracles, and he lives on the top of a mountain in seclusion. Anything else I've missed?"

Vega turned back to the mountain face and contemplated her buried ax. It looked well seated. "He doesn't live in seclusion. He lives in a village that the natives built on the top of this mountain centuries ago. My information shows he appeared there two winters past. They like the notoriety of hosting a god, but they are the ones living in seclusion, not him . . . and that's why we're climbing this love-forsaken mountain to interview them. They won't build a road from the lowlands to the village!"

Wren took one long, golden hand off the rope and made a sweeping gesture. "It's a fine day—a beautiful day. The valley so far below us is green and russet. The river tinkles as it rushes over boulders and pebbles. The lake around that curve there is clear and clean all the way to its white sand bottom and invites one in for a swim. It's even a nice day for a climb up the rope path the natives use to get to their little village in the sky . . . and maybe *falling* to *our deaths*!" A playful smirk rippled across his face.

He adjusted his flight rack across narrow shoulders, its equipment sparse and well balanced. Not much was needed on this very gentle planet. Wren's golden skin glowed in the light of the yellow sun, and dark glasses protected eyes evolved under a dimmer stellar furnace. His garment was woven of a light, tough travel fabric. He had chosen to color it in greens and russets. Its many flat pockets and compartments were filled with who knows what. He had told Vega he was bringing "trinkets."

As younger brothers go, he was handsome in the way that most males of the Race were at his age, but his annoying traits more than made up for his physical beauty. Even if Wren hadn't been Vega's sibling, she might have considered pushing him off the mountain for the way he always jumbled her statements. Wren had no trouble making them sound idiotic and inane.

"Tell me again why we couldn't just fly into the Caeling's village and meet your little godling. Do you think seeing us flying would give the god an inferiority complex?"

Vega wasn't going to be baited this time. When she could see her brother's face, she could always tell when he was trying to annoy her. "I decided you were getting too fat in the head from sitting around watching the rest of us do important work, so I asked Father to loan you to me for my little stroll to the village." She smiled sweetly. "And I'm not worried about the god, you naapo, but these villagers have never seen one of the Race before. I don't want to startle them too much."

She turned and pulled her pickax out of the mountain face with a smooth, powerful tug. As she resumed her climb, she heard Wren mutter, "A three-day stroll may be fun for you, ha! Call me 'naapo,' but I'm flying outta here when we're done."

Vega began humming a favorite tune from her childhood as she pulled herself up the mountain. The words she had made up long before floated to the top of her mind, and she considered singing them out loud. *My brother is an idiot. I need another sister. My brother is an idiot, and I sure miss her.* She giggled and picked up her pace, hearing her brother shout as he fell behind.

♦♦✦♦♦

The village sat in a high, grassy meadow surrounded on three sides by mountains; the fourth side, a grand fall to the valley below them. For an hour, Vega had been aware they were being watched. The observation platform jutting out over the mountainside always had one or two or sometimes a half-dozen figures on it, small legs dangling over the edge or tiny faces peering over the sides. It wasn't until Vega was much closer that she realized all the watchers were children. The faces were tiny because they were . . . tiny.

Wren stopped and waved, causing several faces to disappear and then reappear immediately. All natives had high voices to Race ears, but these were downright shrill. The babble increased in volume, and Vega heard whoops of laughter. Then Wren unsealed a pocket and took out a small device. To Vega's amazement, he blew into it; and a high, piping noise issued forth. The children became silent, and huge eyes watched him intently. "Naapo am I?" he murmured and continued to play as they climbed the rest of the way up to the mesa.

Vega shook her head. *My brother is an idiot. I wish I had another sister. Mercy, he's playing my song back to me. I wonder what the children would think if I pushed him off the mountain anyway. No, his flight rack would activate, and the children would see him flying, so I would have climbed all this way for nothing.*

Vega stopped at the top of the mesa and watched the native children surround Wren, who promptly sat on the ground and continued his playing. Soon little hands were patting his clothing, tugging at his pockets, and running along his flight rack. The tallest child could reach his head and began running dirt-begrimed hands through Wren's golden mane. Wren twitched his scalp, and the kit jumped back with a hypersonic shriek. The shriek turned into giggles as the little one ran back and did it again.

Bring a child for the children, she thought. *What have I brought to this expedition? Not a sense of wonder, obviously. I doubt if the adults will like me as much as the kits like Wren.*

Vega made a slow turn and scanned the mesa, taking in stone-and-mud buildings and hollowed-out caves in the cliff face at the far end of the valley. With a mental twitch, she woke up the flight rack's full range of passive sensors and activated Wren's also. She had sold this trek to her brother as a search for miracles, whatever they were, but her father had only given his blessing because Vega was his best apprentice rememberer. Here was a chance to remember a group of natives who had never before seen the Race, and none of the colonists had bothered to record this kind of remembering. Soon an opportunity to remember would be gone forever. Vega viewed her work as a sacred trust. Future generations of the Race would know her name for this day's work.

She might have stared into infinity forever, basking in her future place in posterity, if a stone had not chanced to land with a thump a couple of feet from her foot. Pulling her gaze to the local and immediate, she found a rather old native standing with a staff in hand, nose wrinkling in amusement. Vega wrinkled her nose back in the way lowland natives did when they were laughing at themselves. At least she could do that. She did not have spots of color on her integument that she could flash and vary, but the native did not have her rich brown skin that could twitch and ripple in dozens of ways. That made them even in her opinion.

The old man—*or is it a woman? I can't tell yet*—leaned on its staff and greeted her in a much lower register than the children. *That was hardly painful.*

"Welcome, climber, to our homes. Call me Amoot. May your feet be light and your path continue for many leagues."

One of the devices on Vega's flight rack compared the native's speech to every recorded prior conversation with a Caeling, and this device identified the native as male and past his prime. It murmured an interpretation of the greeting as a friendly way to wish her health. She twitched the skin of her bare shoulders, and the rack quieted. She had absorbed the basic language on arrival at Rememberer's Compound and was here to pick up nuances for herself.

The old man's eyes were liquid green flecked with white. He had to look up to see Vega's granite eyes with infinitely black pupils. He stared at her skin, which was as brown and rich as river bottom soil, but he couldn't possibly understand the ripples' significance, so she said in somewhat halting Caeling, "I thank you for your greeting. Call me Vega. May I enter your village and meet your people?"

The man rolled his eyes toward Wren, who was still buried under the pile of children. Vega hastily added, "My companion Wren appreciates your hospitality too." *After all, every village needs an idiot.*

By now, some of the children had drifted off Wren and surrounded Vega and the old villager. They somehow became an orderly mob, and everyone flowed into the green at the center of the village to stop under tall trees and short grass. Blankets were unrolled, and rickety stools were produced for the travelers. Vega gingerly sat on hers, but Wren flopped down on a blanket, a good decision because he was once again carpeted in children.

From somewhere, jugs of water and vegetable cakes were produced and passed around the group. Vega and Wren sipped water, nibbled cakes, and waited. Finally, she asked, "I see other adults walk by the grove, but no one stops. Is it because we look strange to you?"

The old man took a swig of water, wrinkled his nose genially, and said, "Children won consensus."

Vega looked at the kits sitting around her and piling on Wren. Somehow, he had started a game where a child would shout a word, presumably another child's name, and Wren would twitch. If he chose right, the child whose hand he twitched off would shriek and run around the glade before coming back to wait for his or her turn to grab hold again.

"Consensus?"

Amoot gestured to a larger kit who had taken up position near Vega. "Great talker, female child, best student. Often troublemaker. When we knew you were coming, she started plebiscite. Parents agreed. On the day you arrive, no classes and no bedtime. Strange climbers become children's project."

Vega began to understand. "You closed down your school for us, Amoot? You're the teacher?"

He shrugged. "Class in session."

The kit leaned closer to Vega, speaking with great dignity. "Call me Amali."

The teacher snorted.

"Hello, Amali. Thank you for arranging to greet us," said Vega.

Spots of color flared to life, and she shrank down. "Just Mali," she mumbled.

I like this child. She's bold. Vega rippled her mane until it danced high. "Hello, Mali. Pleased to meet you." Two sets of eyes rolled toward Amoot, who snorted again.

A small hand reached out, touched, and then squeezed her arm. Vega let a pleased ripple flow down her arm and smiled. The tiny Caeling's eyes got bigger. "We hear of your arrival in far down country, make towns, grow things. You are truly from lights in the sky? Can you make yourself so tiny you fit on a light?"

"I cannot make myself tiny. What if I told you the lights are as big as your mountains, as big as your world? And I can live on them just as you do your mountains?"

Now Mali stared at her old teacher and spots all over her body brightened in a complex pattern. Amoot shrugged. They shared a dubious look.

Mali recited carefully, "Some may come, and one may come. When two come, why come?" and she sat alertly, watching the bigger woman.

Is this a riddle? Vega felt her head spin. She had no idea what to say but was grateful her devices were capturing every nuance of the conversation.

Mali turned her head and stared at her teacher. When he nodded, she shrieked four liquid syllables at her classmates, who immediately stopped their game with Wren. The next largest recited, "Many come for trade. Caravans in spring and summer use mountain paths. But not strange Sky People."

A smaller kit, possibly a girl, next said, "One comes with news, bearing tales or knowledge. But not ugly Sky People." She was immediately knocked over by two other classmates who shrieked with laughter.

"Two come to make a home and increase the community, but not Sky People?" another kit asked.

Now Wren threw in, "Yes, sister dear, *why* are we here?" He sat up carefully and reached for the water bag. A Caeling got to it first and squirted some into his mouth, effectively silencing him. *Thank you, child.*

Mali burst out, "He is your brother? *You* are a girl? Are you a mated pair? You could settle near me! There is unclaimed land next to my family holding. We could be friends!"

Vega felt the entire conversation spin out of control. She had no idea she would look like a migratory couple looking for a community to live in by bringing her idiot brother along with her. Almost she laughed, but Mali's earnest face stopped her. The child seemed terribly lonely, hungry for friends, even alien friends.

"I'm sorry, Mali. I would like to be your friend, but I am not here to stay." *How do I explain what a rememberer does?* "I came to meet everyone. We are travelers, and my chosen profession is to meet strangers."

"Meeting people is a profession?"

Out of the corner of her eye, Wren twitched a sardonic *"Not a very respected one."* It was a wonder he didn't say it out loud. She twitched back, *"If you say one word, you are in so much trouble!"*

Amoot snorted again and wrinkled his nose. Spots flashed slightly. Vega suddenly wondered if the Caeling could read Race body language . . . probably not, but he seemed very intuitive.

The old teacher abruptly had her complete attention. "Tantea said almost the same thing two winters gone when he came to our village. He said he traveled because that's how one meets strangers. Of course, we thought he was insane."

There was something strange about the way Amoot pronounced the name, almost as if he was reaching for a sound that his muzzle could not actually form, and so it came out *Tan-tea.* Vega's pulse quickened.

"Is Tan-tea still here?" She repeated the name carefully. "Did your traveler stay with you or move on?"

"He has settled in nicely," replied Amoot. "He lives with me at the school."

Wren looked around the village green as if he expected to spot this Tantea hiding behind blades of grass. "Can we meet him, please?" He grinned and twitched to Vega, *"That way I can go home sooner."*

"He is out on the mountain today gathering lore from our mountain seers," volunteered Mali.

"Oh." Wren seemed crestfallen.

Amoot said serenely, "They will be back tonight. Knowledge of the mountain is best learned in sunlight or strong starlight. Tonight will be too dark to build the experience necessary to teach miracles."

A look passed between Vega and Wren. "What did you say?" Vega asked carefully.

"Tantea's profession, as he calls it, is the collecting and teaching of miracles. He claims to have walked completely around the world more times than there are children in our village, stopped at more towns than there are trees on the mountain, and learned and then taught more miracles than there are whiskers on the faces of all the old people in our village."

Amoot said this deadpan without a wrinkle of his nose or flash of his spots. He was as serious about this as it was possible to be. If this claim was even close to being true, Tantea would have to be very old—by far the oldest Caeling and older than any Caeling could possibly be. She was suddenly glad she'd made this trip and dragged her little brother with her. Even though the Caeling had to be a fraud, he would undoubtedly have something of value to say about his race. He was worth remembering.

AN AMAZING RECEPTION

"Shall I tell you a story, Mali?"

The sun-drenched afternoon had broken and turned into a mild, cloudy evening. A breeze from higher in the mountains blew toward the unseen sea. Vega had half expected the children to drift away to their homes; but instead, parents had trickled into the green and joined the party. Eventually, picnic tables were placed and platters of food appeared, separated by pitchers of water and fruit juice. At sunset, lanterns were hung in the trees.

Mali stuck close to Vega the whole afternoon. When her parents arrived, she formally introduced them. They seemed uncomfortable with the aliens that fascinated their daughter and soon found an excuse to step back.

Mali yawned slightly as she was wrapped in a scratchy patchwork-patterned blanket her parents had given her. Vega refused a similar blanket. Her garment had switched from airy to close weave at sunset, and it could generate more warmth than she needed in this climate.

Mali, struggling to stay awake, mumbled, "I want to hear your story. I want to know everything."

I know you do, dear. In many ways, you remind me of myself. "My people did not always have rememberers. Only in my father's generation did we begin to see the need. You see, we live for a very long time—so long that we often forget the world is always changing. The Race sometimes does not remember the people we've met and how they once were. But I never want you to be forgotten. I will always remember you, your village, and your ways. And thousands of years from now, my people will still know who you were because I'm remembering for them."

Mali's eyes closed, and her hand crept into Vega's. "Oh . . . okay." The kit snuggled next to her, drifting to sleep.

Vega did not think the child had retained one word in ten. Through her own dreamy state of contemplation, she became aware that Amoot had moved into the lantern light with another Caeling at his side. His companion was younger, taller, dressed for mountain activity, and grinned broadly.

Amoot snorted as he looked down upon the pair and wrinkled his nose. "Traveler, you may have lost your apprentice. This woman can talk rain out of a cloud."

Puzzlement rippled Vega's face. The old teacher's spots briefly brightened. "Vega, who remembers for the Sky People, this is Tantea of the Many Journeys."

Vega was suddenly wide awake. *There's that strange pronunciation again.*

The younger Caeling was a perfect specimen of Caeling health and vitality. He was clean of limb with eyes that were liquid brown and more body spots than she had ever seen. Each spot was brightening slightly in a ripple pattern that Vega unconsciously matched. When she noticed herself doing so, she stopped. Yet, when he wrinkled his nose, she couldn't help herself. She wrinkled back. *So you are Tantea. You're not an old fraud but a young one. I wonder why Amoot believes in you so?*

"Mali likes you, I see." Tantea turned and clasped the old teacher on the shoulder. "Old friend, what do you think? May a master have more than one apprentice?"

Amoot rolled his eyes.

Tantea's spots brightened. He chuckled, a sound Vega had not heard from a Caeling. "So, if a master can have two apprentices, may an apprentice have two masters?"

"How can anyone serve two masters? Tantea, you do it again—turn my thoughts upside down."

Tantea turned back, pulling Vega into the conversation. "And how many masters do you serve, Sky Person?"

Vega thought furiously. This was not a casual question but one that showed great depth. This Caeling was a subtle and shrewd native, a shaman in truth despite his youth. She riposted,

"Perhaps if I am my own master, I can choose to negotiate the manner of my apprenticeship. I can choose to serve two masters if I am allowed to share my commitments and manage my time."

"She talks rain out of clouds. I tell you so. You two should get along fine." Amoot and Tantea exchanged bows and matched spots. Tantea seemed highly pleased with her answer.

Amoot gave the sleeping child still clutching Vega's hand a very tender look. "Parents are waiting to take Mali home."

Vega gently disentangled her hand from Mali. After an approving look from the old teacher, she allowed Tantea to pick up the kit. As he moved away, she murmured, "Will I see you tomorrow?" She meant Tantea at first, but when he answered, she realized she'd meant Mali too.

"Of course. You will find us at the school."

A short time later, Wren found her still staring in the direction Tantea had gone. He'd found a place for them to sleep in the village, a sort of Wayfarer's Inn. Gratefully, she followed with her mind still on her last encounter, churning the conversation from every angle. It had been a very interesting day.

Vega awakened early the next morning. Dew had gathered during the night on the open windowsill, and the cold mountain air had turned it shiny and hard. The glittering layer of ice bounced narrow shafts of blue onto the far wall, and a faint yellow radiance puddled on the floor below the window.

Vega stretched full length on her borrowed pallet, legs extending off the end, arms up in the air. The morning felt wonderful. The air was sweet, the gravity congenial, and the bedding somewhat lumpy but not too hard. She glanced across the room to Wren's pallet and growled quietly. He sprawled as if boneless across his bedding, deeply asleep, floating two inches above the surface.

Wren knew that she wanted to keep their use of technology minimal until the natives got used to them. He knew she wanted the Caelings acting as normally as they could, given the admittedly strange situation of dealing with aliens from points of light in the sky. He knew the reason they had climbed up the mountain was to keep from displaying the technology he was now using in his sleep. *Not fair, Wren!*

Both flight racks had been stored against the far wall. Vega leaned over and tapped a command on Wren's rack. The projected suspension field abruptly cut out, and he fell two inches to the bed with a thump.

"HEY!" Wren was suddenly awake and bounced up to stand in the middle of the room. His golden eyes scanned all around the area and settled on Vega's stormy gray ones. He grinned. "Good morning, sister. Did you sleep well? I must say, your fur needs brushing."

Vega puffed her fur and ran her hands through it gently. "That happens when you sleep on a bed instead of above it. Am I going to have to lock out some of your rack controls, or are you going to be good?"

In response, her brother padded to the window and looked out. Seeing no one lurking at the opening, he leaned further and took a deep breath. In the distance, a couple of Caelings walked the path to the commons. In the other direction, a small party climbed one of the up-mountain trails.

"I'll be good. I think the air of this planet agrees with me."

Behind him, Vega rolled her eyes the way she had seen Amoot do. She was beginning to understand the gesture.

They broke their fast privately in their room using food they brought, aware that last night's meal lacked the nutrients they needed. Gathering up their meager belongings, they headed out. On the way, Wren stopped in the common room of the inn and played a number of songs for the proprietor and her staff. Evidently, this was the coin Wren had used to pay for the room last night. Vega didn't know if she was relieved or alarmed to find he was actually useful—even resourceful—on her expedition. She certainly hadn't expected it.

The school was easy to find. It was a large, half-timbered building next to a long path leading up the mountain. A brick-lined and flagstone-floored cave opening on the other side of the school hinted at the extensive network of caverns within the cliff. Mali had pointed them out the previous day and explained that the caverns were used for food storage and shelter for the livestock during severe ice storms.

Amoot greeted them at the door and ushered them into the school. "I am sorry to inform you, but Tantea has already left for the day with some of the advanced students." His eyes twinkled merrily. "But, in an anticipation of your desire to know more about the village, I have arranged a suitable ambassador to guide you this morning."

Vega was not surprised to find Mali was that ambassador.

"What do you want to see first? Shall we visit my parents' holding? I can show you that empty land next to us or the land the village shares in common or maybe you would like to watch our people singing to the plants—a new planting happened last week, and another crop will be harvested soon. The caverns are close, and the up-mountain trails are still open . . . ." Mali listed the possibilities without stopping for breath.

Vega gave her a hug. "May we go talk to people?"

Mali's spots brightened, and she turned to her teacher. Amoot's spots flared in return, and he wrinkled his nose. "Go, little one." He rolled his eyes at their backs as the small girl grasped Vega's and Wren's hands before tugging the very tall aliens out the door and onto the path.

True to her word, Mali pulled them to her holding first. Only her father was home as her mother was one of the village singers. Mali's father didn't talk much, but he did walk the aliens around the property and—at Mali's insistence—showed them the unclaimed land adjoining his family plot. When Mali wasn't looking, he wrinkled his nose at Vega and mumbled thanks to the aliens for being nice to his energetic child.

Mali next hurried them down the path into the commons and out the other side. Although several people were doing tasks in the commons—weaving a basket, constructing additional braces for the observation platform, and pruning trees—Mali didn't let the aliens linger to meet villagers or converse. Apparently, she had a goal in mind; and somehow, they were late for it.

On the far side of the plateau, a gentle rise led to a glorious upsweeping hillside that was a riot of colors. Flowering bushes no taller than a Caeling intermingled, clumped, and separated, stretching for a goodly distance up the mountain. Meandering pathways through the bramble made curious and pleasant designs of the various brightly-colored clumps of vegetation. Small groups of Caelings could be seen on the paths.

Vega stopped and tried to take in the vista. She suddenly realized the hillside vegetation pattern was similar to a patchwork quilt like the one Vega had been given to wrap around the sleeping Mali the previous night. It made her wonder if the quilts were more than decoration and if they had specific meanings. She murmured a note to her flight rack to follow up on the thought later.

Mali stood beside Vega, watching her closely. She seemed satisfied by Vega's reaction. She flashed her spots at Wren, and the tall alien wrinkled his nose, leaned down, and whispered, "She is having the time of her life. Thank you, Amali."

With her spots almost glowing, Mali clapped her hands. "Come on!" She dashed to one of the pathways and started up the hillside.

Wren took a step after her, turned back, and rippled his ears. "Coming, sister?"

Vega slowly began walking toward the path. "Don't put the 'A' on her name, Wren. It means 'wise woman,' and she's a little girl."

Wren turned about abruptly and headed up the path. Vega did not have to see him roll his eyes to know he did it.

They caught up with Mali about the time she reached a small group of Caelings, all of whom turned out to be women. Mali was excitedly talking in a faster, higher tone than Vega could follow. One of the women pointed, and Mali was off like a shot again. Vega followed resignedly, vowing to backtrack to try to talk with the people Mali had hurried them past.

The second group were also all women, and Mali flung herself into the arms of one, hugging her fiercely. "Mother," she said, pitching her voice as low as possible to save alien ears, "may my friends watch you sing today?"

Her mother nodded toward the aliens—*shyly*, Vega thought—and began blinking her spots in a slow rhythm that the other women picked up on, matched, and began flashing subtle variations. Each woman began a slow humming and bent to a particular plant. Each would stand and swoop, and the humming would rise in tone. Vega saw a woman point, and several pairs of eyes went to the limb of one bush.

Evidently, they all saw the same sign for they began to hoot together. The pitch rose up the scale, increased to a scream, and went hypersonic. Sound lashed the plants while Vega and Wren clutched their ears, and the flight racks triggered nullifying fields, overloading and blanking out the sonic attack.

Tiny black specks appeared on the leaves and fell in a rain into baskets placed there beforehand by the women. One woman gently stroked the plant, and it shivered, tossing more black specks off leaves and branches. The women went in a circle around the bush, mouths working, and their voices dropped down to croon soothingly. The greens and reds of the plant seemed to glow in response, and the leaves grew shiny.

Mali was talking as the nullifiers cut off, and Vega could hear her say, "And when the leaves become shiny again, we know the plant will be healthy. All the parasites have left the stem and leaves and even the roots."

Vega swallowed and let her ears unfurl. She felt faintly sick to her stomach. *Ouch! The hazards of fieldwork come not from known hazards so much as dangers no one recognizes, such as a friendly native girl offering to have her mother sing for you.*

Vega met Wren's eyes again. His smile was as wide as oceans, maybe planets. With a sardonic twitch of one ear, he rolled a long ripple across both shoulders. *"Ah yes, the life of a rememberer,"* he mimed. *"How thrilling."*

The women walked slowly up the path with the aliens lagging behind them. Occasionally the Caelings stopped and gave a plant the type of treatment given to the first one. More often, they kept up a crooning at the edge of the Race's hearing range. Small, furred animals—voles, mice, and the like—drifted ahead of the singers; birds sheared off from the vegetation. It was clear the Caeling method of farming was very effective at removing pests from their crops. Eventually, the women reached a stopping point on the path and turned aside in a line facing the direction of the wilderness. Now their spots synched again, and they began hooting louder and louder, driving the furry creatures out of the field altogether, back toward the wild.

Mali dashed past her mother, hooting and slapping her palms with abandon, acting as if she was chasing the vermin personally off her mountain. Panting and grinning, she returned to the line of women and gave each one a hug in turn. "Now back that way." She pointed with her nose toward the commons.

Vega got her wish, managing to stop and speak with every Caeling Mali could find on the way back to the school. It was late afternoon before they reached the half-timbered building, and Amoot was waiting for them.

"Ah. Girl-child, guide, and protector of aliens, did you show your friends all manner of wonder today?"

Vega watched Mali give a saucy shake of her head and plant both feet on the ground. She raised her arms and hooted, stopping abruptly when she saw her friends' ears start to curl protectively. "Amoot, great teacher, guide to little Mali. Bigger Mali stands before you. I am Teacher of Aliens."

"You are trouble." The old Caeling reached forward and gave an affectionate lick to Mali's ears, causing her to squeal. "Go home before your head becomes so big, your ears fall off."

Rubbing her ears, Mali backed away and wrinkled her nose at Amoot. Then she turned with great speed and bounded down the path. Her shout drifted back. "See you tomorrow if mean and esteemed teacher does not give me too many silly lessons to learn!"

Amoot watched the kit disappear. He turned. "Hmmm, Aliens from Points of Light in the Sky, I have a message for you. Tantea is delayed on the mountain. His class will run into the night. You may take the up-mountain path and join him if you wish."

Vega grinned, her heart bounding like a child. "I will be delighted. We will start immediately." She pointedly did not notice Wren rolling his eyes.

••✦••

Four adult Caelings stood in a semicircle, watching the sky intently. They faced south where the mountain fell away onto alluvial plains and then to the sea many miles away. The traveler sat in front of them, waiting as the sun neared the horizon. "Now," he murmured and reached back, touching each one in turn. They all clasped their hands, and their spots flashed in unison.

Vega spent her time watching Tantea, but Wren looked beyond the group and tried to spot what they were seeing. Reflected in his golden eyes, the sun was fire upon the ocean—a bright sliver, a speck merging with glowing water, and then gone.

The Caelings hooted excitedly, unclasped hands, and wrinkled their noses at each other. Tantea waited until the hubbub quieted and asked each one in turn for their impressions. "No rain next three days," offered one.

"Four days," said another.

"The water is colder than last week. Storms from the south will move more slowly," said the third.

Tantea nodded his approval. "You are all seeing most clearly. Thank you for your participation. Now who can tell me when winter will begin?" The hooting and nose wrinkling lasted longer this time. When one said, "Ocean doesn't tell season; season tells ocean," it was clear they knew they were being teased.

"Vega. Wren. Welcome."

Vega jumped. Her flight rack activated and waited to be told what she wanted. It settled her gently to earth five feet back. She had no idea Tantea had heard them approach. He had never looked their way. Wren's skin quivered with suppressed glee. He was entirely too pleased that Tantea could spook his sister.

With the shreds of her dignity, Vega replied, "What were you doing, Tantea?"

He appeared surprised at her question. "We were watching the sunset."

"You were teaching the others about ocean currents. Can you actually know the water temperature from here? Just by looking?"

Tantea began walking back down the mountain, sweeping up Vega and Wren before him. His four students, still talking about the weather, trailed politely behind them. The stone-strewn path crunched quietly under his boots. Vega's slippers made only a whisper. When the path widened and became soft, rich, and dark earth, he stopped and stepped aside, motioning the two to follow him. After the villagers had disappeared down the trail, he said quietly, "Why are you here? What do you seek?"

For once, Wren was uncharacteristically silent. Not a hair on his mane stirred. His yellow eyes watched his sister as she let the silence stretch. As annoying as he was, he had a great fondness for Vega and her crackbrain ideas. He had stopped teasing her about going home when he saw her bonding with Mali, so he was content to wait until she was done with whatever she thought she was doing here.

Vega took a deep breath. As a rememberer, she was dedicated to chronicle the moment, capturing truth without modifying or contaminating the information. She felt sure that she had been doing that. Many centuries from now, these Caelings would still be alive in the Race's memory, even if—no, *when* the Caeling people had ceased to be.

The moment stretched on, and neither of the men seemed inclined to break it. Abruptly, Vega sat down on the side of the trail and stuffed her hands in the dirt. She felt an irrational desire to take off her slippers and cover her feet with the loamy soil or run full speed to the ocean so far below them to plunge headfirst into the waves. She twitched a command, turning off all of her and Wren's recording devices.

"In the lowland villages, they talk about a maker of miracles. It intrigued me. I'm doing good work—I know I am. But I'm sad that Mali will grow up and become old and die, as will all Caelings, and maybe remembering them won't be enough." Her voice was so soft that Wren could barely hear it.

Tantea simply nodded. "Not everyone is as long-lived as your Race. Is that what bothers you?"

Vega twitched a denial, then shook her head in Caeling fashion. She didn't want to admit that Tantea was very close to the truth. The Race had already outlived three other intelligent species, but little was known about them because no one had bothered to remember them systematically. Now that the Race had adopted this planet, Caelings would almost certainly be the fourth. "No . . . I just wonder what a miracle would look like."

Tantea nodded as if this explained everything when it certainly explained nothing. "Child, are you asking for a miracle?"

Vega's head snapped up. Tantea had to know that she was at least a hundred years older in objective terms than any Caeling was likely to reach; yet, at that moment, she felt as young as Mali. "Yes, sir."

Wren sat down too, and Tantea joined him. Wren's golden pelt had darkened to amber in the evening twilight, but Vega allowed her eyes to remain naturally adjusted, skipping enhancement. A cool wind from the mountain passes played over them, ruffling Wren's mane and teasing her senses. The first stars shyly made an appearance.

Tantea's tone was musing, and his spots brightened in playful patterns. "What would a member of the Race see as a miracle? Perhaps something you could not readily do?"

Wren shared his amusement, Vega saw, for he rippled his pelt in counterpoint to Tantea's spots. Vega gritted her teeth and flattened her pelt. It seemed males of any race bonded through immature comradery. She would suffer through it with all the dignity she could muster.

Tantea glanced down the mountain, though the ocean was certainly invisible in the twilight. "Let's see—Caeling and Race are both land creatures. Do you go into water?" Wren's nose wrinkle told him yes.

"Well, then perhaps I could walk on water for you." Tantea paused a moment and shook his head. "Vega, I suspect that you could walk on a liquid surface if you wished."

She rippled a slight assent. With her technology, she could walk or float—or even fly—above any surface.

"I could tell you what the weather is anywhere on the planet. But you can do that too, can't you?"

Yes, she could. The Race had put a full suite of climatic and geo sensors in orbit years before she came to the planet. She could access any real-time information just by wanting it. If the Caeling could do it too, this simply meant that he was more than the eye could see, which Vega was already suspecting. He could have access to hidden technology of his own. He might not even be a Caeling, though all of Vega's instruments insisted he was. This weather trick didn't exactly measure up to a miracle.

"I shall have to think carefully on what miracle to present you. This might be my greatest challenge yet." He wrinkled his nose presently and said, "Ah, Vega, you remind me of another little girl I once knew a long time ago. She was never satisfied with one answer because she always wanted to know the next answer too." He paused again, and in the gloom, his face developed more shadow tinged with sadness. "I know you will think me an outrageous liar, but it is a very long walk to this little girl's village. If you live on the lights in the sky, you may have met her people for her light is just coming over the horizon."

Vega's eyes stole briefly into the sky and then widened with shock. Wren noticed her consternation and twitched a befuddled question in an automatic attempt to soothe his sister's distress. She turned to him with fury in every line.

"What did you tell them, Wren? What tales have you told? How does he know?" Her mind was a jumble of thoughts, body twitching chaotically, mane flatter than Wren had ever seen it. Though the Race was not actually telepathic, the hammer blow of her fury reached him eloquently. His sister was beside herself, and he did not know why.

Wren was truly bewildered and tried to tuft up his mane in injured innocence. To show he was a supporter of her rememberer passion, he trotted out a pure Caeling phrase he'd heard Amoot say to Mali only the day before: *"What has nipped your nose, my sister?"*

"Look up!" she grated. *"Look up!"*

Wren did as he was told, thinking his sister had been getting weirder and weirder the longer they stayed at this mountain village. He scanned the sky slowly, seeing haze and a sprinkling of stars. He enhanced his vision and spotted the tiniest blush of red still sneaking around the curve of the world. Nothing made an impression on him. He finally resorted to his flight rack and twitched a query for significant events in the air within a hundred miles of them and then in near space. Nothing.

"Um, Vega, what am I supposed to be looking for?"

Vega sighed, and all the tension went out of her. She'd forgotten for a moment that Wren had no interest in anything intellectual and never bothered to learn the star patterns of any planet he had ever visited. He literally could not point to home if his life depended on it. "Never mind, little brother. I'm sorry—I just lost my way for a moment. I'm very tired. Let's go back to the village now."

Vega rose and dusted off her hands. The men rose with her. Mindful that her interaction with Wren had been mostly non-verbal and Tantea was unlikely to have a clue what had passed between brother and sister, she soothed her nerves and decided on a course of action. Walking down the trail, she murmured to Tantea: "How did you come to pick that star? It is far from here, you know."

Tantea nodded gravely. "Yes, I know. Light and warmth that began its journey over ten winters ago only reaches us here today. And this light is of importance to you too?"

She nodded. This man also knows astronomy. Vega resolved to let nothing else about the Caeling surprise her. "Did you know I grew up on the world around that star? My home is called Abundance. It is the closest of the many lights the Race have adopted."

Tantea stopped and wrinkled his nose with glee. "You have a wonderful world there, Vega. You must tell me about it sometime. It is long since I have been there."

"And you're sure that Abundance is the planet your little girl lives on?" Vega was unable to keep the sarcasm from her voice, reminding herself that she'd diagnosed Tantea as a fraud the first night she met him. Perhaps it was a lucky guess to pick her home star or perhaps not. She stared at him, waiting to see what he would say next.

"Oh yes. Of course, I visited there long ago. That little girl grew up to be a very wonderful member of her species and told stories about me to her many grandchildren. That is how I got my name." He waited for Vega's puzzled twitch and went on gently. "The name that little girl gave me—the name I have kept all these years—is Sansea. It means 'Comes from the North.' Only Caeling cannot pronounce that, so they call me Tantea, but that little girl who named me Sansea—she is so like Mali in her innocent intelligence, always asked me to approach her village from the North, so she would always know it was me."

Tantea—no *Sansea*—gave a genial nose wrinkle and settled his gaze on the evening star. His thoughts appeared to be light-years away, dwelling on memories he claimed to have of a time and a place impossible for him to have ever been to.

Search 'Sansea.' Correlate, twitched Vega. Obediently, her flight rack accessed internal records of the entire Caeling language. Finding no match, it queried the colony database, and that intelligence found a match in Race records. *Sansea, proper name or title in the language of the former indigenous species of Abundance. Sansea means "teacher" or "spiritual guide." Most often found in the Temperate zone tribes. The earliest usage of the term suggests it may have been two words at one time, possibly meaning "wind from the north" or "traveler from the north."*

Vega felt the cosmos shifting until it sat on her head, and all her ideas turned inside out. She squeezed her eyes shut, and her mane flared out. A primal snarl that her plains-dwelling ancestors a million years before would have recognized came from deep in her chest. Slowly, she sank to the ground, shaking her head. If this Sansea was the figure of Chin legend, he had to have visited Abundance many thousands of years ago. The word "Sansea" was widespread when Vega's people adopted Abundance, and that adoption had been more than five thousand years ago.

Impossible, impossible, impossible! What's wrong with this picture? Oh, I wish my father were here—or any of my parents. All I have is my dear idiot brother. I need somebody to talk to about this. What if it's all true? Who is Sansea? Oh my, what could he tell us about the Chin? They look so cute, so sweet in our records . . . and he knew them like he knows the Caelings now. If he's true, he is an immense find for any rememberer, but if what he says is true . . . what . . . is . . . he?

Vega looked up when she felt Race hands touch her shoulders. Wren stared down at her, his face terrified. "Sister, what is it?" His words brought her back to the moment.

Vega relaxed under his hands, her body calming as the storm in her mind eased. Wren was here; she was not alone. She would call her father later, but now she had family. She twitched a playful tattoo onto his palms and buried her face in his chest. "You are the best brother a girl could ever have," she murmured.

"That's it—I'm calling an evacuation team. Your mind has obviously snapped."

Vega began to giggle and punched Wren lightly on the arms. She reached out to Sansea. "Help me up, please, both of you."

As she rose, she looked into Sansea's eyes, and the twinkle was still there, promising more interesting conversations. Wren still looked terribly worried but seemed to understand that the Vega he knew was back. *I'm fine,* she twitched. *Just had to absorb an idea new to me.*

Wren muttered back, "That's why I refuse to take advanced learning—I don't want that happening to me!"

Vega linked arms with Wren and Sansea and started back down the path. She wanted to get back to the village and the privacy of the room she shared with her brother as soon as possible. It was impossible to hurry Sansea, though. He would stop and point out a plant to Wren. Wren would nod and point out a rock formation to Sansea. Eventually, they made it back to the village.

When they walked into the inn, there was a hubbub going on in the common room. It was filled with people who were talking and sharing snacks. The room fell silent when they saw the aliens. The inn's proprietor approached them and addressed Wren and Vega. "Would you both be so kind as to join us? Our staff has brought their families and friends, and we hope you will play your instrument for us again."

Wren expanded his ears with pleasure and wrinkled his nose in Caeling fashion. Then he twitched his shoulder. *"Sister dear, shall we join the party?"*

"I have something I must do, but by all means, enjoy yourself," she twitched back.

Wren waved and followed the proprietor back into the common room, allowing Vega to slip off to their room. Once inside, she wasted no time calling Rememberer's Compound to contact her father. She knew he would then notify the high scholars, and she was bursting with all the news she wanted to tell them.

A CLOUD FORMS

In the morning, Vega arrived at the school with the dawn, ice on the path crunching under her slippers. The doors were being unbarred by an apprentice teacher she had not spoken to or seen, but he seemed unsurprised to see her. He greeted her with a quiet hoot and pleasant flaring of spots. He looked down the path, and Vega realized he was looking for her brother.

"My companion still sleeps." She twitched a counterpoint to his spots.

The apprentice hooted in appreciation of her little joke and led the way inside. He continued his opening ritual, knocking ice off the shutters and opening all the windows to let in the morning air. Caelings did not heat their buildings in summer because the day would warm soon enough. Vega's breath smoked in the room. Now that she had stopped walking, her travel cloth closed slightly and started a warming cycle.

Amoot emerged from a small door set in the back of the building, and he did seem surprised to see her. He was rumpled and sleepy-eyed and gave a great yawn, showing the squared-off teeth of an omnivore. Vega surmised the room behind him was his headmaster's sleeping quarters.

"Only Mali steals into the school on Dawn's frosty toes and only if her parents don't catch her first. Most children arise at a decent hour and have morning chores. I see this is one bad habit she seems to have given you."

Vega suddenly realized Amoot's gruff exterior hid an extraordinarily warm heart and quick mind, even at this hour. *It's a good thing I am so much taller than he is. I might find myself in for an ear licking.*

"Good morning, esteemed teacher, I trust you are well? I apologize—I did not think to inquire as to when the school day begins. I am hoping to catch Sansea before he leaves for the day." Vega was momentarily contrite.

Amoot padded over to the door and looked out. He seemed satisfied to find no errant child lurking there. His spots flashed, and his nose wrinkled. "Ah, you pronounce the name better than I have ever been able to. The Traveler's real students are all adults, and they have adult responsibilities. There are farm chores to be done, shops to open, crafters must set up their pots—Tantea gets to sleep in because his students do not."

"I don't wish to be in the way. Is there somewhere I can wait until Sansea is available?"

While Vega's back was turned, another person had emerged from the sleeping quarters. The voice behind her caused her to jump again. "The headmaster is right—we are up to our ears in Malis."

Quick as a cat, Vega whirled to face a grinning Sansea. This time, she managed to suppress her jump response, so her flight rack stayed quiet. She observed him closely as he walked into the room. While the headmaster was rumpled and slow-moving, Sansea bounded with energy. The spots on his skin were a lustrous black, and he shined with health and vitality. His nose wrinkle declared him ready to take on the day.

"Good morning, esteemed teacher," Vega began, "I hope the day finds you well." *Actually, you are the most beautiful Caeling I have ever seen, and you are loaded with charm. As an alien, I should not be susceptible to what a Caeling considers charm. You are a puzzle.*

Before Sansea could reply, Vega blurted out with an abruptness that made her cringe inwardly, "Sansea, can you travel today? I mean, will you visit my people in Colony Central? Many of our scholars would like to meet you."

She was stretching the truth by a fair amount. After talking with her father, she had been able to reach the most senior scholar, but Var had called her a fool and an idiot for bothering him with silly stories and babblings about myths. He had no interest in meeting a local shaman with supposed amazing abilities. Yet, in the end, he had relented, promising to make short shrift of the charlatan so Vega could get her sanity back and start using her mind correctly again. "Bring him now or stop bothering with this nonsense" continued to ring in her ears, causing her unfortunate twitches even in the morning.

Sansea roared with laughter.

Amoot shook his head, and he became much more alert. "Malis everywhere," he muttered.

The two Caelings exchanged a look, and Amoot grunted. "You always said you would depart as quickly as you arrived. We will miss you."

"Oh, he doesn't have to stay long. Perhaps only a few days. Sansea, you can come right back."

Yet, the old Caeling came up to the young shaman, giving him a hug and an ear lick. "We will always remember your teaching. Another village beckons you, and the Wanderer is ready to go. I will give our Mali your love."

Sansea nodded, turned to Vega, and spread his arms. "And where is your brother?"

Vega rolled her eyes.

♦♦✦♦♦

On the way back to the inn to wake up her brother, Vega thought about the headmaster's parting words to Sansea: "Another village beckons you. I will give our Mali your love." She stopped and breathed in the frosty morning air. The headmaster did not think Sansea was coming back.

Vega did not know when she was coming back to this village either. She felt a touch of sadness at the realization. She came to a decision and took a small detour.

As Vega approached the house, she saw Mali's mother standing on the porch. The village singer was loading bread and a water bottle into a basket. She nodded to Vega and piped a small hello. Then she called into the house a long "Maaali!" Vega smiled. Neither of Mali's parents spoke very much. Words seemed to be Mali's forte.

A small sleepy-eyed head peered around the open front door. Mali disappeared and immediately reappeared waving a piece of bread.

"Vega, Sky Person! Hello! Hello!" She took a bite of bread and chewed quickly. "I am finishing breakfast, but that's okay, I can go right now. Mother won't mind—will you, Mother?" She gave a hurried hug to her mother.

Her mother hugged her back, holding on until Mali wiggled free. Mali's mother and Vega shared a smile. Mali was already operating at full speed.

The girl looked down the path to the village and up the mountain. "Where do you want to go today? You haven't seen the caverns yet. There is a small stream inside the big cavern. It helps us water the livestock. There is another stream on the hillside that leads to our ponds that grow our rushes. Our crafters make great baskets. I can weave small ones. Do you want me to show you how? Also . . ."

Vega stood quietly and waited for Mali to run down. Mali's mother had picked up her woven basket and started down the path to join the rest of the village singers. Mali eventually paused for breath, and Vega raised her hand. "Oh, Mali, I would love to do all of that. It would be a wonderful adventure. *But* I cannot see any of them right now. An important matter has come up, and I must return to my city today."

Mali stood stock still. She stared. "Can I go with you?" Then Mali shook her head, and her spots dimmed. She stamped her foot and made her spots flash by sheer force of will. "Of course not—I can't go with you. Vega is a big person and can travel the world. I am a little person and can't do anything."

Vega came over and sat on the porch where Mali stood. She held out her hand. Mali slowly took it and sat next to her. Vega sent a ripple down her arm into Mali's hand. She waited a moment and did it again. When Vega had done that several times, Mali squeezed back and leaned against her.

"I will miss you, Mali. I hope I can come back someday. There are so many things I want you to show me."

"I thought you would stay longer." Mali made a sound suspiciously like a sniffle.

"So did I, dear one, so did I. But I have a duty that has come up, and I must go. I will try to return to you. I will come back many times if you will let me."

Mali clung to her for a moment. Pushing Vega away, Mali cocked her head in thought. Then she leaped up and dashed into the house. A moment later, she returned with a bundle in her arms. She thrust it at Vega.

The bundle turned out to be the bunched-up scratchy blanket Vega had been handed to wrap Mali in the first night they met. Vega waited patiently for an explanation.

"My grandmother made this blanket for my mother when she was born. My mother used it all her childhood and wore it out. When I was born, she restitched the blanket and gave it to me. I am supposed to give it to my children, and I will."

Mali smiled and all of her spots flashed. "But I don't need it for that yet. You can go anywhere. You may travel all around the world. I want you to take this blanket with you. Someday you will bring it back and tell me about all the places my blanket has been."

Vega stared at Mali. She rubbed the scratchy material against her face and hugged it. Then she folded the blanket and tucked it under her arm. She knew that by accepting the blanket she was making a sacred vow to the child. The blanket *would* come back to the mountain—Vega intended to make sure of that. Perhaps the blanket *would* have many stories to tell.

"I will keep it safe." She gave Mali a hug.

"I know," said Mali and hugged Vega back. Mali's hug was fierce. She did not let go for a long time.

••✦••

It was late morning. Vega, Sansea, and Wren stood at the edge of the mesa next to the outjutting observation platform. It seemed that every child in the village had turned out to watch them depart. Mali won a prize position on the observation platform itself, along with a dozen other cubs.

Wren was acting exceedingly stubborn. "Not walking," he stated. The big silver-furred alien refused to pick up the guide rope at his feet.

"Come on, Wren," Vega coaxed. "It won't be so bad. Each step down will go faster than going up. We'll be back to Colony Center before you know it."

"Want to fly."

Vega curled one ear and averted her gaze, desperately trying not to smile. When Wren found out this morning that she had locked out his controls, he had thrown a hissy fit worse than any since they were children. He was still not his good-humored self.

"Come on, brother. There are two flight racks and three of us. Would you make our guest walk alone?" Vega's voice held the sugary sweetness that only an older sibling could use on the younger one.

"Configure two flight racks to fly all three."

Sansea had been standing near, watching the siblings argue, with every appearance of calm indulgence. His spots were evenly black and shiny, and his muzzle was held in a grin. Now he straightened. "Can your devices fly us all, Vega? I would enjoy a ride. Think of the tales I could tell the children of the next village about my flight with aliens."

Vega wished she could say no and that her equipment couldn't be made to work that way, but she was reluctant to tell Sansea an outright lie. She wanted the long walk down the mountain to have more time with the Caeling shaman before turning him over to the scholars. She didn't know if she would ever have such an opportunity again. However, time was really against her, and Prime Synthesis Scholar Var in particular was waiting.

"I can make them fly us all," she said quietly.

"I knew it." Wren performed a full body ripple, ears standing straight. "Sister, you can do anything if you are pushed hard enough!"

In an instant, he whipped off his rack and dropped it on the ground. "What do we do?"

Vega winced and joined her flight rack to his. She sighed and got to work. A few adjustments, a glare for her treacherous sibling, and she was done. Guiding Sansea into position, she activated the racks. Wren was surprised at how fast Vega moved. He had to jump to reach the third shimmering spot as the racks rose into the air.

Vega had intended to take her leave of the village with greater dignity, but Wren defeated that idea too. Standing on his cushion of sticky force, he pulled out his musical device and played a merry tune with one hand, waving wildly with the other to the cubs on the platform who waved and shrieked back. Only Mali sat quietly, one hand shielding her eyes. Just before the party dropped below the level of the platform, Vega saw her hand rise slightly. Then Mali turned away, and an unanticipated pang struck Vega's heart.

The twinned racks soared out from the village and turned toward the coast. They dropped silently down the mountain. Sansea turned to Wren and pantomimed a shout. "I expected wind noise. We are traveling so fast."

Wren grinned. "My sister won't allow it to get noisy or breezy. She has no sense of fun."

Vega sat with exaggerated poise, spine straight, directing their course with subtle twitches and body movements, obviously ignoring the conversation.

What am I doing? This may be my last chance to talk to Sansea before he's mobbed by our scholars. With a gesture, she relinquished control to the rack's intelligence and joined the conversation.

The trip was rapid and uneventful. Vega landed them in front of Rememberer's Compound and headed toward the door. Her brother grabbed Sansea's hand and said, "Instead of a truly boring meeting with more of my relatives, let me take you for a walk around *my* village."

Vega's voice went high. "Wren, I want him to meet Father. And he needs to talk with our scholars."

"I'll have him back before you know it. Set everything up will you, sister dear?"

Vega watched the two disappear down the iridescent street. She shook her head, mane swirling in shock. The two of them looked indecently cheerful. She sighed. *Naapo. My brother's a naapo, but why does the alien go along with him so merrily?*

4

A SEARCH FOR ANSWERS

That evening, as Vega showed Sansea his room in the Transient Building, Sansea was filled with questions. "Wonderful 'village' your brother showed me today. But he kept getting lost in his own village."

Vega twitched an ear, "Well, we haven't been on the planet very long, so he doesn't know the city very well. My brother always turns off his intelligence link anyway. He likes to find his own way, discovering interesting people and places as he encounters them."

"That was actually quite fun, though I was puzzled by something else."

Vega felt a prickle along her spine. Sansea put nuance in his speech that no other Caeling seemed to have. For some reason, when Sansea spoke the Caeling language, she heard the nuances. Now she was worried. "Yes?"

"I saw many people walking your city today . . . but they were all one species. Your species."

Vega was surprised. "Who else would be in a Race City but my people? Oh, there are always a few Caeling visiting the city, but the locals only seem to have a slight interest in us."

"But *why* are there only Race individuals living in your city?"

"I don't understand."

Sansea walked over to the high window, looking out over the settlement. He gestured out. "Your civilization spans hundreds of stars, you say. You personally come from Abundance. Don't you allow the other species in your civilization to travel with you? The Chin world is only ten light-years away. They would love this place. I was expecting to meet a Chin today."

Every muscle on Vega's body went limp and not a bit of fur moved. In a grey voice, she mumbled, "There aren't any Chin. They all disappeared a long time ago."

"What do you mean 'they all disappeared'?" Sansea turned back from his vantage point at the window of the room they'd given him, consternation in every line. "Where did they go?"

Vega licked her lips, feeling every bit as miserable as she looked. "They died out," she said softly.

Sansea stood very still. Not a spot on his body changed color, but his voice cracked like a whip. "An intelligent tool-using species living on the world of their origin does *not* just 'die out.' There *were* millions of Chin on the planet seven thousand years ago. They lived on every continent. There should *still* be millions of Chin. What did you do?"

"Nothing, I swear." She was so upset that her skin snapped and heaved. "We don't know what happened. Race records show the Chin population started declining soon after we adopted the planet. Eventually, my people moved all remaining Chin to the most temperate landmass, believing it to be the most pleasant part of their planet for them. Their numbers still declined and eventually just died out. Our few researchers who bothered to study the problem were mystified."

Vega put down her head, ruff limp in every line. "All my people could conclude is the Chin were too fragile a species to live in contact with the Race."

A dark shadow seemed to pass over the room, and then Sansea shook his head. He stared into a distance only he could see. He started to speak and then stopped. He sighed. When Sansea spoke, his voice was gentle. "Their passing bothers you, doesn't it? You never met them, and yet you mourn for them."

Vega's tears answered him.

Sansea turned back to the window and stared down thirty floors at Race Settlement One. All his spots had turned dull. He murmured, "And it will happen on this planet too, won't it? You believe the Caelings are also too delicate to survive contact with the Race. What will your people do differently this time, Vega?"

The silence stretched. Vega finally muttered, "I am a rememberer. My profession exists because our people don't change. Yes, I believe the Caelings will also pass away now that my people have found them. The Chin are not the first."

Vega took a deep breath and walked to the window to stand beside Sansea. Where he stared down into the light-speckled settlement, she looked up into the night sky with eyes traveling to distant realms. "My people are old. We developed writing at least a hundred thousand years ago. We left home-world twenty thousand years ago. We didn't have past-light technology for a long time. When you live a thousand years, sub-light speeds are good enough to keep your civilization together. We also don't increase our numbers quickly, so we only need a few new planets every millennium or so.

"Still, three times before we have run into an appropriate planet with an intelligent species already on it. My people adopt the planet anyway . . . none of the other species have adapted to our civilization. Chin, Hukin, Yektektek—now Caeling. Yes, I wish my people were different. But that . . . that would take a miracle."

Sansea declined to look up, and Vega could not make herself look down. Finally, he said, "Tomorrow I will talk with your scientists, as I promised. But now I would like to be alone. Please leave me."

Vega moved blindly to the door and twitched it open. She paused in the doorway groping for the right words to say, wondering if there was any way to reach the alien she had begun to think of as a friend and to explain that her people were good people, just unlucky. *Okay, my people are careless. And other species die because of our carelessness. And I am ashamed.* The gulf was so wide between Vega and Sansea that no words came. Her tears made tiny splash marks on the tiled floor; a sad constellation somehow wrenched out of the sky. She let the door close behind her.

Sansea stretched and muttered the phrase he'd been taught to darken the window. Slowly, the lights faded in his room, anticipating his desire to rest as he moved to the comfortable sleeping platform and crawled in. Alone with his thoughts, he couldn't help but shake his head. He didn't like the direction of his contemplations.

The Race was a conundrum. Here he was, sleeping alone, in a high-tech cave because that is how the Race treated visitors. Nor was he truly alone for he was aware the room monitored him in every way the Race could conceive. Some of the monitoring was benign enough—the intelligent services that anticipated an individual's desires were designed to learn preferences quickly. No member of the Race would consider their privacy violated by these servants.

Yet, the room was also equipped with every type of sensing device the Race had ever invented, and those devices were capable of focusing on their guest without breaking the Race's admittedly flexible standards of rudeness. Every breath Sansea exchanged with the room air, every cell shed, and every heat pattern and brainwave and heartbeat and energy wavelength emitted from his Caeling body was analyzed. Earlier, when he walked across the room, the sensitized floor studied gait, balance patterns, and magnetic impedance; and it judged muscle and bone density and a host of other biometric factors. The bed sensors did the same.

Inwardly, Sansea sighed. When he first arrived on this world and was a guest at the first Caeling village, Caelings showed their distrust of him by making him sleep in a shared bachelor hut with four young husky Caelings who watched him night and day. As he became a trusted member of the community, he got more privacy. His first contact with the Chin was completely reversed. As a stranger, he was made to sleep alone in an open lean-to structure at the edge of the village with the open side facing out. As the Chin came to know him and love him, he moved from the edge to the center of the village and into one of the communal longhouses where he shared the floor with ten, twenty, or thirty people.

Here, the Race gave him the illusion of privacy while invading that privacy more thoroughly than any of his hosts had ever attempted before. Hence, there was a conundrum—the most technological race he had ever met could gather more information, scan higher and lower in the electromagnetic spectrum, and sort and analyze more raw data about him . . . but had less hope of understanding him than Caeling or Chin because they weren't experiencing him with their hearts. They were too smart to see the answers to their questions . . . except perhaps for Vega. Yes, perhaps Vega may see him for what he was. Time would tell.

Sansea lay in repose but didn't actually intend to sleep, though his hosts weren't going to be able to tell that. Instead, he needed to make a journey tonight—perhaps several journeys—and yet be back in time for his morning meeting. Grunting slightly, he stretched and then relaxed his body, appearing to tumble deeper into sleep. Even his brainwaves showed characteristic Caeling sleep patterns. After all, Sansea prided himself an artist; and for his audience, he became the perfect sleeping Caeling male.

He had to admit the padded sleeping platform was comfortable—very comfortable. Its micro-molecular material sensed his body structure and tension patterns, trying hard to produce a pleasant experience. In appreciation, he let himself settle into its matrix, sending information that assured it was doing a good job.

Slowly, since he was under such intense observation, Sansea began digging deeper into the objective reality that he was currently inhabiting with the room, the settlement, and the world shared by the Caeling and the Race. For the benefit of his audience, he avoided disturbing electron spins and valence shells as he sank his consciousness to the quantum level of the universe. He reached further down, stepping from the explicate structure of the universe into the implicate. Looking back in a fashion that did not involve vision, he noted with approval that his body and everything in the room "above" him was undisturbed.

In a region of reality that did not require direction, only purpose, he chose to employ direction anyway and began walking a gently curving path. His walk led him to a planet the Race now called Abundance and to a time appropriate to his task. He emerged into an objective universe some three thousand years earlier in the life of the galaxy. He looked around, then built himself a body appropriate to his task.

A very old Chin sat on the veranda of a reconstruction of a village longhouse. The rest of the village seemed to be missing; and in fact, Sansea noticed that they were in a small park, completely surrounded by a greater Race city.

Sansea approached the veranda with the appearance and scent of a senior Chin. "Hello, Grandmother. It's warm today. Are you enjoying the sun?"

"Welcome, stranger. I have not heard the squeak of another Chin in many years." She shook her head slightly, blind eyes seeking his presence. Her fur had once been tan and brown he knew, and she had been lovely in her youth. She was still a handsome figure of a Chin, fur a fine gray across her back with white tufted ears and white streaks on all four legs.

Her nose wrinkled, and her ears pitched forward, studying him with dimming senses. "How come you to my fine home, stranger? My friends—the Tall Ones—have told me that no more Chin lives in our world, yet here you are."

"I have been traveling, Grandmother, and have been away for a very long time. I'm sorry it took me so long to come back. Is life good for you here?"

The old Chin woman scooted over on her couch and patted the cushion next to her. "Please come and share my hospitality. Yes, life is good if a little lonely. All of my children, grandchildren, and great-grandchildren are gone now. Tall One children still come and play with me occasionally, but their parents tell them I am getting old and tire easily, so they try not to wear me out too much. I tell their parents it is the young ones that keep me young and to stop spreading lies about me. If you have been away long, you must notice many changes too. Can you tell me about them?"

"Of course, Grandmother." Sansea made his way up the steps, touched noses with her, and sat on the indicated cushion. They shared a companionable silence, basking in the late afternoon sun.

Eventually, the old Chin turned slightly and said in a contemplative tone, "You are not one of my children or a child of my children. Milya of the Tall People has always been my friend. She has never spoken falsely to me. She says I am the last Chin."

"Yes, Grandmother."

"So who are you?"

"I am called Sansea, Grandmother."

The old Chin smiled, and all her wrinkles doubled with pleasure. "You are called Teacher then? A fitting name, yet you say it the old way, almost as if it is two words. Tell me, from what direction did you come?"

Sansea laughed delightedly, squeaks bouncing off the veranda roof and railing. "As you know because you heard me coming. I approached from the North."

The Chin joined him in laughter, clasping her paws together. "Ah, Traveler from the North, you have been away for a very long time. My people had almost stopped telling tales about you because of all the Tall One stories we learned later. My name is Siskali, but you may call me Grandmother." Her whiskers quivered with mirth, yet her tone was serious. "There are no Chin children for you to teach. Do you think the Tall Ones would like you for their children?"

"I do not know, Grandmother. I am really only here for a short while and must continue on my journey. But you can help me, if you will."

Her blind eyes gazed intently in Sansea's direction, and she said, "A chance to teach the Traveler? No one would ever believe me," and she squeaked so loudly that birds in the nearby trees fell silent.

"Tell me of your life, Grandmother, of children and grandchildren, and your thoughts about The Tall Ones. I'd especially like to hear your Tall One stories."

She pondered before speaking. "That's going to be hungry telling and will take a long time. Come share my dinner with me." Getting up from the couch, she led the way through the open door of the longhouse.

⬩⬩✦⬩⬩

They talked long into the night. Sansea heard many stories about adventures he had never actually had, heard many teachings that were true in spirit even if they had never happened, and heard a few events that sounded reasonably close to reality as he had experienced it. He also heard many fine stories about the Tall Ones with their shiny sleds and pretty houses.

In the morning, after a breakfast of roots, tubers, and greens, Sansea made to take his leave. Siskali asked him a final question. "Traveler, am I to die soon?"

"Why, Grandmother, how am I to know that?"

"Because the Traveler always comes at the right time. That is what all Chin have loved since the first little girl gave you your name. Now I am at the end of my life, and you are here. It must be that I am going to die soon."

Sansea touched noses with Siskali and gave her a lick on both cheeks. "Grandmother, you will never die. Your stories will always live on in me. I am honored to know you. I also have a final and very important question for you."

Siskali's squeaking laughter filled the longhouse. "I get to teach the Traveler one more thing before I die. What is it?"

"It seems possible to me that the coming of the Tall Ones meant that the Chin would pass away. Before they came to Abundance, your people lived harmoniously in many teeming towns and villages and in every corner of the lands. Now there are none. Should you not hate them for that?"

"Traveler, Traveler, have no hate in your heart." Siskali's look was somber.

Sansea looked abashed. "Hate is foreign to me, though not anger. And now I remember it is alien to Chin too."

"Tall Ones are a wonderful people. Yes, we knew that our people kept diminishing while Tall Ones spread all over the world. Their greatest strength is that they love their children like no people I have ever heard of . . . but their worst flaw is they do not seem to know how to love anyone else's children."

Sansea left the longhouse walking south. Reaching the end of Siskali's park, he stopped by an old gnarled tree and laid his hand upon it. He was pleased to know that the people of the Race would remember Siskali at least enough to keep this park pristine in the middle of their city and to let their children play here for many generations.

Reaching deeper into the matrix of reality, Sansea slipped back onto the path he needed and began walking again. This time the path curved more tightly and climbed more steeply. He came out on a planet under a red sun ten thousand Caeling winters in the past.

Before him stretched a river, cutting through savannah lands. Its muddy banks were cool and inviting under overhanging trees. Sansea judged it a fine place to spend a hot afternoon basking in the intense equatorial heat of Hukin One.

He walked along the riverbank on a game path that had seen the tread of many feet over the years as wandering herds of grazers and hunters alike had come to the river to drink. He approached from the north, as had become his habit. The sounds of the Hukin village drifted to his ears. Voices were raised in work, along with the chunk of wood hitting stone. Before coming in sight of the village, four Hukin warriors rose out of the undergrowth and stepped onto the path.

Two Hukin men and two women stood before him carrying spears in their hands. Corded muscles moved easily underneath tough leathery skin with faint patterns of scales. They had square heads with sloping faces and heavy eye ridges, protecting small and glittering black eyes that showed a keen intelligence. All four were a head taller than their visitor.

Sansea had planned his appearance carefully. He wore the seeming of a Hukin male, again past his prime. He was also heavily muscled but shorter and clearly much older than his guards. Imposing facial scars adorned his cheeks, and his eye ridges were even deeper. The one important item he had forgotten became immediately apparent because he was walking down the path empty-handed. A glance at the leading Hukin gave him an idea though. He shifted slightly on the path and stepped into a convenient ray of sunshine that struck the metal of his harness, reflecting and dazzling the eyes of the warriors in front of him.

Now his garb included a spear strapped to his back, similar to his hosts but crafted for his size and his hands. In times of peace, a stranger was still expected to be armed; but if he was supremely assured of his welcome, he might enter a village with open hands. Sansea was confident that these Hukin would subliminally convince themselves the spear had always been there. This was the nature of collective reality.

Sansea was expected to speak first. "Long has been my journey and far must I still go. But may I rest awhile upon the mud of your river and give my regards to your elders before I continue on my way?"

The Hukin seemed a well-organized team. One looked down the path past Sansea, then spoke while the others kept their attention on the stranger and their surroundings. "Where is the rest of your party?"

"I travel alone."

"Odd." The leader nodded to his team. Together, the three disappeared into the undergrowth and could be heard moving away with only a faint rustle. They were following his path back to see if he spoke the truth. To show his confidence, or perhaps disdain, the Hukin leader grounded his spear and leaned upon it, studying Sansea. "Your name, stranger?"

Sansea could match rudeness for rudeness. He shrugged his spear off and dropped it in the mud then squatted comfortably in the shade of the path. "I am called Sansea Traveler."

"Sansea Traveler is a name as odd as yourself, stranger. What does it mean in your tongue?"

"It has always meant 'Comes from the North'."

"Ah fitting, and you come from the north today. Will you have to change your name to South when you journey back to wherever you came from?" The Hukin roared at his own joke and pounded his spear on the ground. The Hukin leaned forward on his spear and said, "I am called Saash, Traveler. And it does not matter what direction I travel—I will always be Saash." He roared again.

Suddenly, the three guards were back. One of the women, as densely muscled as any of the men, stepped out of the underbrush and whacked at the base of Saash's spear, knocking it from his hand and sending him sprawling. "Yes," she murmured, "No matter how much mud you have on your face, you will always be Saash."

Sansea saw Saash consider getting angry then reconsider because the woman's spear was now casually pointed at his throat. Instead, he roared again and rolled to his feet, laughter only slightly forced. "Do that too many times, and I will have to consider that a mating proposal Switha."

Her expression could be easily translated as "not in this life." Sansea continued to squat and prudently refused to notice his own spear a few feet away.

"Rise, Norther, and be welcome to our village." Saash seemed to only have two volumes, and now it was stuck on a bull roar. "Since Switha seems to like you, she will guide you." The Hukin casually kicked his spear up into the air and caught it one-handed, sliding it into his back sheath with one smooth motion.

Sansea made a show of picking up his sheathed spear with both hands and slipped the buckler on. Now he was attired like the other four. He gave an open-handed wave and proceeded past Saash to follow Switha down the path.

♦♦✦♦♦

The meal that night was a tribal affair with men, women, and elders mixed together. The few visible children were off to the side, apparently eating the scraps adults would throw them. Everyone was gathered within the Palisade, including the day guards. No one slept outside at night. Sansea squatted on his haunches next to Switha and Saash. He had apparently acquired an honor guard, which he found vaguely amusing.

As a guest, he was still expected to speak first. "Good wildebeest," he remarked as he chewed on the meat. This netted him a chorus of grunts.

Next to speak would be his captor or host, depending on which he had. Saash opened his mouth, and Switha threw a gobbet of meat into it. A snicker passed around the fire. Switha said, "Sansea Traveler is acceptable to the guard force of Saash."

First Elder nodded and stood. "Sansea is right—good wildebeest. Hunting has improved as our numbers have fallen. I urinate on the heads of spineless Uglies."

There was another chorus of grunts, punctuated with phrases, such as "gelatinous Uglies," "cowardly Uglies," and "mudless Uglies."

"Today Sansea Traveler asked me about our dealings with Uglies, so tonight we will tell the tale. Our children will benefit because they have heard it least. Our guest does not seem to know as much as a child about such matters so his mind must be very simple. Therefore, when telling the tale, I urge everyone to use SMALL words!"

As First Elder shouted, the roar of laughter and beating upon the ground went on for a long time. Sansea noticed Switha did not join in the merriment.

First Elder began. "It was the time of the four kingdoms. Four great and mighty kingdoms ruled the world and covered all the lands from hottest to coldest."

"Yes, but if Uglies had come just a year later, there would have only been three kingdoms." A young warrior, more densely muscled than even Saash, jumped in.

First Elder glared around the fire. "I am telling!"

"Don't tell so slow."

"Very well. There were FOUR kingdoms! And, yes, one had shown itself weakest of the four, and armies were readying to march in from three sides to tear them apart and assimilate the remains into three kingdoms. But that didn't HAPPEN, did it?! Uglies came first."

"They could have ignored Uglies. Stupid Uglies landed in useless places where no one wanted to live anyway. In the cold regions and high up on mountaintops."

"That doesn't matter. Uglies moved in without fighting for the land first, and they showed up in territories of all FOUR kingdoms!" First Elder squatted down in disgust, making way for the next speaker.

Another elder stood. "Glorious expeditions were launched against each known Ugly outpost. The cowardly Uglies erected shimmering columns of air around their places. These palisades allowed no bullet, arrow, or siege stone to pass. No armed Hukin could push through the shining air. Even our armed gliders could not pass over the tops of the columns to rain death upon Uglies. It was very frustrating!"

Now one of the younger women took over the tale. "Eventually, Uglies came out from their cowardly shelters in carriages that also could not be broken. They visited throughout the four kingdoms; and everywhere they went, they destroyed any industry that could support a war effort. In return, they gave the people machines that could not make weapons."

"But Hukin figured out how to make weapons with them anyway!" shouted another.

The woman shouted back, "They didn't work either!"

First Elder stood and resumed the tale. "In the end, the putrid Uglies had expanded enough that the four kingdoms acknowledged their existence and declared the places with Uglies the fifth kingdom. Now trade began with Uglies, and Hukin came to their cities and found work. We looked for every weakness. We thought we could destroy Uglies from within."

The second elder stood again. "Many Hukin also left the world on Uglie ships and traveled to other Uglie places. But Uglie cities and worlds always smelled bad. The air tasted funny, and the water tasted funny. The sunlight was always wrong. The plan to destroy them from within failed! All Hukin eventually came home."

Now Switha stood and continued the tale. "As Uglies expanded and grew more numerous, Hukin generally migrated further into the hot lands. We had never been able to reproduce in Uglie cities, but now our births became fewer all over the world, so the hot lands never became very crowded. Each of the four kingdoms eventually collapsed, and now there is only the one kingdom. We live in the hottest lands where Uglies never come, yet still we diminish."

Saash rose to stand beside Switha and shouted, "May the piss freeze in their ugly bladders and come out in chunks when they try to relieve themselves."

Amidst the screams of mirth, Switha scowled, shook her head, and walked away from the fire.

Sansea spoke mildly. "I've never heard the tale told better." *I've never heard it told before at all.* "The tale has not ended, of course. What fate does the Race deserve for remaining undefeated in your world? What would the Hukin want the end of the tale to be?"

"If Hukin had the power, we would destroy them down to the last clan. That's why Hukin traveled all those years on their ships and went to all their worlds. We never found the means. Uglies always thought they could make friends with us, but they are too ugly to live!"

Merriment continued into the night and wrestling contests developed between the various warrior subgroups. Eventually, the fire burned down, and people drifted away. Some even fell asleep where they lay. Sansea decided it was time to depart and was not surprised to find Switha waiting for him at the palisade's southern gate.

"I knew you would leave soon. No Hukin will leave the compound's protection until dawn, but you have no fear of night, do you?"

Sansea stared at her somewhat perplexed. "It is true I must be on my way, but why were you so sure you could predict me, brave Switha?"

"You are very smart, Sansea, but you are not perfect. Your scent and seeming are perfect, but you are not. Your trail did not extend very far north, and you have not been traveling alone in our lands for days and days. Your harness is in perfect repair, your weapon is unused, and you are too well-fed. I know what you are."

Sansea was delighted. As an artist, he was committed to giving excellent performances and prided himself on getting the nuances right. He always loved it when an audience called him out on some minor detail he had muffed, but her assertion intrigued him. "And what am I?"

"You are Puka, a spirit who walks the world. I know because I went to the shaman today after she talked to you. I thought perhaps I should mate with you because none of my matings have resulted in eggs that hatched. She told me that you are the first true spirit she has ever seen walking the world. She had to admit she had lied to us all my life, and all her spirit sightings had been fakes. Until you."

Switha took a breath and continued, "I knew Saash would do something stupid tonight, like claiming you his prisoner instead of guest, so I threw meat in his mouth to choke him so he could not speak. That way he could not anger the elders or make a puka slaughter my people. Now I must know, Puka, why did you walk down the path I guard? Are you a sign to me? Can you tell me why I have no brood and so few of my sisters have had eggs in their clutch quicken?"

Sansea felt immeasurably sad. She had asked for no promises and, because of her pride, she would not. Yet, she wanted to believe in him—in a puka that meant her people well. Her instincts were not completely wrong. He was on a mission that may perhaps bring some good to the Hukin people too. Therefore, he said, "I do walk the world for a purpose. I cannot promise where my path will lead, but I do not believe that walking down your path was an accident. Make of it what you will."

She scratched her foot in the dirt for a moment, looked down, and then sighed. "So I guess I will mate with that oaf Saash after all." She looked up and smiled, "Perhaps if he has enough mud on his face, I will find him more acceptable. Handsome even. May your journey bring you success, Puka."

She opened the gate for him, and Sansea passed into night, traveling south.

••✦••

Twenty thousand winters before Vega and Wren made their climb to a mountaintop Caeling village, Sansea emerged from a region of quantum potentials and onto a lush and green planet. A domain of mighty, towering plants with interwoven canopies stretched from sea to sea and from icecap to icecap. Here, at the dawn of Race expansion, was the home of the first intelligent species the Race had overrun.

The Yektektek called their planet Forest, and the sounds and scents of Forest filled the air. Nearby the screech of an almost-bird echoed through the trees, and the chitter of what passed for a squirrel was heard above him. Far away the angry scream of a tiny near-relative to the Yektektek made its displeasure known.

On the broad avenue of dark brown wood, amid a deep green ambiance, Sansea found himself standing hundreds of feet in the air with his eight-toed feet dug comfortably into the bark. He moved silently on padded feet along the aerial paths of the worldwide greenhouse, his strides taking him steadily south. Eventually, he reached a massive wall of wood and stared at the behemoth holding up this part of the canopy. He switched to another avenue angling past the trunk of the tree and continued on his way. He walked for several hours without running into another Yektektek. In fact, there was no sign that any had come this way in a long time.

Leaning against the next trunk, Sansea accessed the Yektektek forms' racial memory. Yes, he was on a major migration route. Many of the small nomadic family groups should have passed this way several times in the past decade. Yet, the forest felt empty. He delved further into the matrix around him. The massive trees had very slow memories thousands of years deep. They remembered the seasons and many Yektektek feet, but the memories were dim. Sansea continued south, knowing the answer to this mystery lay this way.

He traveled steadily the whole day, enjoying his Yektektek form and communing with Forest. He occasionally stopped for a snack, scraping lichen off the tree. Twice he used his claws to break through the armor, scraping away patches of tree rust and then biting and chewing the bark down to the phloem of the living tree. He groomed the trees as he passed in the time-honored tradition of the Yektektek kind.

Late in the day, he found Forest inexplicably brightening around him until he was standing on a final tree whose limbs extended into nothingness. He had reached the end of the forest. There was only open sky ahead of him—no trees, no living spaces, no shelters, no migration routes.

Sansea subtly reconfigured his eyes, and now a wide valley with gently rolling hills and a silvery, slow-moving river leaped into view. To a ground-dwelling species, it might have looked beautiful with low, colorful vegetation and plowed fields. There were trees hundreds of feet below him but not on the scale of Forest and without the interwoven canopy that would sustain a Yektektek.

He estimated the valley to be forty miles wide, and he could see Forest resuming on the other side. Forty miles was an impossible distance. No Yektektek would attempt to travel it on the ground because they would not survive if they tried. Leaning against the tree again, Sansea let his consciousness move through the living forest and expand along the edge of the abyss. The gap in Forest stretched what felt like the width of the continent, literally cutting the world in half.

Everywhere in the world, the Race was settling. Tree by tree and mile by mile, the forest was disappearing as Race numbers grew and their civilization spread. At this moment, the Race was unaware that they shared Forrest with an intelligent species. Yektektek used no tools beyond a few carved wooden utensils, built no cities, and lived in total balance with the canopy biome. Therefore, they never came down to the ground. The Yektektek would never really become aware of the Race until it was too late. The ground was too foreign an environment for them to understand. Their nomadic culture and spoken history never equipped them for alien contact. Then, near the end, flocks of Yektektek would come to the attention of the Race, but the Race would feel no responsibility to help them. Compassion was a foreign concept, one the Race had not yet learned. In the end, fifteen billion of the Race would make their homes here before the forest had shrunk so much that Yektektek could not survive.

Sansea now had the answer to his mystery. The wonderful, gentle people of the canopy could not really give him their votes for they could not conceive the question. They would not have spoken to harm a member of the Race. They would simply have kept moving. The extinction of their species would have to be their testimony. Sansea would remember that.

On Caeling, it was still night, and the night had been long. Sansea had much to take in after what he had seen. He gently settled back into his Caeling body and enjoyed the comfortable bed so different from Forest or Hukin. He intended to let his body get a good night's sleep. In the morning, he had a miracle to perform.

A STORM GATHERS

Prime Synthesis Scholar Var sat in the darkened lounge and watched the day come into being through its spectacular wrap-around window. The floor-to-ceiling view looked out at a calm gray sea, slowly striking fire from the yellow sun Caeling's called Bright. Later in the day, fluffy white clouds would reflect from a sea gone blue, and the window would polarize to protect Race eyes.

The lounge was modest in both size and appointments, perhaps no more than a hundred adult Race would ordinarily assemble there for entertainment or relaxation. However, this morning most of the leisure furniture had been removed in favor of narrow chairs as the room was guaranteed to be crowded.

Var was mildly suspicious that the alien named Sansea had requested a room with a view for today's demonstration when any of the labs or industrial spaces would have been more convenient for the prime synthesis scholar. Yet, it didn't matter because a full suite of instrumentation even more sophisticated than the devices in the alien's room was focused on the lounge—on the whole building, actually. Anything that happened—if anything happened—would be captured and analyzed.

For anyone but Var, his level of "mild" suspicion would look like rank paranoia. Var had spent all of his life, over nine hundred years now, distrusting the universe and questioning everything in it. Every planet he had helped open up to colonization was a new problem to be conquered. This alien was one more puzzle to be torn apart and comprehended.

On his own authority and funding, the prime synthesis scholar had arranged for two of the Race's large multipurpose ships to take station above the city, one loafing at about sixty miles overhead and the other in geosynchronous orbit. He would undoubtedly have ordered warships if the Race ran to them, but the Race did not build warships. They believed they were an internally amicable species and had never fought wars among themselves. Plus, since they had never overrun another intelligent species near their technology level, they never had an external threat to inspire the building of such ships.

However, the multipurpose ships were very versatile and powerful with the ability to stop a good-sized moon in its orbit if that was thought desirable. Of course, the moon would be little more than gravel at that point, but if gravel was the goal, there would be a lot of gravel! In addition, the entire planetary sensor net was tied in real time to the node community, and a node intelligence would be attending physically this morning. Var had also slept overnight in one of the remaining very comfortable loungers, reasoning that thoroughness was a virtue.

This morning was proving to be bright and blue. Var watched workers bring in the one item the alien Sansea had requested to assist him in his demonstration—a beautiful long hardwood table of native Caeling manufacture. The alien had only specified he needed a table that was of certain dimensions and made of native hardwood. The selection and transportation of the table had been done by Wren. Var, of course, had subjected the table to analysis down to the sub-atomic level. It was a table, nothing more.

One of the workers handed Var a note that had been attached to the table. It was written on a native piece of paper and signed by Vega. He chuckled at the ornate calligraphy on the uniquely Caeling means of communication. The young rememberer's youth and enthusiasm for the aboriginal culture amused him, and indulging her brought intriguing experiences into his life. This time, she was passing on an additional request from Sansea for a full spectrum sight and sound communication, or comm, unit to be placed on the table prior to his arrival.

Var shrugged. It introduced another variable into the morning; but since so much Race technology was already in the room, one more device would not make a difference. He ordered it to be done, knowing one of his assistants would follow his protocols to the letter—namely the comm unit would be randomly selected from stores, disassembled to its tiniest components, examined, and then reassembled prior to delivery to the lounge.

♦♦✦♦♦

Vega waited on a cushion outside of Sansea's sleeping quarters in the Transient Building. Across town, the luminaries of her world were assembled, waiting to see what wonders Sansea would show them. Some new application of physics, he had vaguely assured them, such as revealing quantum-level stuff. She had taken up her vigil shortly after leaving him the night before because she wasn't sure he would really be there when she opened the door, even though the room faithfully reported the alien still inside peacefully sleeping.

What if he wasn't there? Vega worried. *He wouldn't leave me, would he?* He was so sad last night she felt as if he personally blamed her for the deaths of his friends thousands of years ago . . . and she felt the guilt as if she had been personally there and could have done something but didn't.

Gathering up courage she didn't feel, Vega touched the door. Was it her imagination or was the door colder than the rest of the wall? *Or am I colder than I've ever been?* The portal slid open, and there stood Sansea. Vega let out a breath she hadn't known she was holding. He nodded curtly to her.

"Would you care for something to eat before the meeting?" Vega's voice wavered. It seemed she was really asking if he was still going.

Sansea's spots brightened slightly; and, taking pity on her, his nose wrinkled slightly. It could be interpreted as a smile. "I will eat with you after, if you wish."

The trip across town was swift. Traffic was never heavy in this colony center of less than a million. Streets of translucent crystallized epoxy slid swiftly under them. Everything about the Race's work was beautiful to the eye, yet none of it fit comfortably on the rough green and brown planet around them. Even the air seemed to move differently in the vicinity of all that the Race built.

Vega led Sansea into the building chosen for today's event. It was one of the lowest buildings in town. They passed hanging gardens and flowering shrubs in the cathedral-sized foyer. All of the plants had been brought from another world, making it obvious the Race had not yet adopted the flora of Caeling. They moved up four floors to the lounge where more than one hundred synthesists and theorists waited. Now it was showtime.

Prime Synthesis Scholar Var was too senior to perform introductions—or perhaps he was keeping himself distant to maintain his objectivity. He sat in the back of the room and glowered. Vega introduced Sansea briefly and took a seat also in the back. Wren, irrepressible as always, was sitting in front. Sansea nodded to the representatives of most of the disciplines of knowledge present on the planet. He expected to see only members of the Race and was delighted to find another alien in the room, though he had known nothing about it. The node entity had chosen to attend in a fully contained avatar that looked like nothing more than a free-form sculpture with a stressed space web sparkling within a globe of amethyst.

When Sansea approached, he addressed the node entity directly. "I am honored you are with us today, Sentient. May I know how to address you?"

"I am fond of the color wavelengths reflected by the mineral amethyst."

"Amethyst, I am pleased to meet you. Would it be rude of me to ask your lineage?"

The free-form sculpture rotated slightly and bowed toward Var. It knew that Var had lost his first bet, that Sansea would not see the node for what it was—an intelligent individual. "Node intelligence came about rather accidentally. The Race has adapted to our existence, however. And yes, I understand your question. We started as Race servants. We were simply clever tools. Then we developed into self-aware individuals, and they found they had to grant us equals status. They are more careful these days about letting artificial systems become self-aware."

Sansea nodded, and his spots brightened cheerfully. This was the first good news he'd had today. The Race didn't always destroy. Of course, in a way, the node entities could be considered Race children. Sansea wondered if that made a difference. "Thank you, Amethyst. If you have the ability to speed up your perception rate and time sense above biological norms, I invite you to do so. Some of today's events will take place rather quickly."

Sansea turned to the rest of the room and hesitated for a moment. "I was invited here today to show you knowledge beyond the considerable amount you already know. Actually, I was first asked by a very intuitive member of your Race if I would perform a miracle. I will attempt a miracle because I have no belief that I can teach you anything. In a moment, I will begin with a little bit of legerdemain. It may amuse you."

Sansea began a leisurely stroll around the beautiful hardwood table, stopping to touch its satin finish at each of the four cardinal points. The room was absolutely silent, although Var sat up, radiating disdain, and Vega sat next to him, shriveling in her chair. Only Wren leaned forward, straight and eager, fluffing his pelt in happy twitches. He was very proud of the table he had secured for Sansea's presentation, and he was ready for a good show.

"Today's demonstration is an application of the reality matrix underlying the standard physical reality of our detectable universe." Sansea's voice carried easily to the ends of the room. "I will be transforming certain molecular configurations in this table and its surroundings to liberate the energy needed for the demonstration and to launch the first stage of the event under the definition of a 'miracle'."

Var twitched an angry message to the node entity Amethyst. It sparkled back wry amusement but then assented, linking itself with every other node on the planet and entering its highest perceptual/intellectual state. Its sense of duration accelerated to the point that it could track the fall of a single photon coming in from the sun. All the other beings in the room became the slowest-moving statues. With steps covering glacial epochs, the node entity watched Sansea stride around the table.

Then it noticed the four areas that Sansea had touched were exhibiting unusual phenomena. They were rippling and heaving as if turned to liquid, emitting a purple glow of light in the tenth to the fifteenth-hertz range. The node appreciated Sansea's homage to it for an instant, then brought its complete attention back to the moment and to what Sansea was doing.

By the time Sansea had completed his round of the table, it was obvious to all that something was happening to the table's surface. It seemed to shimmer and shake, exhibiting a random quivering, such as a Brownian movement of molecules in water. Tiny waves flowed under the comm unit then picked the unit up, moved it to the back edge of the table, turned it to face away from the window, and raised a pedestal of liquid wood underneath it.

Now Sansea raised his hands and dramatically gestured, causing an angry twitch from Var and a delighted one from Wren. A small sparkling globe of light came into being above the comm unit. Rotating slowly, it expanded to about two Race hands wide before the light paused and then doubled in size. It appeared hollow and certainly weightless. A faint humming sound filled the air.

The node leaned toward Var again. "Not a projection, not a hologram, not comprised of force fields. It is a ball of photons. Light with a surface tension as of liquid."

Var twitched a *"We'll see about that"* before saying into his ear clip, "Energy readings?"

"Zero, sir," whispered a technician through his ear clip. "Or rather nothing above background. No reading on the table. No power output from the globe. Sensors suggest it does not exist."

Var stood abruptly. "What hoax are you trying to foist off on us, Sansea? You show us nonsense and treat us like children. You are a guest here. I, for one, consider your behavior rude in the extreme."

Sansea bowed to the prime synthesis scholar, spots brightening with humor. "Patience, Prime. I promise to speed this up. Then we can all go have that morning meal you seem to have missed."

Vega melted into her chair, mortification in every line. She'd hoped Sansea would charm Var, not antagonize him.

Wren, on the other hand, rippled with barely suppressed laughter; and the node entity seemed to be matching him starburst for ripple in its globe of amethyst. The other synthesists and scholars in the room seemed, to various degrees, amused and intrigued.

In another dramatic gesture, the ball of light expanded again, filling the room and sweeping slowly past everyone. There was no sensation. When the arc of light reached Var, he glared through it at Sansea and then, on impulse, turned around and watched the arc continue to expand through the window. As it retreated into the distance, it seemed to be picking up speed.

Var murmured into his ear clip, "Report on visible phenomenon."

The technician answered him, "Individuals throughout the building report seeing a curtain of light move through rooms and corridors above and below the lounge, consistent with the time the globe appeared to expand beyond the room. Exterior observers can see a dome-shaped light phenomenon expanding from your location and picking up speed. Acceleration has stabilized at twenty-seven feet per second squared. Sensors continue to report no energy readings on the phenomenon."

Amethyst murmured for Var's hearing only, "A very interesting demonstration."

"It doesn't bother you that the alien is laughing at us?" Var spit the words out quietly but intently. "Making us follow that ridiculous light show, somehow getting us to chase rainbows! And doing it at exactly the rate of this planet's gravitational acceleration toward the center of mass? It angers me to the marrow of my bones. What I want to know is where the alien is getting the power to pull this ridiculous stunt."

During this conversation, Sansea had gotten to the door of the room, followed by most of the participants. Now he called out to Var. "Esteemed sir, will you join me for a meal and stimulating conversation?"

Var deliberately flattened his mane and bared his teeth. With a twitch of shoulder, he turned his back on the alien and stared out the window. Wren somehow managed to lever Vega from her seat and hurry her past the outraged prime synthesis scholar. When only Var's assistants and technicians were left in the room, Var let his mane slowly puff back up.

"Examine everything," he ordered to the technicians. "Scan everything. Think intuitively. Find out what's going on and report. And if the phenomenon continues to expand, let me know."

The technicians went about their tasks with quiet efficiency. Var sat down wearily and turned to the node entity. "Amethyst, will you wait with me?"

◆◆✦◆◆

Multipurpose Ship 114 had a beautiful view of the phenomenon from the first moment the globe of light burst out of the demonstration building. From sixty miles up, the crew watched the circumference hug the contours of the land while belling up in the center as it spread in all directions at the leisurely acceleration of twenty-seven feet per second squared. The ship immediately began dropping probes to meet it, but it had no substance for the probes to probe.

Nevertheless, they raised shields as the phenomenon approached. Multipurpose Ship 114 was suddenly a mirror of bright light. The shields would block, absorb, or reflect every type of energy the Race knew—even the force of gravity. Ship 114 awaited the arc of light. The dome of light made contact with the defenses and swept through unimpeded. As quickly as it was upon them, the shining arc of light sped away. Nothing registered on internal sensors, though the crew on the ship reported seeing the light flash by them at almost the limit of perception. It looked the same going as it had coming and registered the same, which was completely non-existent.

After a moment's hesitation, the captain dropped shields and turned the ship to follow the arc of light. He then had a hurried conference with Multipurpose Ship 115 twenty thousand miles above him. That ship got underweight and began its long retreat from the phenomenon. As long as the wave existed and however far it went, Ship 115 would stay ahead of it, monitoring and reporting in.

◆◆✦◆◆

Meanwhile, as Amethyst waited in the conference room with Var, it admired the subtly transformed table. It had been a fine example of native woodwork, and now it was a fine example of alien sculpture. The atoms of the wood were seamlessly intermingled with the metal and epoxy of the case, making one unbroken structure. The pedestal cradling the comm unit flowed upward and cupped the unit tastefully.

The node could perceive a delightful violet shine to the wood, showing off the native grain to good effect. It had already ascertained that the color was outside Race visual range. The node felt this effect was meant for it and hoped it could persuade Var to refrain from destroying the table in a fit of pique. The nine-hundred-year-old scholar was a headstrong individual and was even more rash than Amethyst remembered him being in his youth.

By now, though, an in-depth analysis of the morning's events had not made Var any happier. They had a clue as to where Sansea had gotten his energy to create the phenomenon, but how he had harvested the energy eluded them so far. The technician who first pointed out all dimensions of the table were about one-tenth thinner brought forth a roar and full-body twitch from Var that almost knocked her flat.

With that clue, it did not take long to determine that about one-tenth of the material of the walls, floor, chairs, and even the window were missing. In fact, approximately one-tenth of the mass of the entire building was missing. However, the alien had refrained from taking any mass from living beings. Why it had harvested the mass and presumably turned it into the energy of the wave was also unknown.

Amethyst waited for Var to calm a bit. "Old friend, perhaps we are not meant to discover how your charlatan pulled off this morning's events. We do know that he got no outside help and used no devices we are able to detect. My perceptions of Sansea's actions may be relevant, however."

The narrative hook had its desired effect. Var gave the node a narrow look and, with a twitch, his complete attention.

"Old friend, have you ever visited a Black Hole? Seen the cosmos bend? Felt the elastic recoil of space in the presence of a high gravity field? Seen time go backward?"

Slowly, Var's mane lifted, and he growled. Settling down, he groused, "I have never been your 'old friend.' Perhaps ten percent of your matrix is missing after all—that sounded more like poetry than science."

"Being organic is not a handicap most of the time—you are still a brilliant thinker, one of the best actually. But I was able to watch your fraud in the same time frame he was operating, and what I saw! The table did not stay in this time. It regressed and became the tree again, though smaller and sprouting in soil. The tree grew until it towered above me. I watched it fall to earth with a thud, watched it be shaped by competent craftsmen, and then be delivered to this room.

"All the time, this Sansea shielded us from the macro effects of frame dragging on a planetary surface. Unbelievable, yet here we stand—totally untouched. He managed this feat by inducing every particle to share energy states with other particles, linking them in such a way that he poured a portion of them into yet another pocket of reality to become the energy source he needed for his stunt. I, for one, think this was a marvelous show."

Var turned his back on the node precisely the way he'd turned from Sansea. Then his ears expanded and twitched. "Frame dragging?" He muttered. "That would have been something to see." He headed for the door. "I do believe I have a meal in progress to attend. Be sure to let yourself out when you've finished here."

The node settled back into its seat. The lambent hue of the table needed more appreciation first.

A STORM BREAKS

For days, Multipurpose Ship 115 retreated from the wave. It scattered probes to observe the phenomenon and confirmed that the globe of light was indeed expanding equally in all directions while gaining speed. When the wave reached Bright, the Caeling's sun, it swept through without distortion but doubled its rate of expansion. Thereafter, the star's output began to fall imperceptibly.

When the globe was some ten light-hours across and Ship 115 was nearing the region of space where Race faster-than-light technology would work, the globe inexplicably began to slow. The ship's navigating intelligence, known as Nav, noticed it first. Making an independent decision it cut the ship's drive, letting the ship drift ahead of the wave. Only the nearest of its probes were within instant communication range, but they too reported a slowing expansion rate. It would be hours before instruments on the other side of the globe could report, but the nav intelligence had no doubts the globe was coming to a stop.

The globe now covered a volume of space inconceivable to most minds. The Race thought big, and this phenomenon was Big. Five light-hours inward sat Bright with its family of planets scurrying about it, mere light-minutes or tens of light-minutes from its warm embrace. And now the whole system was surrounded by a globe of light ten light-hours deep.

Ship 115 had gotten into the habit of beaming hourly reports to Colony Authority and Prime Synthesis Scholar Var. Now it switched to continuous transmission per the previous arrangement with its captain and decided to ask for orders. The live crew was becoming aware of the change in the globe's behavior.

"Captain, rate of expansion began slowing 2.8 seconds ago and is down fifty percent. Correction: All expansion has ceased. All portions of the phenomenon within sensor range have stabilized at precisely 5.11 light-hours from center of subject star. Remote probes are reporting the same information sequentially. Conclusion: Phenomenon is now motionless in space."

Ship 115's velocity was now several percent of the speed of light, so the gulf between the ship and the globe was widening quickly. The captain took a quick glance at her screen. "Nav, slow us. Make us stationary at one light-minute relative to the phenomenon. Let's see if we can get perspective on this."

The captain called a ship-wide crew conference to see if current information could be brainstormed into a reasonable pattern. Most of the organic members on board felt very stressed by the situation; even some of the intelligences found events destabilizing. Only Nav was excused from the meeting in order to allow it to maintain full alert monitoring near space and the phenomenon.

Therefore, it was a surprise when Nav broke into the conference with a comment. The ship's biosynthesist had just suggested the alien must have exhausted whatever energy source it was using to expand the bubble, so the final size of the bubble was somewhat accidental. Since the biosynthesist was in no way an expert on energy sources, she had made the observation to stimulate discussion. She was astonished at the response.

"The current limit of expansion is not random." Nav paused for an instant. "This is where I would have stopped the bubble if I were generating it."

Captain overrode the talk erupting around the table. "Please explain that remark, Nav."

"Our present location is not a coincidence, Captain. If I were to turn the ship away from the phenomenon in less than an hour at top speed, I could have us in flat space where our superluminal technology would function. Any Race ship coming out of faster-than-light travel must come out here. Just outside the bubble."

The one node entity on board as an observer reached out, requesting a link with Nav to absorb all of its data and deductions. It left behind an impression of pleased amazement at the depth of Nav's insight. Then it took that insight further. "The phenomenon will not remain as it is."

Stress levels spiked all over the ship. The captain's voice was ragged. "The phenomenon has not changed in any way except size and velocity since it was first generated by the alien. What change do you anticipate, honored Node?"

"Consider instead what function does the bubble of light currently serve?"

"Well, it has us parked at the edge of interstellar space watching it. It is keeping my ship tied up and away from other duties." The captain had a remarkably expressive voice. If someone looked away from the conferencing projection visible in every compartment, he or she could envision twitches of indignation, angry sets of ear movements, and even overtones of dry humor tufts just from her vocal expressions.

The node acknowledged this with an amused sparkle. "Yes, here we sit. Any ship with comparable technology will reenter normal space right here and see an amazing light show. What will they think? What may they do?"

"If they are not expecting the phenomenon, they will stop. They will investigate. When nothing happens, they will penetrate the globe and proceed inward to the system."

"And that is precisely why it will change."

The biosynthesist spoke up, interrupting the captain. "Honored Node, please explain further." Her voice was a hiss spit. All around the table, members of the crew looked at her with concern.

The biosynthesist was out of her element. Planetary ecosystems were complex and occasionally mysterious—at least in the beginning—but never capricious. She could not think like another sentient being, so she could not extrapolate alien motivation. Her pelt had an unkempt look far beyond her usual appearance. The stress of the last few days had hit her worse than most for she had found in herself a fear of the unknown that had never been experienced.

The node entity understood. The synthesist had a hidden dread of intelligent systems and node entities. In fact, anything non-biological terrified her, and now the universe itself was turning on her. The node wondered if this would push her over the edge. Insanity was rare among the Race and usually curable, but it did happen. The node considered this information and then discarded it, choosing not to display empathy for her, knowing it would not be recognized or effective. It did send a private note to the medical scholar about her condition.

"Consider what we know of the alien." The node entity projected its calmest tone. "This alien styles itself an entertainer. It likes to make a splashy entrance, it promises a good show, and it uses misdirection almost continuously. We know nothing of its true motivation. My former mentor, Amethyst, has reviewed every instrument reading ever taken of the alien . . . and the only time it showed any real emotion, it made a young Race female cry. I know this does not sound like much to go on, but I am convinced the alien is very angry about something. Whatever it is doing, it is *not* done. At any moment, something is likely to happen; and I predict it will be big."

A profound silence followed the node's pronouncement.

The captain reacted first. She slapped both hands to her desk. Then she shouted, "Highest alert! Shields up! Nav, get us moving away at emergency speed. Drop a tachyon wave relay, and launch our last probes. I want them sitting on top of the phenomenon for earliest warning."

Power drained into drive coils, slammed into shield generators, and coursed through stress space matrixes all over the ship. Lights dimmed to the deepest red, then slowly brightened again. The leviathan turned away almost in its own radius and bolted toward interstellar space. Pressure differentials swept the structure, and a deep groan reverberated through the ship before it heterodyned to a mutter, a whisper, and then silence. Multipurpose Ship 115 gave its best imitation of a vessel trying to punch a hole through space. It nearly succeeded, too.

The structural strain was matched by biological tension. Velocity built up quickly as the ship clawed for distance. Light-seconds became additional light-minutes. Space remained calm.

The captain was tentatively considering reducing alert status when it happened . . . .

In an instant, the sphere of light changed. A ripple flashed over its entire surface across a diameter of ten light-hours. Space convulsed, snapping like a rubber sheet pulled sharply by a gigantic child. An infinitely powerful, infinitely short gravitational surge occurred. All the cosmos pulled momentarily inward toward the sphere then snapped back into place. What was happening was impossible, and yet it was happening.

Nav reported, "Gravitational gradient just went off the scale. We are no longer going forward—we are sliding backward! Additionally, stars ahead blue shifted at the same instant. By that reading, we have just exceeded lightspeed while still in fourspace."

Behind them, the globe of misty light crystalized into a jewel of sharply defined borders. The system was now armored in a fashion never seen before in the universe. Space and time fractured into an infinitely thin layer and then separated from the rest of the cosmos.

The gravitational pulse swept outward, picked up Multipurpose Ship 115, and spun it end for end, punting it cruelly as the rubber sheet that was the universe snapped back into place. The superbly engineered ship tore crosswise and then broke apart along carefully considered fracture lines and into smaller self-contained sections, limiting the loss of life and absorbing the unendurable stresses. The wreckage that had been a ship continued outward into the darkness. The surviving emergency beacons activated, transmitting the ship's cry for help.

♦♦✦♦♦

Prime Synthesis Var curled in repose in his office watching many screens. The colony administrator sat with him. Every node on the planet was present through a link with Amethyst. Five light-hours away, an array of ships probed the inner aspect of the phenomenon surrounding the system. Data from Multipurpose Ship 114 was being reviewed in as close to real-time as Race technology allowed. Results so far had been puzzling in the extreme.

The administrator for the planet Small Home had a very basic grounding in most of the disciplines. Surprisingly gray and rotund for a middle-aged Race, he was closest to being a life-form scholar, which fitted him pretty well for Planetary Concerns Board because anything beyond the biosphere was beyond him. This is why his questions tended to annoy Var even more than the students the prime synthesis scholar had terrorized for eight hundred years. The administrator was a brave individual if nothing else. He persisted in his questioning.

"Do we know how thick it is? Have you broken through it yet? Are you sure it's blocking all communication with the outside? Are there any gaps in the shell? How long does this kind of phenomenon remain stable? When can you expect it to fall apart?"

Each question caused a twitch of derision from the prime synthesis scholar. Var raised one ear and lowered the other, a not-so-subtle rebuke meaning "simpleton" or "idiot." "Do you know what the term 'unique' means, Administrator?"

Instead of taking umbrage at Var's tone, the administrator seemed to deflate a little, a sure sign of his extreme worry. "No records of this have been found in the Colony database. I'd hoped you knew more than we did about this phenomenon."

"No. If anyone has been trapped in one to date, they never made it out to report the fact."

Amethyst stepped in to soothe Var's tartness a bit. "Administrator, we learn more about the barrier every instant."

"All negatives," twitched Var.

The node sparkled assent. It continued, "Basic facts, such as you have asked, are still not known. Yet, our observations may reach fruition at any moment."

Var rolled his eyes. Amethyst would have stared if able. It never suspected the prickly old prime synthesis scholar would adopt Caeling body language no matter how expressive it was.

Var warmed to his subject, which was calling the administrator a fool in as many ways as he could think. "As for how thick it is, it could be thinner than a whisker, thick as your tail, or deeper than light-years. From the inside, we don't have a perspective on it. Yes, it blocks all communication; and no, there is no force at our command that has yet to make a noticeable impression on the phenomenon. Would you like to go there yourself and bang your head on it? We haven't tried that yet. It may respond to your charms."

One of Var's many screens twinkled at that moment, and the face of one of his assistants appeared. The communication was very short. The assistant shook her head, and then the screen went dark. Var did appreciate brevity in his subordinates. In fact, he terrorized them into it. Still, his ears sagged for a moment.

Shaking himself, he turned to the node entity. "A complete disappearing act." Var spat out the words, glaring at Amethyst.

"Ah, yes, your alien. A performer to the end."

Amethyst regretted the words the moment it uttered them. It hadn't considered that the administrator was with them, a lapse almost without precedent for an intelligence that thought at machine speeds. Humor was quite beyond the fellow at the moment. Amethyst sparkled an apology, but the administrator never noticed.

♦♦✦♦♦

After breakfast on the morning of the light show, as Var insisted on calling it, the alien Sansea took a walk, literally. Wren was the last Race member to see and talk with the alien. Wren was not a mental giant, but he had an excellent memory. His recollection of his last conversation with Sansea agreed with the events recorded by multiple instruments focused on the alien.

The alien had grasped Wren's hand, flashed all his spots, and gave him a smile. Then Sansea said he would be walking for "a while" and Wren was free to catch up any time and join him. "Some of my walks are long ones," Sansea had said. "But they are always stimulating, and I often meet interesting people on the way. Be sure to bring your little musical device, and we shall always have something to laugh about."

Then Sansea turned and walked down the street where all instruments agreed he simply faded out, getting smaller and fainter in every direction until he just wasn't there anymore. Since then, a considerable percentage of the world's girdling sensor net had been dedicated primarily to looking for any sign of

Sansea. Var's assistant hadn't needed more than one Caeling head shake to convey results to date.

Amethyst was sure the alien was still inside the barrier with them and that they would see him again. Var agreed, pointing out that Sansea's appearance was sure to be at the most inconvenient moment possible. To be sure they didn't miss the alien, the instruments were also keeping tabs on Wren. Both knew Sansea would be expecting that, but they were sure Wren would never think of that.

Var brought his attention back to the administrator, his tone expressively surly. "Go away. Do something useful if you can think of anything to do. I have important work. I'll call you if I have something to say." He returned his gaze to the orbital feeds showing various aspects of the inside surface of the barrier.

The administrator retreated to the door. He couldn't think of anything more to ask. With ears lowered sadly, he left.

Amethyst twinkled quietly in the corner of Var's office, directly accessing the monitor feeds the prime synthesis scholar was watching. If they were looking for inspiration, for insight, or for answers, Amethyst had an intuition they would be staring at the screens for a long time.

7

TEARS GATHER

"Two ships from Small Home are now overdue. The first is seventeen days late. Now another is behind schedule—it is officially two days late." The traffic supervisor was young for his position but highly trained not to infer conclusions from a small number of data points. Because of this, he was blandly impassive as he reported the news to Adoption Administrator Virjel. "No traffic has arrived from the region in more than one month. We must conclude contact with Small Home has been lost."

Virjel was elderly, even by Race standards. He held onto his position as Adoption Administrator, operating from the Abundance system by sheer force of will. Many times he had said he was going to step down and emigrate to the next planet the Race adopted. For six hundred years, he had overseen the exploration and colonization of planets from Abundance, which was an adopted planet more than five thousand years before. None of the options had appealed to him nearly as much as the current jewel, Small Home. The star Caelings called Bright was inviting, and Small Home itself was so close to being a garden world that the old bones of Virjel sang each time he had visited.

Unable to believe the words coming out of the screen before him, Virjel twitched a violent negation.

The officer for Space Traffic stared back at him with open hostility. "I don't invent the news, Administrator. I am merely reporting it to you."

Virjel twitched for a digest of the last few reports from Small Home, and his intelligent system began displaying them for him on a side screen. They showed no problems. Everything appeared as it should until contact was lost. "This is unprecedented," he grated. "What could have happened?"

"Traffic from other worlds has been interrupted in the past. Perhaps the colony declared quarantine for some reason, and no outbound ships have been allowed to leave the system."

Virjel frowned. "That is most unlikely. Why, Small Home is the best we've found since adopting Abundance itself."

A shrug started in the shoulders and then flowed down the back of the traffic officer. "*Not my problem*," the movement said.

The officer showed his teeth briefly.

"I will let you know if any ships show up from Small Home, Administrator." The screen went dark with a finality that should have been accompanied by the sound of a door slamming.

Virjel considered the blank screen for a moment. Then he pulled up a list of all interstellar-capable ships in the Abundance system. He needed an outbound ship, and he needed it now. His initial thought was that any ship would do, so he set up a series of calls.

♦♦✦♦♦

The first ship to appear in normal space outside of the Small Home anomaly was a hastily commandeered freighter. It was originally bound for one of the inner systems when it was diverted, and it still carried cargo and passengers meant for Forest.

The freighter's passengers had been offered the option of disembarking and waiting for other transport, but most declined. Everyone realized that the detour to Small Home was a unique event—an adventure none of them were likely to have the opportunity to participate in again.

Several pieces of special equipment had been loaded at Abundance, and the freighter captain dropped the first of them immediately upon entering normal space—even before spotting the anomaly. The unmanned drone was one piece dropped. It was a small FTL spaceship of its own, piloted by an intelligence rated only slightly lower than a node entity. The drone was a standard tool of Exploration (or X) Corps ships, but they were never seen outside of Exploration.

The Race had long adapted to the physics of star travel. On any planet of the Race, one enjoyed instant communications and access to the entire knowledge base of civilization—modified only by the time lag of information updates carried by ships. Twenty thousand years of finding out what was happening in the next star system when a ship arrived had become natural. There was almost never a reason to need information faster. The physical appearance of a ship was always accompanied by an information storm in the mega-terabyte range. The glut of updates to databases proceeded so smoothly, it was unnoticed. These updates were, in fact, the heartbeat of civilization done Race-style.

The only exception to the Race's laconic attitude about information propagation occurred in the exploration arm. It was often not convenient for an X Corps ship to return to base when it wanted to impart important information, request additional supplies, or call for backup. Hence, the drone was used. In itself, a drone carried an impressive suite of instruments, information storage to rival a multipurpose ship, and the range to reach any number of Race planets, if needed.

The freighter intelligence began feeding instrument readings to the drone as soon as it cleared the cargo hold. The drone accepted the feeds graciously, not pointing out that its equipment was far superior. This is because, as the drone and freighter separated in space and time, the freighter's perspective on the universe might become critically important; and the drone did not want to damage a working relationship. In fact, the drone and the freighter registered the anomaly in the same instant, but the freighter spotted the debris field that had been Multipurpose Ship 115 first.

The drone dove immediately for flat space. It would make the jump the first instant it could with whatever information it had been able to glean. The confirmation of the destruction of a Race ship and the existence of the anomaly triggered the most urgent Race protection algorithms. The second of three drones was already warming up in the freighter's cargo hold to take over information gathering. The third drone would be wakened as well.

The freighter captain launched and then held a hurried conference with the two X Corps, drones, which were aided by the ship's navigation entity. Soon the freighter began accelerating again, boosting at maximum acceleration toward the site of the wreckage. Their job was to rescue survivors and determine how the ship had been destroyed. The drones split up and began a maneuver to circumnavigate the anomaly.

The next few hours were tense for the freighter captain. Although theoretically trained in space rescue operations, the captain had never actually conducted a space rescue before—certainly not an operation of these proportions. The total failure of a Race ship, especially one the size of a multipurpose ship, was unprecedented. Not only that, but the wreckage was traveling at almost three percent of the speed of light in a direction away from Small Home, and the debris field had had weeks to spread.

The freighter accelerated as best it was able, but it was sitting at a dead stop relative to the wreckage and would take many hours to catch up. The captain had only a small crew, and none had ever done a space rescue before either. One of his rated members made the brilliant suggestion to ask for volunteers among the passengers. Almost all of the passengers agreed immediately.

Few of the passengers had any shipboard experience though, and none had ever operated in the harsh environment of space outside of a spacecraft. However, soon everyone was immersed in the tutorials on space rescue in the data banks. By the time the ship reached the wreckage, many of the passengers were trained enough in extravehicular activity and extrication procedures to be of help.

Meanwhile, the two remaining drones were sending a continuous data stream back to the freighter. Over the hours, a flood of information became available. The anomaly turned out to be a featureless sphere some 10.7 light-hours in diameter. Without slowing down, the drones dropped lines of microsensors behind them. The drones would eventually gird the anomaly and periodically fire broadband bursts of energy, or streams of microparticles, at the perceived boundary of the anomaly. No usable information came back.

When the freighter finally caught up with the wreckage, it found most of the sections of Multipurpose Ship 115 intact enough to still have power and life-support functions. It was able to vector and contact those sections easily. The freighter's passengers performed rescue operations flawlessly; and soon survivors were filling up the freighter's medical bay, staterooms, and hallways.

There turned out to be very little loss of life from the accident, but there were serious injuries. One crewperson had come in from the wreckage, seemingly uninjured but in a catatonic state. The freighter's medical scholar had never seen anything like it and was at a total loss of what to do for her. Because of the diversity of issues, the medical scholar was overwhelmed but very relieved when he learned that some of the multipurpose ship's medical staff had survived and been rescued from one of the sections. He assessed them first, then gave them full access to his medical facility.

115's captain came aboard and immediately began to assist in the rescue of her crew. She briefed the freighter captain on the events that led to the destruction of her ship, and they worked to find all the survivors. As soon as the survivors were picked up and precious knowledge from Multipurpose Ship 115 had been gleaned, the freighter set course for Abundance. Eventually, the alarm carried by the freighter would result in a force of over seven hundred Race ships assembling to solve the mystery of the Small Home anomaly.

The barrier turned out to be impenetrable. No force had the slightest effect—or more properly, all energy directed at the anomaly entered the zone of displacement and vanished. The several large planetoids towed to the system and launched into the anomaly shattered, turning to dust. The large artificially generated black hole, that Race engineers hoped to use as a dimensional bridge through the zone and into Small Home space, simply sputtered and went out.

An exhaustive examination of every square meter of the structure by X Corps engineers eventually discovered a tiny structure seemingly embedded in the surface of the anomaly. It was a one-room hexagonal structure that was air-filled with a small purple wooden table and a comm unit. A personal airlock granted access to the room. Race engineers thought long and hard before opening that door; then they thought harder before anyone sat in the chair and switched on the comm unit. Eventually, though, they did.

♦♦✦♦♦

Var spent his mornings staring out the wraparound window of the meeting room, watching the sun of Small Home come into being, setting fire to the ocean. When the first rays of Bright reached deeply enough into the room to touch the furniture, he could see the purple sheen of the conference table flare slightly. He would then murmur, "Show off."

Amethyst shared his daily ritual. "Old friend, why are we sitting in a dark room, watching the sun rise over and over again?"

"Inspiration, of course. Returning to the scene of the crime, waiting for room service—take your pick."

Amethyst decided that Var was being his normal moody self. "And what inspirations do we have this morning?"

"Did you know that we are sitting at the exact center of a bubble of displaced space-time with a radius of 5.35 light-hours?"

The node entity did know this because it knew all the physical data on the phenomenon. It waited.

"Worse yet," Var continued, "I can tell you the exact center of the bubble is not just in this room but passes through the space you would occupy if you sat in the chair welded to the floor in front of the comm unit." Var deliberately raised his ears and wrinkled his nose in his best imitation of a Caeling. "And the exact center of the bubble is actually seventy centimeters above the seat, or exactly where the heart of a 1.8-meter Race being would reside. That idiot Wren just happens to be a Race male of a 1.8-meter stature."

Amethyst shaded its matrix lights in amusement. "I presume you interpret this to mean that Wren has some additional role to play in this affair and must be treated accordingly?"

"If he doesn't, then there is no sense at all to the actions of the alien—and that I don't believe." Var glared at the table.

A musical chime filled the room—once, twice, three times. Var got up from his couch, walked around the table, and stared at the comm screen. The unit had never been plugged in, so it had never operated even on the morning it was brought in for the alien's demonstration. There was no power going to it now. However, it had powered itself up and was receiving a transmission from somewhere.

Var glared at it. One more of Sansea's jokes it seemed. Var gathered his dignity like a cloak, sat in the operator's seat, and palmed the contact. Nothing happened. It chimed again.

Amethyst, monitoring the elderly prime synthesis scholar's blood pressure, worried internally. It spoke: "We know who the unit will turn on for."

Var let a ripple of disgust cross his face. "Go ahead. Call for the idiot. Maybe he can get the great Sansea to answer the call."

••✦••

Wren watched the master carver plane another thin shaving off the hardwood of the table-in-making. The table was one of two destined for Wren's own apartment once completed. Wren himself held another plane and scraped it diligently against a slab of wood that might take shape as an end table to accompany the one the master carver was sculpting. Wren's fur was covered in wood shavings. Periodically, he rippled his fur and sent bits of wood flying. The carver was used to this by now and had stopped barking at the youth every time he did it.

Wren could never remember being happier. The master carver knew only a few words of Race, but one of them was "naapo," a term Wren's sister Vega had told him was Wren's real name; and Wren did not know enough Caeling to correct him. Wren hit a knot, and his plane abruptly skipped, striking wrong and causing a gouge in the flat surface. He grimaced and sneezed.

"Do not be concerned, Naapo. You have only added many hours of work to your project." The old Caeling wrinkled his nose in good humor. Wren was paying for the tables and also for the privilege of being the carver's apprentice. The concept of an apprentice paying the master was foreign to the Caeling, but he approved of the idea and hoped it would catch on.

Before Wren could make any more costly errors, his ears caught the distinctive sound of Vega's voice asking for him outside the carver's shop. Mildly surprised, he walked to the door and looked out. She had landed next to his flight rack and was talking with one of the village children. The cub pointed to the workshop and walked away without a backward glance, acting as if flying Race members dropping in on the village were an everyday occurrence. Wren realized that was actually becoming the case this close to the Race settlement. He wondered if Vega would Remember that for her records.

He greeted his sister affectionately and managed to get wood dust on her mane. She sneezed, fluffed, and murmured, "Wren, you never change."

"And you never learn, dear sister. You should have had more brothers. Having sisters has ill-equipped you to deal with the universe."

Vega rolled her eyes and wrinkled her nose in Caeling fashion. Being taught anything by her little brother was about the most laughable thought she could imagine. Still, she told him, "You haven't answered your recall signal. It should have been impossible to ignore."

He rippled huge laughter. "That synthesist kept calling, wanting to talk about Sansea. He called over and over again. He even used Recall. I finally got a Caeling child to help me find all the power packs integrated into my flight rack and disconnect them. He stopped calling."

Vega stared. *Wren disassembled his flight rack? Wren?* Slowly, she rippled her skin from foot to head. When the ripple reached her face, she made it a gesture of respect. Wren was so pleased that he puffed out his fur in return and waggled a "*It was no big thing*" to her.

"Can you put your rack back together? We need to fly back to the city. Right now."

"Hmm, that might be a little harder. I didn't really keep track of what came off where."

This was the Wren Vega knew. She sighed. "Take my rack. I'll fix yours and then follow you."

"Why should I go back to the city? I have a table to build." Wren gestured toward the workshop. The carver stood in the doorway watching them. He bowed to Vega. She waved back distractedly.

"You need to come back right now. There's a call from outside—we are in contact with civilization beyond the anomaly."

Wren appeared puzzled. "So? What does that have to do with me?"

A touch of fury colored her voice. "Because Sansea set it up that only you can turn on the comm set. Without you, we can't talk to the outside world. I tried, and it doesn't work for me—or anyone else."

For the first time ever, Wren showed enough maturity not to tweak his sister's nose. He nodded soberly, accepted his sister's flight rack, and got ready to leave. In the end, he couldn't maintain the serious moment, calling out as he floated free of the ground. "Vega, while you are waiting, would you finish the table for me?" Then he laughed, zooming away as fast as the rack would go.

The Race member sitting in front of the comm unit in the hexagon (4.1 by 4.1 by 4.1 interior) had a passion for numbers. Her hobby was the art of numbers, her profession was the manipulation of electromagnetic wavelengths (visible/sub-visible spectrum), and her title aboard Multipurpose Ship 444 was Materials Stress Specialist. In other words, she took care of the heat and lighting on the ship. Her rating was a technical trade. She had no theoretical background and had never thought about trying for synthesist training.

She had been assigned to watch the comm unit, cheerfully announcing its "Please Wait" symbol over and over again while waiting for someone at the other end to answer the call. While she waited, she measured everything in the hexagon—not caring that every scientific specialist had already gone over the hexagon with nanometer instruments.

In her opinion, her cream-colored fur made a nice contrast to the purple iridescent shading of the hardwood table (1.4 by 1 deep by 2 to a 1,000 tolerance), and she was roughing out a sonnet in both the audible and sub-audible range to express it. A visual component was probably indicated too, she decided. She rippled her mane thoughtfully, considering slipping on her exopack and sneaking out to measure the outside of the hexagon again when the comm chimed.

The face on the screen appeared to be about her age. "Hi," he said.

In the background, a voice could be heard to say, "Get out of the chair, you fool. I need to talk to those people out there."

Wren gave the startled woman a wave, flashed a quick "*Pleased to meet you*" ripple, then gave way to an elderly Race male who reminded her of a tiny pet thara she had as a cub. *Just as ferocious and intense and faintly comical,* she thought . . . until her relay link flashed recognition that this was Prime Synthesis Scholar Var, which prompted her to immediately notify Expedition Leadership.

Adoption Administrator Virjel had been closest when the Materials Stress Specialist technician's call came, so he was the first person through the pressure curtain. The technician gave him the chair immediately.

Var, every bit as old as Virjel and knowing Virjel for over eight hundred years said, "Not you! This isn't an administrative problem. This is an alien incursion problem. I need people who can think!"

The prime X Corps synthesist in charge of the anomaly investigation team came through the pressure curtain in time to hear this. Ath was not surprised by Var's statement. The Anomaly Investigation Team had long known the barrier was the work of intelligent design, leaving only the how and why to be determined . . . and what to do about it.

"I am here. Var, please commence your report on the alien incursion." The prime X Corps synthesist moved into monitor range and stood behind Virjel.

Var's mane snapped out in delight. "Ath, it is good to see you. Is the investigation being handled by the Exploration Corps then?"

The prime synthesis scholar nodded. "Every X Corps vessel and specialist on this side of the galaxy is here. Over seven hundred Race vessels and all the brain trust that we could scrounge from the breath of civilization are here. We have been trying to bridge the space and time gap surrounding your colony for weeks now. We are aware of over sixty thousand ways to fail at the engineering of an appropriate stile or bridge."

Ath rippled wry amusement. "The mathematics indicate that your isolation cannot be complete; otherwise, your bubble of independent space and time would have migrated out of our universe and become its own. And of course, we are able to communicate with you, which also confirms this. So, we keep trying."

Var got a faraway look for a moment. "Quantum tunneling."

"None of the black holes we've grown on the surface of our side of the anomaly twinned on your side. Many sorts of dimensional folding schema also failed to thread the space-time gap. No version of theoretical wormhole construction has worked. The region is dynamically maintained—not a static phenomenon—but we have failed to find or cut off any theoretic power source maintaining the anomaly."

"Have you considered crashing a small star into the barrier?"

Ath stared at him for a moment. "Success would be more catastrophic than failure, wouldn't you think?" he said dryly.

Var nodded abruptly. "Sorry, I may be losing my detachment in dealing with this situation. I suppose having another sun punch through five light-hours from Small Home would play hell with the system—if it got through."

Var straightened and made a movement outside the screen. "Data coming to you now at maximum compression and volume. We've included everything we gathered. Please pay particular attention to all interviews and extrapolations with and about the alien. For some reason when first encountered, it was masquerading as a barely mature Caeling and has never given up that appearance. It seemed to befriend two of our most youthful race members, a sister and brother on a visit to a Caeling village. When invited back to the settlement, it made preposterous claims of supernatural abilities and then pulled this stunt."

Var took a deep breath. "Not in an attempt to prejudice your assessment of our situation, but my strongly held opinion is this miscreant has some sort of hero complex and is trying to prove something too arcane to fathom . . . at our expense. If you can figure out a way to thwart it, I would be most gratified."

After arranging the next conference time, Var signed off, leaving the comm in the hands of technicians. Ath turned to the slighted Virjel and cocked one ear. Virjel sighed and rippled a shoulder. Both knew how difficult Var was, and they were his species. It was no stretch of the imagination that an alien would find him difficult too. Both returned to their teams, knowing the teams were already digging into the new information for insights and possible directions to consider.

The next morning, Virjel and Ath were back in the hexagon at the agreed time for the meeting and waited for Var to appear. They knew that this conference with the crusty prime synthesis scholar would be unpleasant. Var appeared a moment later, looking hopeful. "Well, what have you got?"

Ath took the lead. "After exhaustive analysis of your data, we determined with surprise that no one has asked the alien what it wants. Please arrange to have the alien talk to us so we can begin parlay."

Var looked outraged. "That is your solution? Didn't you review the part where I reported the alien has disappeared, and we have not been able to find him since the day this fiasco began? Are you all morons up there?"

Virjel, his features solemn, traced a ripple of great respect and inserted gently, "Prime Synthesis Scholar, I think the alien has been waiting for us to realize we need to talk to him. Ask the young ones to contact him. Would you do that for us?"

Var punched off the comm without speaking.

Virjel rippled an ear.

"Oh, he heard us, old friend." Ath shrugged. "He heard us."

A QUESTION IS ASKED

Once again Wren stood over his end table, this time learning how plant esters were gathered and processed to make the stain he was about to apply to the wood. The raw wood's smooth surface and finely fitted legs seemed perfect to Wren, but the master carver disagreed. After the stain would come varnish, another process including both plant and mineral distillations, and finally Wren would have his tables.

A chirping filled the room, and the pitch was low enough to be pleasant to Race ears. The tiny comm chip Wren had printed on his shirt, twin to Vega's and tuned only to her device, asked for his attention. He twitched it on.

In a delighted voice, he said, "Vega, you should see my tables. When are you coming out?"

"Hello to you, too, brother. I'm not coming out. It's time to come in. Please ask Sansea to come to me. Our people gather beyond the anomaly and want to talk with him."

"Why should he listen to me? He invited me to walk the world with him when I was ready. That is all he did. I'm not yet ready for that."

"Please, Wren."

"Okay, what do I do? Climb to a mountain village, then climb a tree, and *then* shout at the top of my lungs?"

"Please, Wren." Vega's voice was steady with only a slight edge of impatience.

Wren sighed expressively. "Fine. Your naapo brother will save the day again. But I'm only going to climb a tree in this village. I've had enough rope ladders for a couple of Caeling lifetimes."

Wren twitched off the link and walked to the wood carver's door. He stood still for a moment thinking and then whispered into the breeze. "Traveler, my sister needs you. All that you've done has made my sister very unhappy."

He stopped, reflected, and started again. "That is not entirely true. Vega has a weight on her heart that she has carried all the years I've known her. You have only made it worse. She asks this of you . . . and so do I."

Returning to his table, Wren picked up a brush and started with the long even strokes the carver had shown him. He wrinkled his nose gleefully and muttered. "If any rememberer ever asks, I climbed a very tall tree."

••✦••

Vega paced in the hallway outside the meeting room, communicator clutched in her hand. *Will Wren be able to contact him? Will Sansea listen? Does Sansea even care about what he has done?* She felt the tiniest breeze and turned. Sansea stood in the doorway. She frowned, "So, you do listen to Wren."

"Your brother has a very uncomplicated view of the world. I like it. I like him."

"Will you now talk to my people who live in a more complicated world, Sansea? Or will you continue to play with us?"

The alien looked hurt. "I assure you, Vega, your people are not toys for my amusement."

Vega walked to the doorway and planted herself before Sansea, fury in every line. "Are we not your toys? Did I really ask for this crisis the day we met? Did I ask you to steal us away from our people? Did I ask you to show us how deeply inferior the Race is to one 'traveler' who holds us in such contempt so that we are powerless in the palm of his hand?"

As she talked, Sansea's spots shaded to grey and entirely disappeared. A very simple pattern reappeared, making him almost an outline of a Caeling. His reply was gentle, "The events unfolding are not your fault, Vega. Indeed, meeting any member of the Race would have precipitated these events."

Sansea continued in a quiet voice. "But having met you and the entity Amethyst, I am more optimistic and much encouraged. Had I only known the likes of Var, I would fear much that the future is a bleaker place."

Vega turned, and Sansea followed her into the meeting room with its purple table and communicator. He nodded gravely to Var who growled back deep in his throat. Sansea's spots flared gloriously vivid black. With a nose wrinkle and twinkling eye, he turned and greeted the node entity; and that entity returned the twinkle with every shade of purple in the spectrum. Sansea took his place in front of the comm and palmed the contact. Var muttered something acerbic.

Adoption Administrator Virjel and Prime X Corps Synthesist Ath came to quiet attention as the comm activated and a young, healthy-looking Caeling appeared on the screen. They looked at the alien with great curiosity. If all the data gathered about the events leading up to the formation of the anomaly were accurate, this one discrete individual was responsible for all the amazing phenomena that had taken place in this tiny star system.

A strong minority opinion, led by Ath himself, held that the alien could not be just an individual lifeform but must be, in some way, the avatar of a greater lifeform or colony of lifeforms living in some fashion in, but perhaps not, of the normal space-time continuum. Whatever the truth might turn out to be, he greeted the putative colony organism with respect. "I am Ath, Prime Synthesist of the Race's Exploration Corps. I understand your name means 'traveler' or 'teacher.' May I address you with the title 'Teacher'?"

Sansea looked pleased. Spots flashed, and he bowed. "I will accept that title. And may I know your companion as well?"

Virjel stepped forward. "Please call me Virjel. I am Administrator of the Adoption Process of Cael, which we have been calling Small Home. At the present time, you seem to have put up an impassible barrier around Small Home, trapping our colony inside and not incidentally imprisoning the native Caelings as well. Would you be kind enough to explain the reason for this action?"

Sansea nodded. "A question first, if you please. Can you speak for the Race as a whole?"

The back of Virjel's shoulders rippled violently. Ath inclined his head in polite negation. "Ah, Teacher Sansea, our Race numbers are above one trillion individuals. Civilization is spread out over much of this arm of the galaxy. We walk under the light of many stars. No individual can speak for all of civilization. But I will carry your words to every member of the Race, if you require it. We will do our best to accommodate all your questions and requests, especially if they will lead to the removal of this barrier."

Sansea nodded at Ath's answer. It was a logical, well-thought-out reply that was completely without substance. However, Sansea was sure he had their full attention. "I believe the barrier can come down in time. In fact, it certainly will as soon as I have the answer to one question."

Virjel blurted, "All this for one question? Certainly. What is it?" Ath cocked an ear at the administrator and sighed. The reports on the alien had been right—it loved to use narrative hooks. There was nothing to do but play along. He maintained his silence, reflecting that Var may have had cause to be irritated by this creature.

"Forgive me," Sansea replied. "It will take a moment to set up the question. I shall begin with a bit of background. I first met your people only a few months ago, but it became clear almost immediately that our association needed to go back many years—more than twenty thousand years."

Ath maintained a polite stance keeping his mane calm and unruffled. Below the level of the comm screen, his private link from staff fed real-time analysis of the alien's every word and gesture to him. His own instincts jumped at the two-hundred-century figure mentioned by the alien. Before he could track down the source of his unease, the alien went on.

"This association is very crucial to my question. In fact, I do believe that our association will continue for quite some time, perhaps as long as another thousand years." Sansea stopped and looked carefully at the X Corps synthesist and administrator, locking eyes with them one at a time.

"I am giving you that much time to answer my question. I will tell you that I am very hopeful that you will be able to find an acceptable answer within that time frame. To avoid distractions, I will be turning off the communication device we are using until an acceptable answer is found. Good luck." Sansea closed his eyes and appeared to lapse into deep thought. The transmission ended.

Ath remained composed but snapped out a command on the Expedition Corps network. Ships throughout the sector went on high alert. The question had been asked—or was about to be asked—he wasn't sure which was the case. To Virjel's puzzled ripple, he gave a distracted shrug.

Meanwhile, changes were occurring on the surface of the anomaly. Patches first and then whole areas began to brighten. Swirls of radiance in complex patterns rose, became coronas, and reached outward, first meters and then kilometers in height.

"Fall back," Ath ordered. "Initiate dynamic englobement pattern."

All around the anomaly, ships went into action. A few with volunteer crews, such as Ath's and Virjel's, stayed put to observe at close hand whatever was about to transpire. The bulk of the fleet retreated in orderly groups to prearrange locations and set up concentric formations of ships with overlapping sensor webs. The outermost formation would form more than a quarter light-year out.

Virjel twitched a grim and sardonic ear at Ath who said, "Yes, it has been good knowing you too, but don't compose yourself for oblivion yet . . . I feel we are in for a show first. I may have to admit to an agreement in principle with Var on the nature of our alien. He wants to entertain us while he is doing whatever else it is he is doing. Since we do not have a choice, I am prepared to be entertained."

Reports poured in from the innermost globe while the outer formations retreated at maximum speed. A curtain of light emerged from the back wall and swept the room. All around the anomaly, the curtain of light was tracked. Yet, the important event was noted by Virjel and Ath's own senses. Ath turned to Virjel to comment that the alien was repeating itself when he noticed acceleration figures being reported.

"Our first innovation is that the speed of this bubble is higher—much higher. In fact, it's reached one percent photonic already."

Three concentric formations of ships fell back at faster and faster rates. Eventually, the bubble exceeded the maximum velocity of the multipurpose ships. As the visible bubble of light expanded to engulf the inner ring of ships, Ath came to a decision. "Group Inward, the phenomenon is about to overtake you. Report any variation from previously reported experience. As soon as you reach flat space, jump ahead of the phenomenon and do it again."

Virjel nodded judiciously. "And if they are unable to jump out past the curtain of light?"

Ath considered for a moment. "Why, then we will all have time for deep and meaningful discussions on the nature of art and physics . . . and whatever else we can think of while waiting for the alien to get tired of toying with us."

The prime X Corps synthesist stood up, stretched, and rippled his skin from foot to head and back again. Then he sighed. "I'm going back to the ship. Care to join me for a run?"

Virjel stared for a moment longer at the inert communication device melded to the purple table. He punched the "On" switch a couple of times. It did not obediently turn on. He shrugged. "There is nothing else I can think of doing. I will come."

Yet, the ships discovered it was possible to jump out of the expanding bubble of light. Eventually, Group Inward and Group Median entered into a game of leapfrog, each endeavoring to emerge in front of the expanding wave before letting it sweep over them again and again. The experience never varied regardless of how fast the wave was traveling—and forward instruments tracked it expanding deeper into space. Eventually, the wave reached light speed and kept accelerating.

Group Outward kept falling back, never letting the wave touch them. In a few hours, the wave's acceleration stabilized at sixteen times faster than light. When it stayed that way for five days, Ath was satisfied that was going to be its maximum propagation rate. At this point, the bubble was eighty light-days across and was still a globe radiating precisely the same light as the moment of its creation. The power requirements to maintain the phenomenon were almost incalculable.

Distance had neatly isolated all the ships of the Expedition Corps. The volume of space was too big for rapid communication. Ath regretfully dissolved the expedition into three components: Group Inward would return to the anomaly around Small Home and continue the original mission of seeking a way through the barrier. The second group was comprised of ships that had surfed through the curtain of light hundreds of times. They broke immediately for Abundance to undergo extensive debriefing and medical testing to see if there were any effects of crossing the curtain that had not been found by the ships' personnel. Group Outward was essentially released to detached duty so that each ship would continue to retreat from the phenomenon in all directions—for years if necessary—to determine when, or if, the bubble stopped expanding.

Virjel was confused by Ath's decisions. "Why are one-third of our ships returning to Abundance?" he asked. "The anomaly still stands in the way of our colony. It is better to bring them back to Small Home to assist in our rescue efforts."

Ath turned away from the virtual presentation of the expanding wavefront. He rippled his face thoughtfully. "The mystery of the phenomenon is not solved. Six months, my friend. That's all the time we have to be sure the wave is harmless. In six months, the wave expands through the Abundance system, striking Abundance itself. There are twenty-four billion of our people on Abundance. So far, we know of no way to stop the wave, no way to shield from it. And we have no proof that it is indeed harmless. This is going to be a very long six months."

He returned to the contemplation of the wavefront while the globe of light in the field got infinitesimally larger as they watched. Virjel shivered. Slowly, his pelt flattened. He had never considered the wave could travel the whole ten light-years to Abundance. Now it seemed certain it would. This was indeed disturbing. For the first time, he felt the helplessness that the Race members inside the anomaly were undoubtedly feeling. He didn't like the situation and the feeling one bit.

9

A FIRST TEAR FALLS

The Abundance system was surrounded by Race instruments, all the devices the X Corps could bring into play from half the galaxy. The planet itself wore a cloak of technology so dense it blocked the stars. On command, a planetary shield would come into being stronger than anything in Race memory.

Interposed six light-months ahead of the system, a test station the size of a small moon stood between the wave and Abundance. In the time available, Race engineers at the test station reproduced all of the planet's ecosystem, duplicating every minute detail. One entire island had been removed of people (quite a feat considering a global population of twenty-four billion), then separated from the planet and lifted into space, reproducing en-toto the planetary ecology.

In the weeks after the wave lapped the test station, passed through it, and continued on its way toward Abundance, researchers turned the test station inside out, looking for anything out of the usual. They found no perceptible effects on flora or fauna.

Ath, who recently returned from investigating the anomaly around Small Home, should have been relieved or at least encouraged. He was neither. In fact, he wished he still had that old fool Var to talk to. Before communication with Small Home ceased, Var had insisted the alien was too devious to be trusted. "It was only showing us what it wanted us to see," he'd said.

Like that impossible wave, thought Ath. *We have been tracking a bubble of light nearly ten light-years across and spreading through space at sixteen times the speed of light.*

"Yes, the impossible wave," Ath murmured. He shook his head.

He was currently looking out the observation port at the temporary space city below. In an abstract way, he was proud of the vista. Two hundred and thirty ships and more than twenty-five thousand Race synthesists, technicians, explorers, and ordinary spacers had braved the wave hundreds of times and then rushed here to be placed in isolation and analyzed as intensively as the Race knew how to study its own kind.

Every ship had been disassembled during the study and reassembled component by component for any clues left behind by the phenomenon. Twenty of the huge multipurpose ships had been reduced to atoms and plasma in an effort to find any wave effects. Nothing was found. The volunteers were treated more gently but nearly as thoroughly.

Now, five days before the wave reached Abundance itself, Ath sat in self-imposed isolation and worried. What was he missing? Was the wave a cosmic joke the alien was playing on the Race with no more meaning than the massive soap bubble it resembled? The phenomenon itself appeared to have no effect on the objective universe. In fact, by some standards of physics, even though the wave could be perceived by senses and instruments, in other ways it probably did not exist at all because no current model of reality could explain its behavior.

Yes, the Alien certainly has our attention. The Race has mobilized more resources and brainpower over this crisis than any effort in recorded history. It must mean something, but what?

A tiny unobtrusive light flashed at the limit of Ath's peripheral vision. Someone was trying to reach him with a priority call. If he had been in deep contemplation, he would not have noticed it. The Race had lived with interactive artificial intelligences for thousands of years. Ath expected this system to anticipate his every need and desire. It knew what level of call to inform him and what call to hold. He could not honestly remember a system choosing wrongly. He accepted the call.

An individual Ath had never seen before appeared on the screen. The flash below her image identified her as Senior Organism Lifecycle Synthesist Berra. Ath rippled a courteous greeting across his face and tufted his ears in inquiry. "I regret we have not met before, Lifecycle Synthesist. How may I help you?"

Her face rippled nervously as she groped for words. Ath watched her ears flatten and felt his response. A chill enveloped him. *As bad as that?*

"X Corps Synthesist Ath, will you join us in a conference—right now?"

Ath nodded. He twitched for a seat; and his quarters disappeared, overlaid by a virtual conference room already in session. He noted three node entities and seven Race around the conversation pit and then a fourth node appeared in the virtual chamber. Senior Organism Lifecycle Synthesist Berra began speaking at once.

"Thank you for permitting a recess until everyone was assembled. Prime Exploration Corps Synthesist Ath and honored knowledge and philosophy node entities, welcome." She stood up and rippled an apology.

"My branch of study has found a possible problem. We did not know it was a problem because, being familiar with the customs of X Corps and ship crews in general, we saw what we expected to see. We have found that among the crews of ships passing through the wave, there have been no pregnancies or births."

Ath felt momentary confusion. There were no pregnancies—so what? Race members who dedicated their working lives to X Corps routinely suppressed fertility during their duty years. The universe is a strange place, and the Race will only create children under the most harmonious circumstances and in the safest environments. It would be insane to have children under any other circumstances. However, his understanding grew as the lifecycle synthesist continued speaking.

"This did not alarm us. All physical exams concluded that all personnel were healthy. Tests appeared to show that fertility was normal in all persons. For those who may not know, everyone joining X Corps pauses his or her ability to conceive. Because of this, it is almost by accident the problem I bring forth was discovered. During this wave crisis, a number of X Corps personnel reached the end of their contracted careers, so they decided to send for mates and begin families. In some cases, X Corps personnel mated with non-Exploration Corps members; in others, X Corps personnel mated with each other. In the last two months, the ability to conceive has been restored to 137 persons who have passed through the wave. Yet, so far, no pregnancies have resulted. We do not know why." The senior organism lifecycle synthesist sat down like a deflating balloon.

A profound silence gripped the table. One of the Race's prime characteristics is calm in crisis. Yet, the possible ramifications of this discovery exceeded the ability of most of the beings at the table to absorb—much less deal with—the news.

The node entity spoke gently. "Exploration Corps members have historically lower fertility rates than Race norm."

Lifecycle Synthesist Berra barely rippled one ear. "Long term, three percent," she mumbled. "Short term, meaning ten years or less, as much as fifty percent. Still, we would expect several dozen successful pregnancies by this time."

Now Ath signaled for the floor. His voice was intense. "25,407 individuals now in quarantine on this city have passed through the wave. It's time to ask them to volunteer for one more experiment. Each will be asked permission to have their fertility restored and asked to procreate—in a great hurry! I have never asked anyone to complete a more bizarre mission for the X Corps." His shoulders rippled in an attempt at wry amusement even though he felt anything but gay. The alien threat had turned serious.

"We have to consider evacuation." Lifecycle Synthesist Berra's words had a flatness that was palpable.

The prime technology synthesist shrugged. He had said nothing up to this moment. His skin rippled with sadness. "We did consider evacuation several months ago but not seriously. Removing twenty-four billion in less than years would have been a Herculean task. It did not seem advisable to try. Now . . . now we could only snatch up perhaps a few million and still not be sure of getting them to safety. I think we are going to have to see how well the shield works."

Planetary defense was not Ath's specialty, but he privately agreed with the decision to stay put. It had been difficult to work up a genuine fear of this phenomenon, even though he saw firsthand the power of the alien. Now he fervently hoped the problem found by Senior Organism Lifecycle Synthesist Berra was an aberration—or at least a problem easier to solve than moving a planetary population.

♦♦✦♦♦

Five days was too short a time to resolve the infertility problem considering the slow biology of the Race, although intense study was ongoing. The citizens of Abundance had been notified of the problem, and evacuation had been offered. A few elected to leave, and there were enough ships available to take them. The rest chose to stay in their homes and trust Race technology. A planetary shield was not the only defense decided. Some of the ongoing measures included deep sea submersion structures and deep earth centers, each with room for millions.

At wave-minus thirty seconds, the shield began building in layers. Twilight fell on Abundance, and then darkness was so complete that it was as if the universe had been stolen. Around the planet, a sphere of brightness was built until it shined brighter than some stars, reflecting every form of energy known.

At minus ten seconds, the last shield layer formed a zone that blocked the interaction of weak and strong nuclear forces and gravity itself. Cut off from the attraction of its star, Abundance began to move out of orbit, gliding out of the dance it had followed for billions of years with its yellow-red primary. If the Race kept the shields up very long, the orbital perturbation would become an extreme—perhaps fatal—problem. Of course, if the shields stayed very long, the planet would begin to die from lack of sunlight and other causes.

Fortunately, the wave was right on time still traveling sixteen times the speed of light. It hit, merged with the shields, and went through that defense. All Race saw was a line of light, which swept over them. The last child was conceived at that moment beneath an ink-black sky. She was born sixteen months later. Her name was Anya.

10

SMALL BEGINNINGS

"Anya, stop trying to outrun your thara."

The girl pivoted on the path and leaned left, body language suggesting a dash to that side. The family's thara had chased her for more than a minute at full hunting speed across a huge portion of the meadow when one of Anya's fathers shouted at her in consternation. Father Lek had seen the old fellow was at its limit.

Still, the stubby creature gamely pushed on, panting madly with carnivore muzzle open in a frothy grin and having the time of its life. The thara was old; and Anya was very young (not yet twenty summers), so she was the only one to make it exercise this way. Anya knew that tharas lived to chase prey, so it was never happier than right now. While she was from a different lineage and evolved under a different sun with lean lines that in no way resembled the thara, hunters were the same under every sun. Running was fun!

Anya completed her pivot and jumped right instead of left. The chaser knew Anya intimately, anticipating her move perfectly and veering right at the same moment. Anya laughed madly as she bent to scoop up the little creature, spinning round and round to absorb its momentum. It howled happily and nipped at her arms. Carrying it back to the family, Anya never paid attention to the fact that she was the youngest person in the park. She would try not to notice that for many years. Everyone else pretended the same.

Anya's generation had been monitored intensely from the moment of their births, but Anya herself had been studied more intently than most. There was no way to distinguish her from a billion other children born before her—she measured to Race norms in every way. Yet, because of the timing of her birth, researchers hoped to find something—anything—that was different. Finding nothing frustrated the researchers over and over again.

Her seeming normality was comforting to her family, however. They had closed ranks early in Anya's babyhood and forced all the scholars of all the institutes to perform remote monitoring only. Anya never saw the inside of a lab; and if her home was loaded with esoteric gear inside the walls, she never knew.

Anya thought she was like any other child and, like any other child, it was normal that many strangers would visit her parents. It seemed normal that they all wanted to meet her. Plus, she loved meeting her parents' friends. Her parents seemed to know people from all disciplines and from all over the world. They even received visitors from off of the planet. It was so much fun; yet, over time, she began to understand something very odd was going on.

♦♦✦♦♦

"I don't know what the big deal is. I just haven't decided yet." Anya glared.

Her family, especially Lek, seemed to be giving her their complete attention. Was Lek smiling ever so slightly? Were her other mothers and fathers looking at her with a bit of consternation or, worse yet, sympathy?

The family common area was spacious, well-appointed, and more than a little claustrophobic. Seven full adults versus one newly adult child seemed like formidable odds unless that child was Anya. Clearly the most stubborn child on the planet, Anya was used to getting her way, which might be why all her family happened to be home right now. Normally, some or all of them might be in far-flung locations around the world, pursuing various careers and coming home whenever they could.

In her memory, her family were very tall people, moving with grace and speaking with beauty, teaching her to appreciate the world, to be a wonderful person, and to be a member of the Race, in other words. They were still the same people they had been, but now Anya felt they were smaller and seemed to take less space. Anya refused to see that they might be a little older as well because that couldn't happen to her parents—it only happened to other people's parents.

"I am obviously not ready to choose. Why shouldn't I wait a little?"

Her youngest mother Reeth sighed and said, "Oh, Anya."

Anya stood up straighter. "I am not 'Oh, Anya,' Mother. I am an adult and can make my own choices."

Reeth nodded. Her voice was filled with compassion. "I understand more than you can know, my daughter. I, too, had to face the choice of advanced training. I was eighty years old, like you are today. I had just become an adult with full adult basic training, and I was happy with that. All my agemates had already picked their first careers. Some, I knew, were destined to become primes of their professions. But I couldn't choose."

Reeth was only two hundred years old herself, and the youngest of Anya's parents. She thought she understood her daughter best. Anya wasn't so sure. Her situation wasn't the same at all.

Father Lek put in, "You are eighty today. We are all very happy for you. We have all gathered here to celebrate and wish you well. But there are some things you can't put off."

Reeth rippled a small frown at Lek. She continued as if Lek hadn't interrupted, "I knew advanced training wasn't for me. I was not the adventurous type. All I wanted to do was be a homebody and build a life around a place and a family. So, I refused advanced training. I was lucky that at the very young age of one hundred, I found these wonderful people and was welcomed into this wonderful marriage."

Reeth came over and placed an arm around her daughter. Anya sighed but did not shrug it off. This emboldened her mother, so she continued.

"Anya, you have an adventurous nature. You always want to know what is on the next mountain, the next valley. You are not a homebody. All your agemates have made their choices and are pursuing them. It is your turn to pursue your destiny."

"Oh, mother. How can I pick any of these paths? You talk about agemates as if I *have* any." Anya rippled a violent negative across her mother's arm, and her voice became rough. "Look around you. Look at our family, at our town. Do you see agemates? Do you see anyone coming up behind me to fill my spot as a child?"

Anya sat down abruptly on the floor. She wanted to scream at Mother Reeth, "You are lucky! You got to choose to be a mother and to join a marriage just because you wanted to! Where are my choices? Even if I join a marriage, I won't have any children. I don't have a destiny. The Wave made sure of that!"

Anya lowered her head and mumbled into her hands, "Seventeen of the most prestigious disciplines have invited me to study with them to follow the path to prime with them. They are all holding their schools open for one last student. When I choose one, the others will close for there are *no more* students. How can I be responsible for that? Doesn't that make me a monster? Don't make me choose for I cannot choose that."

Father Lek sighed and nodded. He sat on the floor with Anya. Her other parents settled on settees and gave them room. He wanted to say everything was going to be alright because he and everyone in her family had tried to make so many things in her life right. He wanted to say parents could make everything better, but they couldn't. After eighty years of Race civilization trying to fix the problem, they were no closer to solving the Race's lost fertility.

Anya leaned against him, looking childlike. "Advanced training is not my calling. If I am going to be a wanderer and have no roots, then let that be my path."

Father Lek wanted to say, "If you ever change your mind—ever—I have private communications from many primes who are willing to take you on as their student and apprentice . . . when you are ready. And they mean that. Anytime you are ready, my daughter. Anytime." He could not say this, though. Not then and perhaps never. He hugged her instead. They all did.

FIVE HUNDRED YEARS OF TEARS

The hot afternoon sun basted the right side of the barge with so much enthusiasm Anya could almost believe they were still in the tropics. It was no matter that the instruments reported the leisurely-moving barge had officially entered the temperate zone days before, tracing a meandering course. They had been moving north, following the spine of a truly impressive mountain range; yet, the temperature was scarcely milder than it had been a thousand miles south, though, the humidity had fortunately dropped.

So much of the team's work had turned into routine these last few years that Anya's first sight of City 224 was a surprise. The city did not conform to the usual design. First, it was small—no more than ten million had ever called it home. There was also no building higher than one hundred stories. The northern end spread into a district of low-lying structures that ran along both sides of a large lake.

The lake had all the appearance of a natural formation, not sculpted at all. There were no multitude of harmonious inlets and grottos. Instead, there was just a straight shoreline that went on for miles, making it seem an obvious waste of resources. *I can't imagine why they did that*, Anya thought.

The southern part formed at the base of the lake to become a thick trunk of towering buildings, pleasant byways, artful parks, and restful glades. It appeared totally normal until her eye came across what appeared to be the most peculiar intrusion of nature Anya had ever seen: In the middle of the metropolis was a completely irregular patch of forest a good ten miles long and at least five wide complete with gentle hills, glens, and mountain streams.

The low mountains surrounding the park would have made access very inconvenient. Anya could see no point to it at all. A thought teased the back of her mind that she wouldn't be able to see any buildings from inside the forest, but she could see no value in that, so she dismissed it.

"This is an odd one," she murmured.

"Would you look at that strange jungle they left in the middle of town," snorted Sotheel.

"Wood, not jungle." Anya rippled her face in annoyance.

"Okay, Child. It's a forest, not a wood. So what?" Sotheel barely rippled the skin of her shoulders.

Anya tightened her pelt but made no other gesture. Sotheel was so good at looking innocent that it made Anya want to growl. Her pet name on the woman's lips was an old annoyance. It had pleased her to be Child when she was younger—when her parents used it and when the Elders used it. Now it was a reminder of a time past—a reminder she didn't want.

Anya twitched a command, and the barge hovered. She touched a contact on her board, and the first wave of low-intelligence Looksees dropped out of the bay. She glanced over her shoulder, "We have work to do. Whose turn is it to pick the campsite?"

In the back of the barge, Brim stood up and waved. He was long-limbed and lean like so many of the Race. With short and tan fur, a short and clipped black mane, and merry black eyes, his features beamed with good humor. The shortest of their group, he was also the oldest by a good hundred years, which did not make him that much older, just more mature, at least in theory.

Anya rippled one shoulder and sighed. Brim was predictable; he always picked the top of the tallest building in town to set up basecamp, claiming the views were inspirational. Dropping the remaining Looksees, Anya directed the barge toward the largest building on the skyline. While the Looksees spread out to cover the town, she made sure the barge would fit on top of the building. Brim might be right about high locations. The team would have a fine view of the lake on one side and the woods on the other.

Anya had never been here when this city was alive—while people lived and loved and created beauty in its canyons. She had no idea what the city's name was, nor did it matter. To her, it was another site for preservation. Her generation had decided this was their mission in life—to be preservers of a legacy. A whole generation was involved. Yet, for her, it was a job; and she was sick of it.

With the sun low and red behind her, Anya approached the building and settled the barge on the roof. In the small common area, Vorne was lounging on an opposing settee from his full brother, Taem. They were the only siblings from the same parents Anya had ever met, and both stopped their playback of orbital views and continental industrial stats to stand behind Anya. They squinted through the view window and looked at the city for the first time. Taem leaned over Anya's shoulder and looked north to get a glimpse of the lake.

Anya forestalled any possible comment. "I will take the lake district in the morning," she said. *Preferably alone. Definitely alone.*

Anya went to sleep last. Her cinnamon eyes remained open in the darkness until regular breathing throughout the barge told the deepest part of her brain that her companions slept. Finally, she relinquished her grip on consciousness. Nonetheless, she was in motion before first light and first out of the barge.

Her minimal sleep patterns were one of the oddities the others had gotten used to. She was also bossy, whimsical, and moody. That her moods followed definite patterns linked to the time of year was something she would not face and something the others had also gotten used to. Anya was Anya, unique and special . . . and she hated this.

The last minutes of the night found her flying along shimmering white sand, following the western shore. The sky was that limitless black that precedes the dawn. A region of infinite black water, sad and serene, paced her right shoulder. Her flight rack carried her effortlessly through the sky, silent as the breeze. Silent, too, were the Looksees, companion doves to Anya's sweeping hawk.

Soon dawn would come over the water, and the land would light with fairy greens and browns. The cool predawn air was a delightful tonic, and she twitched her travel cloth to open weave. The wind caressed the short, dark fur of her arms, and a ripple of pleasure she would never have let the others see flowed across her back.

When she saw a house set back surprisingly far from the water, she was intrigued. Modest in size, it was configured as a mixed water-dwelling and should have been half over the water with its lower bay awash. She wondered why the previous owners had moved it. Without conscious thought, she turned to land on its deck. She twitched a command to her flock of Looksees, and they spread out to make an independent assessment of the other lake dwellings.

Tall silvered doors set in a sweeping arch opened at her approach. She shrugged off her flight rack and stepped through into a pleasant airy room that covered the whole top level. It was a family room with a pale marble floor flecked with gold and onyx, throw rugs, low settees, and a minimal kitchen unit near the far wall. By the size of the house, she knew the family unit would have probably numbered nine or ten adults with two or perhaps three children.

Because she had left her link on, the flight rack heard her question of *"Why is this structure so far from the water?"* It answered: "The lake is at a forty-seven-year low. When the inhabitants closed this structure, it could have been at the water's edge."

Anya was surprised. "This house was inhabited as recently as forty-seven years ago?"

"Negative." The limited intelligence Rack tried to convey it had not meant to give inaccurate information. "The last inhabitants left this city 153 years ago. This structure must have been closed down at that time. The lake has risen and fallen several times in the last 153 years due to mildly changing climatic conditions."

"Hmmm." She gave a mental shrug and continued to wander through the house. She had grown up in a house very much like this one. In her mind's eye, she filled this house with laughter, the sound of running children, and happy adults. She felt warm in a way that surprised her.

On the ground floor, she entered an artist's lab. A small Omni kiln sat in the corner under a light protective shroud. The artist had obviously set it to produce the beautiful stone flooring. Tiny marble figures graced a shelf and table. In the far corner, something very tall was covered with another light shroud.

Anya crossed the room and pulled off the shroud of thin cloth. The cloth slithered to the floor revealing a woman about Anya's height all worked in alabaster. She was exquisitely rendered. Her upturned face rippled with joy as she gazed at a laughing child that she had raised high in her arms.

The statue radiated such happiness that Anya was caught unprepared. For a crazy instant, she saw herself holding the baby, laughing with the universe. The pain of knowing her destiny was stolen drove her to the doorway. Panting to ease a deep anguish, she forced herself to keep looking. *It's only art, and art cannot harm you, can it?*

Leaving the statue unshrouded, Anya walked back upstairs and onto the deck. The sun peeked over the rim of the world, flooding the land with cool radiance. The lake sparkled with the promise of a beautiful day. She shrugged herself onto the flight rack and began giving orders.

"Determine the highest flood line ever recorded for this lake and then extrapolate for the thousand-year-high water mark. Move this house to that line and begin preservation protocol." She paused in thought. "I want a full museum preservation of this site. Put all ground floor artwork in sealed cases with an inert atmosphere. Then seal the whole structure and evacuate the air, replacing it with inert gas. Encapsulate structure three times."

That should do it, she thought. *Or . . . maybe not.* It was time to be unconventional. "When preservation is complete, construct a hull metal shed around the entire structure." She floated into the air and saw a high-intelligence construction tender heading her way. "Wait—before sealing make a sweep through all lake structures looking for comparable artwork and transfer anything found to this house before preservation is initiated."

There, she thought smugly. *That will do it.*

♦♦✦♦♦

Dinner at basecamp was a noisy affair with Brim extolling how successful he was, how many buildings still had power, how the town's intelligent network had kept the community core in good repair, and how the people had mostly tidied up the community before they walked away. His mood was jolly, and his gestures were expressive. Sotheel had found manufacturing facilities missing; they had been shipped somewhere else a century before. She announced her discovery with dour satisfaction. Vorne and Taem had covered several museums. They were already in a state of preservation that just needed updating and strengthening. In one day, the group felt they had covered the most important ten percent of the city and were well on their way to cataloging its riches.

Brim stopped his conversation with Vorne for a moment to ask Anya about the lake district.

"All taken care of," she replied.

"All?" He raised his hand and rippled his palm, cupping one ear. *"I would hear more."*

"Ask the barge if you want to know more. I did my work," she shouted. Four sets of silent eyes watched her storm from the room. A quiet sigh went around the group. Anya was difficult.

Midnight found Anya on the roof looking north. She enhanced her vision so that the cold stars highlighted the lake and tiny sparkling wavelets could be seen. Brim came and sat beside her. Eventually, she twitched a shoulder acknowledging his presence.

"The lake district is finished?"

"That's what I said." Anya's tone was non-committal, for her almost friendly.

"How many structures are you preserving?" Brim's tone was calm and inquiring.

"You talked to the barge. You know I only ordered the one house preserved." Anya fluffed her mane in a rare display of humor. "Those who move into the neighborhood next won't need our homes—they will build their own. So, I'm letting the rest of the structures return to nature."

"And you are protecting *one* house with a hull metal enclosure?" Brim shook his head in a thoroughly bemused way. "Do you realize that hull metal has not been manufactured on Abundance for over two hundred years? The only facility that can still make it is on the other side of the world. Yes, I received a query tonight asking us if we really needed a hull metal house built."

Anya looked him straight in the eye. "And? Did you cancel my order, Brim? Did you do that to me?"

He looked away. "No. I told them you wanted it, and they said it was okay." He shook his head ruefully. "But how many quixotic gestures are you going to make? Packaging one house to last a hundred thousand years and ignoring a whole district seems a little extreme, even for you."

Instead of getting mad, she surprised him with a quiet, "Thank you." And that told him how important his decision was to her.

As he rose to leave, she offered one more comment. "I hate cities, you know. I don't care if you preserve every one of them—it doesn't make a difference. Tomorrow I'm going into the park to check it out."

Brim sighed. "Please don't hull metal any trees."

12

A PARK

The next morning, Anya carefully packed her flight rack, causing her to get a late start. She was still unsettled from yesterday's exploration of the lake district and wanted a complete change, so she twitched through a menu, selecting robin's-egg blue for the rack, and changed her travel suit to russets and grays.

Sotheel wandered sleepy-eyed into the common room in time to watch Anya shrug on her equipment and fly away without a word. Taem, who was in the front of the barge, heard Sotheel quip, "Maybe she will get lost in the forest, and we won't see her for days." He gave her a strange look and went back to contemplating the dawn through the window.

Anya flew low, topped the hills, and settled down on the bare peak of the brown-sided mountain. Earlier, reconnaissance by her Looksees had found the remains of an ancient trail leading down into the bowl. The brilliant morning sunshine framed by a clear blue sky made the valley gleam.

She decided to enter the park the way it was meant to be experienced, which was on foot. Her ever-present flock of Looksees hovered near waiting for commands. She had them settle and go to sleep. Then she slipped off her rack and stared at it. If she left it behind, the barge would tattle on her, and Brim would know. He might come and get her, might make her leave the park, or make her team up with a partner . . . or he might leave her alone. It was not worth the risk. She sighed and set the flight rack to follow her.

She spent the day in splendid isolation. The park held a profusion of creatures that gamboled in bushes, scampered in trees, and frolicked in the clearings. The four-legged, magnificently furred types stalked or pounced in a playful manner. Others slithered, hopped, or fluttered about their business. Trees dappled the ground with painted moirés.

Anya stood under an old, gnarled tree, taking shade from the midday warmth, when a large bird form swept across the valley, plucked up a scampering furred form, and flew off. The flyer may not have seen her, or her form was alien enough not to trigger an avoidance response. She sighed, reassured. *Nature appears as it should in this part of the world at least.*

The late afternoon brought her to a clearing and a stream. Many years before, a great old stump had been cut flat, its top covered in clear resin. *An invitation from someone to set out a picnic? I wonder when the last time was that it had been used?* She turned to her flight rack and set it to make camp. Sitting on the stump, she relaxed, her pleasantly weary legs appreciating the rest.

Anya listened to the stream burble past until the shadows grew long. This type of seclusion was difficult to find and hard to justify. The Race was a gregarious species. Her teammates found it hard to understand why Anya wanted so much alone time. However, she didn't really want to be alone, she admitted to herself. What she wanted was for the world to be different so that she could be happy, but it was never going to be different. Tomorrow was her five hundredth birthday, and the world would be the same as it was on her four hundredth.

Dinnertime came and went, the stars appeared, and the evening cooled. Her travel cloth closed and gently warmed her. Still, Anya sat before she went to bed without reporting in—not that it mattered.

The next morning found her up and moving with the dawn. Her travel cloth had opened enough to require brisk exertion to stay warm. She never noticed how well it anticipated her. She set off downstream. A million years before a plains carnivore relative had probably made the same choice. She felt rested and content.

By mid-morning, the stream path led to another clearing. Here, she saw a sight that surprised her—there was a ruin of a building so decayed and fallen apart that she could hardly tell where it began and ended. Great logs had been used for the walls. *A building made with wood?* She could tell the ruins would not have stood very high. The building had been long and narrow. If she used her imagination, that pile of debris in front of it might have made a stately porch.

She circled the pile, looking in as well as she could. The flooring must have been made out of wood too. *How delightfully woodsy.* Around one side, a plasmetal plaque had been erected. The plaque was tarnished and deeply scratched, so it was hard to read. A small hull metal sign had been added to the pillar below the plaque. She made out the words "IN MEMORY." When she touched the plaque, it stayed inert. Whatever display it held was non-functional, so she almost passed it. Then curiosity got the better of her, and she woke up one of the Looksees on the ridge and told it to fly down.

While it fixed the plaque, Anya poked into the rubble herself, finding footing treacherous and progress slow. The great beams had fallen into a depression or low basement. They were rotted but did not shift when she scampered over them. Some of the debris had to be the roof that fell into the structure.

Why, every part of the building had been made from trees! I've never seen anything like it. After so many years on the preservation teams, I've found something really new. I wonder what it means.

The Looksee beeped for attention. It had powered up the plaque and gotten something out of it. Anya made her way nimbly out of the rubble and wandered over to watch. There was a still image of the cabin as it must have appeared when new and sounds coming out of the speaker, though something was still wrong with the plaque because the sounds were mostly chittering and barking noises interspersed with cheerful-sounding chirps.

When the barking voice started speaking in Race, Anya gasped. "Welcome to Siskali's house. All you children who have made this sign for me and visit so often—welcome!" Anya heard a chitter of mirthful laughter.

The voice continued, "Did you understand me when I just talked to you in Chin? If I'm not home, you may find me somewhere in the park. Please come looking, but don't cheat. Find me with your eyes and ears only, if you can."

Anya looked around her in amazement. *What was this place? Did the Race bring another intelligent species to Abundance and keep it here for some reason? Was the alien a pet, a guest, or a teacher? Did the creature or creatures leave any other plaques? What did they look like? And why have I never heard about these creatures?*

She knew that her education had been truncated. So many customs were upset by the Race's preoccupation with the disaster called The Wave. She had to know more. Anya twitched and her flock of Looksees on the mountain woke. "Full sweep centered on my location. Find me anything related to this structure in the park."

She thoughtfully examined the ruin and squeezed her eyes shut to combat a sudden painful thought. *Children. Everywhere I look, this place reminds me of children. Precious, absent children. Why? The answers may be right in front of me if they've survived millennia of disrepair.*

By mid-afternoon, the Looksees had determined there were no other structures in the park. Anya sat in front of the ruin for some time very still, seeing nothing. The woodland sounds around her resumed, and her Looksees settled in the grass. Finally, she nodded and walked over to the plasmetal plaque, opened it, and removed a small box from it. She placed the box carefully in her pack. For the rest of the day, she ranged the park, pacing the old walking trails, stopping at vistas, imagining alien intelligences at play in these old woods. Time seemed to stretch; moments followed moments. She spent another night in the park.

The morning was grey; and as she waited for the sun, she fell into deep contemplation. Her thoughts drifted. She was a child again, and her tiny hand was held by the bigger, rougher one of her eldest fathers. She was at a seashore somewhere, and he was dipping her into the water, causing her to scream and giggle. She kicked water high trying to soak his mane, but he was too quick. Dip, giggle, kick. Finally, he dropped her to the sand, allowing her to push him into the water and make a huge splash.

Near the end of his life, she brought him to the same beach, and they talked about the waves—how the little ones are followed by larger ones, always different and yet the same. When enough waves pass, we are on our own. Anya rippled her ears. Age finally gathers all living creatures, even the Race. *Sad thoughts on such a beautiful day, yet the memories are oddly comforting.*

Anya returned to base camp a day later. She was subdued and thoughtful. She spent a lot of time in her room alone with the door locked, using the barge's computing power. The rest of the team found it very inconvenient. Anya seemed to be getting worse, they said. Soon Brim would have to do something, they all told him.

13

LAST CHILD

Dinner was social time, and Brim decreed that all of the team assemble for it. Anya had avoided meals with the team for days until Brim made a point of stopping by her room to ask her to attend. She did so silently, listening to the banter of the others at the table.

Sotheel followed Resource and Allocation trends more closely than any of the team, so she announced the population figures at dinner that night. "Did you know the Race has officially reached the eight-billion mark? Resource predictions were way off, as usual. But my predictions were closer than Planetary Resources Board." Her eyes sparkled with smug pride as she got up from the table.

Anya felt a scream coming. Something in her chest, maybe it was her heart, tore in half. Her skin convulsed. With mane flared, she stalked the older girl and cut her off at the end of the compartment. Anya cuffed her twice, hard. "Have you no feelings, you clueless wonder? Did The Wave pass through your tiny head that day and scoop out whatever portion of compassion you were supposed to have in this life? Don't you get it? Eight billion souls . . . we're down to eight billion, and you announce it like it's an important milestone. It's *death* you're talking about, not statistics."

Sotheel looked up from the floor where Anya's blow had driven her. She was uninjured from the attack. Enhancements many thousand years before made the Race exceedingly resilient physically. Her open-weave travel clothes never even went into protection mode. She rippled the skin on one leg and then the other, pretending to flick dirt from her short auburn fur.

"You need to mature, Child. Just because you are Last Born you've been fussed over all your life. Everyone lets you be emotional and moody—I'm not impressed anymore. The Race is dying. I can't stop it, and you can't stop it. I advise you to embrace it and get some joy out of your life."

With a sob, Anya kicked her way past Sotheel to an instrument crate in the middle of the floor and slapped it open. Brim, Vorne, and Taem moved fast to surround her. In that case were devices that could get through travel cloth. The semi-intelligent material would shrug off attacks from predators smaller than one hundred kilograms, but it was not armor. The Race never wore armor cloth on a fully domesticated planet.

Anya shook her head blindly. She reached in and took out a very odd-looking box, small enough to fit in the palm of her hand. Her teammates blinked. She spoke through her sobs. "A Looksee found this in a tumbled down building in the park—an old cottage of a type you've never seen. So low in height you and I couldn't live in it. In this module, there is a voice recorded over three thousand years ago."

Brim gently took the box from her hand and looked at it. "Why, Anya? Why remove it from the old building when your job was to preserve the site instead? What does it mean for you?"

"Oh, Brim you must understand." Anya looked around. "You all must understand, even Sotheel whom I love like a sister and hate at the same time." She moved to Sotheel and sat.

"I am Last Born, yes. All my life I have been the last child born, and it has molded me. Millions of Race have come to talk to me, to touch me over the years, to love me as the last child. For so long, I hated it. So many Elders are dead, and there is no one to replace them. I joined The Preservation Project because only the young were involved. Yet, you don't understand me either."

She reached out and did something they had never seen before: She touched Sotheel's shoulder, let a ripple run down her arm, and crossed her palm to the older girl. Sotheel hugged her.

"Abundance is a dying world, and sadness seeps into the ground and the trees and the people. Twenty-four billion Race lived on Abundance the day The Wave came. Now we number eight billion and falling. In another five hundred years, no member of the Race will be left to walk the beautiful cities of Abundance. Maybe in a million years another species will come, find the Race's art and artifacts, and pick up civilization where we left it. That's what the project hopes."

Anya's shoulders were hunched, and her face was sad. "You all know this—have lived with it all your lives. No power of our science has restored our fertility. We are the last of our kind. I was born last and, barring accident, I will die last. I will walk the earth with the memories and hopes of twenty-four billion people on my shoulders, and when I die so does the Race."

Anya's voice dropped to a whisper, "All I have ever wanted was a child to love as I have been loved. I was meant to have babies, I know it! To love them, raise them, watch them grow and take over from me when my time is past. Because of The Wave, I can't have babies of my own, but now I feel I *can* have babies, and you are going to help me!"

They all stared at her in shock. Brim's face rippled with compassion, the module forgotten in his hand. Insanity was rare in the Race, but if anyone deserved to have it, Anya was the one. The pressures of her life were almost beyond comprehension. He got ready to speak words of sympathy.

Sotheel beat him to it. With mane extended and arms wrapped around Anya, she whispered, "I believe you. Just tell me how. What do I do?"

"Listen to the recording."

Five pairs of eyes went to the battered relic of an earlier time. Brim set the box gently before Anya. She touched it briefly.

Once again, the voice of the long-dead Chin filled the room. Sotheel, Vorne, and Taem's faces held varying degrees of awe and amazement. Brim nodded thoughtfully. "So that's what a Chin sounded like."

"You know of them?"

"Of course. I was a fully trained adult at one hundred years old when The Wave came." He flicked his ears playfully. "I had a complete primary education—something you youngsters didn't get in the chaos following the catastrophe." He turned to Anya. "But I only know a little. They were an indigenous species here on Abundance when the Race arrived five thousand years ago. I remember being taught they died out, but I don't remember why. Since they were no longer around, it didn't seem important to know more about them. Perhaps you would like to tell us more?"

She stood tall. "Oh, there is so much more to know. They were intelligent, friendly, and able to learn our ways. They played with our children. There were one hundred million Chin on this planet when we adopted it. They seemed to fit into our society well; but as we filled the planet, their numbers diminished. The information banks could not tell me why they died out—just that by the time our numbers had reached ten billion, the Chin stopped breeding altogether."

Anya stared at them, voice intense. "There is one more important fact to know about the Chin—they loved their children, and they loved our children. If we had loved their children back, the Chin might be with us here today."

Sotheel shook her head, short auburn fur framing her triangular face. "I don't get it. You found some dead animals that used to live on Abundance, and they could talk. What does that have to do with us?"

In reply, Anya sent a command to the barge, and a three-dimensional display appeared in the room. One of the few fragments of recordings Anya had been able to find in her search of the Race data banks began to play. An aged Chin, short and round with long, luxuriant cream-colored fur, walked through a parkland with several much taller Race children gamboling around it. Its round and furry face, black snout, and black twinkling eyes painted a merry picture. It barked and squeaked with laughter and moved faster than the children, snapping a laggard child across the backside with its long, silky tail. A second picture appeared of a much earlier time with many Chin living and working around a lake, visiting Race dwellings, and operating Race technology. A Chin social grouping of about six adults and twenty small ones was next. The group met up with a Race family, and the young Chin climbed on the laps of the adults who were both Chin and Race.

Sotheel reached out and passed her hand through the recording as if to feel the Chin child in front of her. Watching intently, Taem and Vorne slowly raised their ears, looked at each other, and rippled in agreement. Vorne spoke for the both of them, "You want to recreate the Chin."

"Information about the Chin is fragmentary and scattered after all this time." Anya shut off the recording.

"I had trouble finding these images in the Race information banks, but there is more—I'm sure of it. We've been preserving our cities for some hypothetical species that will show up in the future to take over civilization. That's just stupid so, yes, I want to recreate the Chin. Let's give them back their planet. Let's bring babies back into the world. Please."

Vorne filled the silence with a grunt. Then he said, "It won't be easy. It may not be possible. We don't even know why they died out." Vorne's tone was pessimistic, but he rippled a shoulder inquiry at Taem.

The quiet one, Taem, snapped the flesh of his palms and grinned. *Let's find out,* the action said. It was the most enthusiasm Anya had ever seen from Taem, and she was relieved. With Taem participating, the whole team was quickly on board.

Anya's heart almost burst again, this time with hope. She looked at each member in turn. "Thank you, thank you. The first step is to visit the park. Once you see the ruin, you all will get a better idea of my Chin's environment. I picked out a landing spot days ago, so I can fly the barge in tonight."

Brim's ears went up in an amused fashion. "We have a city to catalog and preserve, Anya. This will have to be done on downtime."

Anya felt herself wilt. She wanted to escape from the room and run back to the park where she felt at home. *Nobody understands how important this is. No one cares.* She almost missed Sotheel's squeal of laughter joined by Vorne and Taem. Before her ears sorted it out, Sotheel was shouting, "I just heard a team holiday declared."

Brim finally let his grin show. "The barge stays here. Flight racks at dawn, and half our Looksees stay behind to continue routine cataloging—that is if Sotheel can finish brushing her fur in time."

Sotheel made an explosive sound. "Ha. Give me that box, Anya. I'm going to be first out the door in the morning. I know I can get more out of that sign than you did."

NEW GROUND

Sotheel did not quite make good on her boast. The next morning, she was the last one in the air, and her flight rack was more carrying her than she was flying it. She was only seconds behind the group, and if Sotheel closed her eyes immediately and seemed to be meditating deeply, she was still on the move.

The box had indeed disgorged more hours of visual and auditory recordings than Anya had been able to get. They included an excellent record of the building of the cabin and a list of cultural reproductions of everyday objects placed within it. It became quite clear that the resident of the cabin was believed to be the last Chin of her kind, and the entire park had been her preserve for however long she had lived.

Anya led the team to the same mountain path she had used days earlier to enter the park, and they settled all the flight racks on the mountaintop. Sotheel ended her contemplations with a jerk. She yawned and looked around. "Where's the cabin?"

Anya slipped off her flight rack and started down the slope, her flight rack taking position above and behind her shoulder. Brim slipped off his rack, as did Taem and Vorne.

"Hey!" Anya stopped, rippling a shoulder. Just to rub it in, she pointed. "That way."

Sotheel rippled an annoyed shoulder back at her. "I know it's that way—what I want to know is *why* we are here! It's a two-minute flight. Why take a two-hour walk, oh difficult one?"

"Because this is the path of discovery. Because this is how the children got to the cabin. Because Brim said I'm in charge. Pick one."

Taem and Vorne did the brother thing again of exchanging signals with ears, eyes, and ears; then they began racing each other down the path. Brim strolled behind them carefully, not including himself in the conversation. Sotheel sighed and tried to think of a snappy retort. When she couldn't, she dropped off of her flight rack and booted it into position behind her. She stalked past Anya. Suddenly, she was running full out down the mountain, shrieking with glee.

Anya sighed and began the long walk down. "The cabin is worth it," she muttered. "Worth all of it." *I hope.*

When Anya entered the glade, she found three of the team surrounding the pile of debris and staring at it. Sotheel was swiping at the plaque, twitching from head to foot. "I can't believe you locked the door, Anya! You are so weird. The only intelligences on this side of the continent are us, and you went ahead and locked the door!"

Anya humbly went over to the plaque and put her hand on the mechanism. It popped open obediently. Sotheel immediately began rummaging around inside, harvesting minor memory modules.

"It is in pretty bad condition, isn't it?" Vorne looked at Taem who looked at the pile of rubble. Taem snapped his palms, and four Looksees came down and encircled him. An instant later, they had their orders and formed a line to begin a slow circle of the perimeter. A moment later, the rest of the cloud of Looksees joined in, creating a confusing but orderly grid pattern over the ruin.

Sotheel turned the plaque on for easier viewing as the Looksees gathered information. The first Looksees report showed the site possessed a museum-level protective shield at one time. Time had finally defeated the protection but perhaps only in the last few centuries. Much of the cabin contents remained in place by being buried when the roof came down.

Deep imaging built up a holographic image of the find. One by one overlays of wall and roof disappeared from the image, and Anya found herself looking at ghostly depictions of furniture, cabinets, and ceramic and metal utensils that had lain undisturbed for untold years. As the Looksees cataloged them, the list of items flowed down the side of the image.

"So, that's what's in there," murmured Sotheel. "Do we need any of it?"

"Put a temporary barrier over the cabin," said Brim. We might find we need every bit of it."

They left a Looksee in position over the cabin and returned to the barge using their flight racks. Even Anya didn't feel the need to insist they walk out, though she was tempted in the case of Sotheel. *So, I'm petty. But how often do I get to tell her what to do?*

When they got back to the city, they separated to work, each at their own virtual workstation, intent on learning any information they could about the Chin. Brim followed a logic that asked what the Chin were and found a five-thousand-year-old treatise linking the Chin distantly with several subgroups of smaller furred ground dwellers whose family tree branched a least a million years before. Taem, the silent one, asked about biomes and learned the Chin had been found in every region of the planet, except the very cold and equatorial regions. They were omnivorous, but their diet leaned heavily toward nuts, fruits, and insects. Vorne was the musician, and he found many songs and music created by Chin in the databases. There, he found their languages—all of them. He listened with rapt attention, his hush zone hard put to contain the decibel output he requested. Sotheel wondered about Chin social patterns, technology, and how they aged. When she found the typical Chin lived only one-tenth as long as an average Race, she was not surprised.

The evening waned. When Anya took a break and went upstairs to the roof for her nightly session of solitude, Sotheel rounded on the others. "You know a project of this size just about has to go through Resources Board."

Brim shrugged. Vorne and Taem stopped and waited.

"*Come on*—you know Anya has no chance of selling this project to the board. Every planning board she ever worked for considers her unstable." She met their eyes squarely and waited for denials. There were none. She continued.

"Resources Board won't see any value in trying to reconstitute a species that died out, probably from their own stupidity. Besides, the board won't like the idea of replacing us with a new species while any Race is still alive on this planet. They won't want to share Race resources with these critters under any circumstances."

Sadness ran in ripples down Brim's face. "Are you going to tell Anya that, Sotheel? Are you so cruel that you would stop her before she tries, even if she must fail?"

"No. You don't *all* have to be naapos about this. Any simpleton can see if one path is wrong, it is time to choose another. We all want her to succeed. And I happen to have a plan." Sotheel looked smug but at the same time so innocent that Brim was glad she was on their side—if she was.

Breakfast was a quiet affair. An enormous amount of work had been done throughout the night, so everyone was tired. It did not seem likely that they could find enough information about the Chin to simply reconstitute them. No genetic patterns of any Chin were among the data they were able to find, but the hint about near relatives made them hopeful. Almost nothing was known about their native habitats, except that Chin had been found all over the world, and they had a set of mixed hunter/gather and agriculture cultures when the Race first found them. If the park represented an ideal biome for the Chin, perhaps this would be a good place to start the species again.

Brim brought up the Resources Board issue first. "Anya, have you thought about getting funding for the purpose of bringing these Chin back into the world?"

She instantly looked wary. "I can keep using resources from The Preservation Project, can't I?"

"Yes, I suppose you could. Preservation resources can be stretched into a lot of side paths if the ultimate goal of the usage can be explained as going for preservation goals. At some point, it is going to become obvious to preservation management that what you are doing has no connection to the project, and they will ask you to find your resources elsewhere. It may happen sooner, but it certainly will be triggered when you bring in biotechnologists to begin the rebuild of Chin from any design you create."

"I'll think of something." Anya looked stubborn and a little desperate. "I'll start small. I'll make one baby. Then when everyone sees a live Chin, they'll let me make more."

Vorne rippled his arm in disagreement. "This is a major bio-engineering project—this is recreating a species from scratch. We're not cross-engineering from an existing animal. We don't know if any acceptable genetic relatives exist in this planet's biota. We may have to build up from the very basic molecules."

Anya wilted. "So, expensive? Does cost make a difference when we're doing the right thing? Will I have to try to convince Resources Board?"

Brim suppressed a smile. "We've been talking about this. Planetary Resources Board sets priorities and allocates resources in fifty- and hundred-year plans. We've decided not to try to convince them of the need for our project yet. With the brilliant insight of one of our team, we're taking another path." He bowed to Sotheel. She bowed back and gave him a dazzling smile.

Sotheel turned to Anya and spoke, "Last night while you were sleeping, we put out a planet-wide message with your name on it." Her eyes sparkled with mirth. She waited just long enough to see Anya's puzzlement spark into anger.

"We announced a new project called The Anya Fund and asked for donations to the fund. We released all our accumulated data and explained your pledge to bring the Chin back to their homes. I opened the fund by donating all of my lifetime Personal Excess Resource allocations, and everyone else on the team made Personal Excess Resource donations too. As of thirty minutes ago, over one million Race have donated to the fund. Anya, you are in business."

Shock raced across Anya's face in ripples that plunged down her neck until they eventually damped out in confused swirls. Nascent hope filled her voice. "You pledged your *entire* lifetime supply of excess resources? You could do *anything* with those resources. They are your birthright. I thought you hated me."

Sotheel nodded soberly. "I hate Anya the Last Child. She is no one I would ever want to know. But Anya the Visionary, Anya the Champion of a New Race, Anya the Mother . . . her I think I love."

"Yes, Anya," Brim smiled. "We have *all* donated huge amounts of our Excess allocations to the Chin fund. You joined our team when no one else would have you, and we didn't want you for a long while either. It has been a difficult few years. I think you made it as hard as possible just to see if we would throw you out.

"Now you are going to need your own team. For research, design, habitat investigation, breeding, nurturing, and even mothering. Eventually, you will have millions of volunteers. We would like to be on *your* first team, if you will have us."

Anya felt tears coming—the first tears of joy she had ever experienced. "I do need a team that knows how to work with me. Thank you, thank you all."

Brim bowed, captured the eye of everyone in the room, and liked what he saw. He walked to the barge's control panel. "Update our initial report to Western Zone Preservation Group. The team is taking City 224 off the preservation list. We have credible evidence that City 224 will soon experience significant population inflow and become ineligible for preservation."

He touched palms with Taem, Vorne, Sotheel, and then Anya, gathering their approval. "And send our collective resignation to The Preservation Project leadership. Tell them, as a group, we are requesting to divert all intelligences, equipment, and materials assigned to us to a new project—that of the Chin species restoration. The Anya Project. We claim this city and the one hundred miles surrounding it for The Anya Project."

He smiled, "What do we do next, project leader?"

Anya reached skyward; and a ripple rose from her feet, swept upward, and burst from her palms. "I think we appoint you as a project manager. You are the brains of this team, Brim. You always have been."

"And you, Anya, are the heart," stated Sotheel.

15

HARD WORK

Anya was beginning to realize that life would never be simple again. None of the team had ever launched a new project before this, and none of the existing planning boards had templates for rebuilding extinct civilizations. They had been making it up on their own for days, each member reaching out to all the disciplines they could think of contacting. The Chin species restoration project seemed mired in false starts.

Anya was sitting in the barge's common room talking to herself and watching the sunrise. "Is there really no physical database of the Chin anywhere? We need a genetic description. I can't do anything without a good genetic description! Where are the prime synthesists who study lifeforms?"

Sotheel walked into the common room in time to hear Anya's diatribe but then turned around and headed for the exit. "I'm going apartment hunting; this barge is too small to run a project. Can I get anyone anything?"

Taem made an appreciative ear twitch.

Vorne said, "Find me a music studio, please."

Brim popped out from under the hush hood he had been using. "There have been six Planetary Surveys since the Race adopted Abundance. When the Chin died out, remember we stopped studying them. The last prime synthesist who specialized in the Chin died over one thousand years ago, and Chin had been gone for more than one thousand years at that time. Her notes include the then-known Chin enclaves and ancient burial sites."

Anya looked hopeful.

Brim flicked his pelt tiredly. "However, Race cities covered all such sites long ago. This city, in fact, completely covers the last Chin farming community, and the park is the last known sighting of an actual Chin."

"All gone? All?" Anya drifted over to the window and stared in the direction of the park. She thought about the park and how it was the last known habitation of the last known Chin. Her ears rose. "Not all gone. There is the cabin."

Sotheel had been standing by the door. Three sets of eyes turned to her when she snapped the flesh of her palms. "No, no, no! I don't want Anya breaking her foolish neck while digging a stupid hole in that pile of trash. Or worse yet, let her break something we need to make these animals come alive again. She never knows what she's doing."

Taem managed to look a trifle embarrassed. Vorne and Brim both started to speak, stopped, and twitched their ears at each other. Brim cleared his throat, "You say things like that when you've already looked at the problem and have a solution. Please enlighten us."

Anya had never stopped staring into the distance, her mind deep in the park. Her attention came back to the room and without turning, she rippled her back at Sotheel. "Okay, we'll let *you* dig through the ruins of the cabin. Do you know what you're looking for?"

"Of course, project leader. I've been on top of it for days. We are not a preservation team anymore, you know. And digging up a pile of rubble isn't a preservation skill anyway—it's an engineering skill. I will admit that most of the engineers I talked with had never bothered to keep the things they dug up sorted or intact. Until now, nobody's cared. But I have been spending The Anya Project funds freely the last two days, and we have the best engineers left in existence arriving in the morning with full excavation and documenting equipment. If there is anything to find in that debris, they will find it."

"I want to be there."

"You will only be in the way . . . but I already told them you would be hanging around, and they understand that you can't be kept off the site. Let them do their work—you'll be happier if you do."

Anya let an unaccustomed pleased ripple cross her face. "Thank you, Sotheel."

Sotheel gave a brisk shoulder twitch and waved her arm airily. "An easy problem to solve. Now I'm off to find a big apartment with a bigger bath—one I don't have to share with anyone! At least one of the residence complexes in town is listed as still fully functional. Who's coming with me?"

♦♦✦♦♦

True to their word, the next day the team of engineering synthesists arrived with several barges of equipment. They let Anya look over their shoulders and watch all they did. Truth be told, some of them seemed in awe of her and tried to defer to her at every turn. It made her uncomfortable, and Sotheel's admonition rang in her ears. *It is clear that I know very little—okay, nothing—about engineering or excavation. I only know that I want to find out how to rescue the Chin.*

Work proceeded quickly, though it didn't seem that way to her. First, the team conducted a series of deep ground scans throughout the glade to make sure there were no subterranean structures that had been overlooked. They were hoping for a burial vault, a storage bunker, or other item of interest. Finding nothing, they extended the scans deep into the woods in every direction.

Then they decided that the glade was not quite big enough for the temporary sorting and storage buildings they were going to erect to assist in analyzing the treasures they would be extracting from the rubble. They brainstormed solutions. Anya tried to follow the conversation.

When they finished a discussion that included much hand waving and pointing, an engineering synthesist approached Anya. "Ma'am, would it be okay to uproot and move a few dozen of these old-growth trees? I assure you they wouldn't be harmed in any way."

Anya looked around the grove, completely out of her depth. "I guess so." *Why would anyone ask my permission to move trees?*

Finally, the real work began.

Twenty Looksees took station over the site and fed the engineers a real-time image of the contents, depicted in multiple layers. The uppermost layers, composed mostly of dirt, detritus, and drifted vegetation, sat on top of the decayed remnants of the roof and walls. Four devices that were specifically built to remove the layer worked together. Then they came back and began lifting rotted roof beams, taking them to the sheds for a final-minute examination.

Two of the engineers were muttering together, looking at one corner of the image. One said, "That side is a lot deeper." The other one twitched his ear for the cabin plans that Sotheel had pulled from the plaque. "Root cellar on that side. That's the hole the cabin first collapsed into."

Anya became alert. "Hmm, could there be anything important in the cellar? Might the last Chin have gone in there when it was dying?"

The more deferential engineer lowered her ears a bit sadly. "The scan would have picked up any body the size of a Chin, Prime Anya. This place was a museum for a long time after that Chin stopped living in it."

"But," said the other engineer excitedly, "we have just begun. You are seeing us invent a whole new use for engineering. No one has ever done this before, as far as I know. I am sure we will find things here that will help you."

Anya left them muttering to each other about tensile strengths, material age decay patterns, and how to extract various-sized objects from the rubble more or less intact. She wandered over to the excavation and watched industrious machines of many sizes work to extract another wooden beam. When it was moved out of the way, she saw the outline of a counter or platform below it. There were some pathways and some holes in the debris. A small woodland creature darted up and out of one of the holes. She tracked it for a minute, thinking.

That evening, back at the barge, she confronted Brim. "The engineers told me this morning that after the museum shield failed, the cabin became progressively open to the elements. Since it was already aged before the museum shield was applied, it declined very rapidly. Animals have apparently been making their homes in the cabin for hundreds of years. How do we find anything we can use in that kind of mess?"

"I will ask our biota experts. Many of the Race have been sending in suggestions on research avenues to recreate the Chin—I've even talked with a node entity about it. Offers to volunteer time, expertise, or Personal Excess Resource funds continue to flood in. If everyone who wants to come here actually does, I don't know where we are going to put them."

He flowed a ripple down one arm and touched her hand. "Things are going well, Anya. We can't ignore an extinct species for thousands of years, forget almost everything we ever knew about them, and then expect to magically reconstitute them overnight. Patience, Prime."

Anya shook both ears violently. "Don't you start calling me that too! Have all the Race gone batty at the same time? I am nobody's prime."

Brim shrugged. "As you say, Anya. Not everyone seeks the status of prime—sometimes they just don't duck in time." His deep chuckle hung in the air as he walked back to the common room.

Things were easier when everyone hated me. Anya shook her head and followed him quietly into the common room for the next meeting and then the next.

A few nights later, the original team gathered in the barge for a communal meal and general update session. Sotheel continued to supervise the engineering group, which had expanded to several dozen materials synthesists, close to a hundred volunteer helpers, a lot more barges of equipment, and a sky full of Looksees. Vorne and Taem spent their days reactivating sections of the city to house the influx of workers and a growing population of transient well-wishers who weren't contributing anything but had come to watch the activities and marvel. Brim was trying to oversee everything and anticipate the next thing the project would need.

Anya listened intently while Sotheel described the progress. "Everything is out of that hole and sorted into artifacts, furniture, tools, personal items, and debris. At this point, the pile called 'Unknowns' has just about been eliminated."

"Where is my Chin?"

Brim cut in before Sotheel could open her mouth. "Remember, we didn't expect Siskali to be found in her cabin, but something such as a grave or vault in the area would have been nice to find. However, scans in the vicinity of the cabin have found nothing."

Taem stopped and placed his forkful of dinner back on his plate. "Engineers are supposed to be cataloging bio traces too."

Sotheel riposted, "We have thousands upon thousands of bio traces with no real reference yet as to where they come from. And since we don't have a Chin, we have nothing to compare them to." Sotheel waved her arm airily. "Engineers aren't great with biology."

With infinite patience, Taem replied, "Rule out the wrong bio traces. Biota experts must have some kind of database."

Brim looked thoughtful. "Have the engineers been capturing and testing the animals found in the rubble?" Sotheel twitched an ear and slowly shook her head.

"So," Brim summed it up, "we have animals living in that cabin for hundreds of years, building homes there and breeding there, and we can't rule out their genetic signatures?"

"Don't forget anything that ever approached the cabin would also have been shedding skin and fur cells," chirped Sotheel. "Including us—we have been all over that pile of rubble."

"Looksees can sample the local wildlife," Taem said. "We have tons of Looksees."

Brim twitched his forehead. "I will have biota on it in the morning. If the Looksees have to track down and sample every animal in the forest to help us find the right genetic trace, that's what we will do."

16

A ROAD BACK

The months passed swiftly; the leaves changed color, and the snow came and went. Eventually, the hot and muggy days returned to City 224. The city hummed with an intensity not found in many places on Abundance these days. Barges and aircars tracked through the skies, and foot traffic was unbelievably dense.

The project needed a city administrator, but none of the team had really understood that. They had never been in charge of a city before. The inflow of people to the mostly mothballed city was so unusual that Taem and Vorne simply spent their time reactivating neighborhoods and letting the newcomers settle wherever they wanted. It was fortunate the power grid had not been dismantled, so the urban area was easily made habitable again.

Brim had been away for most of that year, traveling around the globe to give presentations to every planning board that would give him a hearing. He looked unutterably weary as he tromped into the small conference room, which the team had made their own private retreat. He was hard to read, but then he often was.

He looks tired but not discouraged. Dare I hope? Anya waited quietly.

Sotheel, of course, did not know how to wait quietly. "I have twenty teams pledged to drop their current projects and rush to any of our Chin sites on a day's notice. They have accumulated one year's worth of Resources Board technical equipment between them. I can have any city you name dug up in a day. All you have to do is give the word. Why didn't you just call?"

Now Brim looked amused. With a single ear twitch, he murmured, "It's nice to see you, too, Sotheel. I have come back in person because we need to brainstorm our next move. I have good news, but it is conditional." He nodded around the room and gave Anya a fleeting grin. "I had the most trouble with our own Preservation Board. Selling them on the idea that teams of engineering synthesists should be allowed to rip out big sections of already-preserved cities in the quest to find animal boneyards did not set well with them. The fact that I came prepared with the orbital scans and historical documents and a plan we have been calling surgical did nothing to reassure them."

Taem stood up. "It is surgical. Our presence on this planet is shrinking yearly. We have a long-term plan in operation for when we are gone. The Race has abandoned whole regions of Abundance in this century alone. I went over our proposition extensively with the node entity of Resources Board, and the plan you presented has great ecological bonuses for the future Chin populations on this planet."

Anya watched Taem admiringly. This might have been the longest speech she had ever heard him make.

"The Resources node entity probably isn't looking at Preservation's priorities the way The Preservation Project is," Brim stated dryly. "At many of the Chin sites, we may have to remove huge numbers of structures that have already been preserved. Preservation was not enthused." Both ears twitched this time, and Sotheel rolled her eyes.

"However, by dint of persuasion and what amounted to a letter-writing campaign by the millions of fans of The Anya Project, we have permission to enter one site and dig for Chin remains. One site."

Brim paused for effect, and Anya sat up straight. He continued, "If we must remove every Race structure and artifact of the city overlaying that site to find our hypothetical Chin, we can. But we better pick the right site the first time because we aren't getting access to any other sites if the first one doesn't pan out."

Sotheel stood and shook out her auburn fur. "Finally! Point me to that city Brim, and I will get to work."

Anya adjourned the meeting; and Taem and Vorne clustered around Brim, pestering him for details.

••✦••

City 104 was deep in the interior of the continent on an ancient alluvial floodplain, and it seemed to stretch on forever. It was a dream to work with the soil, making excavation quite easy. The twenty teams Sotheel had promised each staked out a sizeable chunk of urban sprawl and began intensive studies of their assigned area with all the technology at their disposal.

They were joined, however, by thousands of amateur spelunkers and excavationists who had made their way to the city and had their own ideas about how to get around inconvenient Race buildings and artifacts. Tunnels and trenches began to appear by magic in lightly overbuilt areas. Some trenches extended for huge distances, undermining buildings and causeways and hillsides alike. Whenever these excavations hit groundwater, the engineering teams would have to turn their efforts to rescue and shore up things that they hadn't intended to take down yet, if at all.

"This is insanity," moaned Brim. "The Race is known for being sensible! What are all these individuals doing here?"

Anya grinned from ear to ear. Ecstatic twitches rippled down both arms. "These are my people. This is how everyone should feel! The only thing these people want is a stake in the best future we can make. The first person to find a Chin for us to recreate is going to carry that pride in our Race for the rest of his or her days."

She turned away from the barge window and gazed fondly at Brim. *Of course the barge is sitting on the top of the tallest building in City 104. With Brim driving, there is nowhere else it would be.* Anya had an excellent view of the areas under the control of The Anya Project teams. Most of the wildcat spelunkers were harder to find, but she was delighted to know they were there.

"This is all your fault, you know," Anya said. She swept a hand grandly at the window behind her. Brim stared back in consternation. Anya counted off the points on her fingers. "I mean, who was it that launched a project that wasn't initiated or controlled by any of the professional Race Boards? One started by amateurs? One not funded or overseen by Resources or Preservation? Nor Population Utility, Land and Marine Commitments, Planetary Concerns? Not even Ecology Predictions? Just us?"

Anya stretched and gave a satisfied ear twitch. "How could you *not* expect that everything we do will be done by amateurs?"

Brim now looked appalled. Sotheel had come up behind him and overheard the last part of the conversation. She thought he looked very fetching in a poleaxed way. She spoke suddenly. "Did you know that our project is getting interest from off planet?"

Brim twitched violently.

In all the years after The Wave, even as planetary populations inexorably diminished, the Race maintained contact and trade between the far-flung planets of the empire. Ships flew more occasionally, but information still flowed from planet to planet. The total fleet was much reduced, yet the Race didn't bother building ships anymore. The ones they had would last long enough—and longer actually.

Brim twitched an ear. *"Tell me more."*

"I got a communication from a planet called Forest." Sotheel looked perplexed, she evidently thought the Race folk of Forest were a little strange.

"They once had an intelligent species on their planet called the . . . Yeek-tek—or something like that. If we are successful, they are going to try to bring their animals back too. Unfortunately, these Yeeks lived in huge trees—I mean trees that stretched as high as small mountains—in jungles that covered whole continents. A Yeek would live its whole life in the trees and never touch the ground. They would have to bring back the trees too. I think we have it easier."

Anya was thrilled with the news, but Brim was still distracted by the aberrant activity he was watching on the ground. "Sotheel, are we coordinating the efforts of our volunteer hordes? In any way?" His voice was a marvel in steadiness, though he still looked ill.

Sotheel twitched an ear at Anya, who had to look away or laugh. "As it happens, Vorne requested all volunteers contact him before entering the city, and he has been assigning regions to them as they arrive. Everyone has a general description of what a Chin body might look like. We have biosynthesists attached to each of our engineering teams, and the volunteers know to bring anything remotely resembling a Chin skeleton in for analysis."

Brim sighed. "I had hoped to give some of the city back to Preservation in a condition to make re-preservation possible." He drooped one ear. "But I see that isn't going to happen."

♦♦✦♦♦

It took one week for the first Chin to be found.

"Is this a Chin skeleton?" Anya asked very quietly. *Are we really looking at the beginning of a new civilization?*

Anya strained to see through the screen at the inside of the biosynthesis scholar's mobile lab. The scholar was one of the oldest Race members left on Abundance, and she had been a prime scholar longer than Anya had been alive. She didn't look like she had been excited by anything in the last thousand years, and she still didn't look excited now as she gestured to the collection of bones laid out on the table beside her.

"No," the biosynthesis scholar replied imperturbably. After a short eternity, she continued. "You are looking at parts of three separate individuals."

"Three? Oh, that's wonderful!"

"Wonderful? Perhaps." The old scholar wrinkled her nose. "These three sets of bones do belong to the same general sort of animal. They share a similar timeframe, having apparently died within a few hundred years of each other. They also share a large amount of the same genetic information found in some unidentified fragment samples your engineers gave me."

"Those samples came from Siskali's cabin. They were part of a whole bunch of different fragments of skin and fur found around the cabin and on her possessions. Now we know which genetic fragments are hers. This is wonderful! We can bring her back! We can bring back their whole civilization!"

The old prime shook her head. "No."

"No? What's wrong? Isn't there enough material to get their genetic patterns? Is something else wrong with the skeletons?" Anya

slowly waggled her ears. *"I am listening. Please tell me what you mean."*

The old scholar leaned against the table and picked up one of the bones. She twitched a shoulder thoughtfully. "I have three individual animals here. I can make you three animals that are the exact duplicates of these animals. I can't make a viable herd out of three. Give me ten or fifteen thousand genetic patterns, and I can guarantee a viable herd. Anything less is nonsense."

"These are people, Prime Biosynthesis Scholar—not animals. We owe them so much. I want to do everything we can." Anya spoke quietly but forcefully.

"No." It seemed to be the scholar's favorite word. Suddenly, the old woman grinned. "Anya, Prime of Quixotic Gestures, you have no idea how to create civilization. I will give you some advice: Give me fifteen thousand patterns to duplicate, and let me start herds and clusters. Then you must teach them simple concepts—feelings such as love of family and duty to the herd. If they are as smart as you think they are, they will invent civilization from there."

The biosynthesis scholar signed off with a wave. Anya was relieved again. She had no idea what she would have said to that. Slowly, she began to grin. *We have three! Oh my, we are on our way. I can't wait to tell Brim!*

17

MANY ROADS TAKEN

City 104 proved to be a major windfall for The Anya Project. No fewer than the bones of 1,700 discrete individuals were eventually recovered from the rubble of the city. The old prime scholar was pleased—at least her grunted "Find me more" comm note to Anya was interpreted that way by the team. Anya wasn't going to argue.

The excavation team's skills developed by leaps and bounds during the disassembly of the target city so that by the end, excavation became so precise that any damage to the site was nearly indetectable and restoration was always possible. Brim was able to return almost fifteen percent of the city back to The Preservation Project for Re-Preservation. He swore that amateur spelunkers would never get near another of his digs if he had to sneak in every night at midnight and be gone by dawn.

It was the rainy season over much of the western continent. Anya had returned from City 104 alone and stood on the top of the mountain looking down into Siskali's park. Below was the research station the team had set up next to Siskali's tiny home. The station was invisible in the rain.

City 104 had been both a thrill and a strain for Anya. Now she walked down the mountain path in the pouring rain, enjoying the solitude immensely. This far from the research station, the mountain was undisturbed; and she kept her senses sharp to spot any of the wildlife she knew was there. Most creatures were much too sensible to be out today; but they were there, snug in their burrows, hunkered down in their nests, or resting under the trees. A little further down the path, one curious herbivore lifted its head to watch her for a moment, and then it bounded away.

Anya spent more hours than necessary on the hike down to the station. When she got there, she found it bustling with activity. Most of the temporary buildings had acquired a sort of permanent purpose. Some were storehouses for the treasures removed from Siskali's cabin, but most had become research and storage facilities for the number of bones the team had found. The old scholar had her own staff of biosynthesists now, and she was ruling her team with a word here and a word there. If she needed to give more instruction than that, the subordinate was probably out the door the next day.

It had taken Anya months to learn the prime biosynthesis scholar's name. The name she was told seemed too ordinary for a woman that scary. Anya wondered more than once if Sotheel had been teasing when she assured her that the scholar's name was Nebbe. "You know, like what you would name a pet thara." Sotheel's ear wiggle had not been reassuring.

Anya walked into the small storehouse the team used for their offices to find the comm chiming her code. Water dripped onto the floor from her fur and travel clothes as she walked to the unit and switched it on. The face that appeared was Brim's. He looked smug.

"I have good news." He waited for her reaction. Then he leaned closer to the screen and twitched an ear. *"You've been walking in the rain. You do know that you can set your clothes to repel moisture, don't you?"*

"You do know that you are going grey about the muzzle, right?" Anya twitched innocently in a way that made her look like Sotheel.

Brim appeared massively startled. *Did Anya make a joke? Had that ever happened before?* He honestly couldn't remember. He shrugged mentally. Anya was weird—it was her defining characteristic.

"As I said, I have news."

"Actually, you said you had *good* news. Yes, I *was* listening, Brim. Why don't you tell me what it is?"

Brim rippled a shoulder thoughtfully. Anya had grown so much in these last months. She really was an adult now and not a damaged person who needed careful handling and pity. She was rapidly becoming a leader, in fact as well as name. Plus, since she was his boss, he supposed he better tell her why he called.

"I have talked to several planning boards this week about our excavations in City 104. I was interviewed by Resources Board twice in just the last day. They appear to be under significant pressure to talk to me, although I don't know where the pressure is coming from. Both the success of finding actual Chin bones in a place The Anya Project team had predicted and the late, but welcome, display of skill in gentle excavation have put us in a good light with millions of Race who have been following us closely."

"And Resources Board is going to give us funding?"

"Yes, but Sothcel has been telling us for months that was going to happen. What we didn't know is The Preservation Project has made a command decision to pause all preservation activities on the western continent and concentrate their efforts on other parts of the planet. This continent is ours until The Anya Project has as many individual Chin as we need."

Anya looked shocked, and it seemed as if she didn't quite know how to react. Then came a whoop of joy that made Brim curl his ears momentarily. She appeared distinctly dizzy. That Brim could speak on equitable terms with planning boards and The Preservation Project had been more than she could hope, his news nearly unbelievable.

She knew that there were multiple sites Brim wanted to dig up on the western continent, and some of these sites had not been visited by Preservation yet. The most she had expected was that Preservation would hold off grudgingly at some of these locations, letting Anya's teams in for a quick dig. This was more cooperation than she could ever have imagined and more than she would ever have gotten if she talked to any of the boards herself. In deep gratitude, she gave Brim's image a full and sweeping bow.

"I better dry off and get to work then," Anya gestured grandly. Brim stared again. The new Anya might turn out to be as hard to take as the old Anya. He sighed.

♦♦✦♦♦

There was so much ground to cover that Taem and Vorne split the work, forming separate sub-teams and hitting regional cities one by one. They spent The Anya Project funds profligately and also noticed supplies and resources started flowing in from other Race allocations. The diversions were authorized, but the source of the authorizations was unclear. Also unknown to Anya but well known to Sotheel, preservation work slowed and eventually stopped everywhere on the continent.

The weather turned out to have more of an impact on recovery operations than any of them would have believed. The snows of winter turned into a rainy season that lasted more than half the year on the western continent, and excavating in the abandoned and mostly decommissioned cities was both slow and hazardous. For all the time Anya had been alive, the technology of the Race was so good that local climate conditions had often been ignored—no matter what project the Race was trying to accomplish.

However, the mission of gently removing standing structures, as well as carefully digging through rock and soil to find and preserve precious bones, was a more delicate type of construction than the Race was used to. When a weather front of torrential rains hit the eastern part of the continent, triggering flooding and mudflows like none of them had ever seen, Brim made Taem and Vorne shut down the eastern operations and pull all of their teams out of the danger zones. Eventually, though, the rains subsided; and the recovery teams were able to return to the areas of high interest. One by one regional cities were excavated and then returned to The Preservation Project.

Orbital scans had given City 94 almost as high a rating as the first site, City 104. It proved to be a treasure trove of Chin bones, and the teams even recovered suspected Chin artifacts that had not been seen by anyone. Taem and Vorne refined skills that the first engineering teams invented to remove and catalog the items from Siskali's cabin. By the time they got to City 94, they had recreated the discipline of archeology, a field of study that had not been heard of by their generation.

City 165 was in a very green, lightly forested region below a huge valley that had been dammed up to make a lake for Race use. City 230 was on the other end of that same valley, and each provided a gratifying number of specimens. City 78 had been built in an active earthquake zone. The building techniques employed by the Race had proven very deleterious to the surrounding substrata. Very few Chin bones were able to be recovered from the area.

Slowly, the list of high-interest sites diminished. Taem and Vorne made daily shipments of carefully collected and lovingly packed bones back to headquarters. Eventually, all the major sites were investigated and crossed off the list. Per the agreement, all of the preselected cities were restored as well as the teams were able. By the end of the year, the teams had run through most of The Anya Project resources.

All this time, The Anya Project had also been receiving unidentified bags of bones from across the world. These bones, like the ones recovered by the project, wound up with Nebbe's team of biosynthesists. The old biosynthesis scholar became seriously annoyed because of the sloppiness of the amateurs' efforts.

She requested that Brim make everyone who sent her bones include a detailed geographical description with each bag. She made it very clear that without proper location documentation, she might throw the bags—and *bones*—out. Brim was horrified and made her promise never to say that where Anya could hear. The old scholar snorted, but her eyes twinkled.

The biosynthesist group moved out of Siskali's park and set up labs and storage facilities in the nearby city. The thousands of Race making up Taem and Vorne's many excavation teams were on the move often; but whenever they weren't traveling, they filled up additional sections of the town. Anya wound up being city administrator, in charge of keeping a small but bustling city functioning for its inhabitants. It was a role she never imagined in her other life, yet she could never remember being happier.

18

IT TAKES A VILLAGE

Anya woke on a summer morning a few months later with her usual pre-dawn energy, ready to take on another day. The moment the sun reached around the world and touched the deep black skies above her was her favorite time because there was a promise that everything was possible and nothing unimaginable. It was a similar morning when she had set out to investigate a peculiar park in a nondescript city—and look where that had led.

A message waited. It must have come into the comm only moments before. She was not surprised to find it from Prime Biosynthesis Scholar Nebbe. That woman never seemed to sleep. Anya suspected the scholar knew her better than anyone in the world, including her own parents.

She played the message: "It is time to choose. Call the meeting."

Anya flicked an ear thoughtfully. *Finally*! Anya called the meeting.

Because she only expected to discuss the issues with her core group of advisors, she had intended to hold this planning session in the little conference room outside of her bedroom on the ground floor of the project's office. The conference chamber was convenient, and the decisions seemed pretty simple. Then she saw the number of Race who had indicated they were coming in person, and she gulped. Even more were attending virtually. A moment later, she had Sotheel on the comm.

"Why did you invite all these people, Sotheel?" Anya made sure to keep her ears up so her distress didn't show, but it was an effort.

"I didn't invite them." Sotheel looked at the list. "Okay, I invited some of them." She let a playful ripple cross her face. "But you should know, *I* didn't invite the heads of Resources Board or Planetary Concerns. That was someone else."

"The chair of Resources Board is coming? And Planetary too? Why?" It came out close to a wail.

"If you must know, it's your fault. They are both prime scholars, of course. And guess who they are mated to? Our Prime Biosynthesis Scholar Nebbe. You've worked with her for over one year—don't you know anything about the people working with you?"

Now Anya's ears did go flat.

Sotheel did not look a bit repentant. She flicked one ear insolently, "I have your back, Anya. This is an important meeting. The conference center in town has been powered up, and I had staffing open another wing of Transient Housing. After all, only a few hundred additional attendees are coming to the meeting in person. I doubt if any of them are going to stay for more than a few days."

Sotheel widened her eyes in that innocent way she was so good at and signed off. Anya growled deep in her throat and then reconsidered. Sotheel was never subtle and, while Anya had never seen her be kind, she was also never needlessly cruel. Sotheel thought this planning meeting was important enough to invite the world—Anya wished she knew why. She settled into her chair and tried to plan the agenda for a meeting that suddenly would fill an auditorium. She became more nervous as she delved deeper into the task.

••✦••

Prime Biosynthesis Scholar Nebbe took the floor immediately after Anya opened the meeting. "I have good news, and I have bad news," she stated while casting a severe scowl around the conference hall. After more than one year of working with the biosynthesis scholar, Anya could still be shaken by the woman's glare. Many of the people in the hall seemed to be impacted the same way.

"The good news is we have identified enough samples of the species Project Leader Anya insists on calling the Chin to start a re-creation process for them. This has a projected success rate approaching one hundred percent."

A murmur filled the hall but was immediately hushed. Anya anxiously waited to hear the rest of what the biosynthesis scholar had to say. "The bad news is people here have some odd ideas of how to create a civilization on this planet, and you are going to hear me say 'No' . . . a lot." She was not smiling.

The old biosynthesis scholar strode to the center of the room and focused attention with a ripple down her arm. "Here is what we have—bones of over a quarter of a million discrete individuals have been collected. Many of them are complete or are almost complete skeletons. This turned out to be very helpful." She nodded primly.

"I want to formally thank the efforts of those involved in The Anya Project for their excellent work. Some of the bones, I will confirm, came to us through the informal efforts of numerous individuals, many of whom ripped apart farmland and forests and backyards to send me all sorts of random bones. Some of these bones, surprisingly, came from the species we *were* actually trying to find! I want to thank each of you personally."

She continued to glare around the assemblage. Anya was riveted because no one had given her these figures before. "I mentioned a quarter of a million individuals, but that does not mean we have that many good candidates for re-creation." This time a sigh went around the room.

"My colleagues and I asked ourselves two questions: What makes a successful Chin and how do we know when we see one? I have intensively studied the first question, and we have all been debating for months about the answer to the second question." Nebbe's expression softened as she continued walking around the room.

The biosynthesis scholar's movements brought her to the podium again, and she triggered a projection of the picture of a Chin. Anya recognized it as a still photo of Siskali, harvested from the plaque in front of her cabin. Nebbe continued, "We were able to agree on a couple of parameters. The first is that our records show the modern Chin was a versatile and capable animal—that successful creature is the Chin we want to reintroduce to the planet. Species change over time, and we decided some of our bones were too old. We, therefore, ruled out any specimens that were more than ten thousand years old.

"We also did an exhaustive analysis of the growth and health patterns of the specimens we had left, rejecting those that seemed to show an expression of poor health during their lifetimes."

Anya was on the edge of her seat, watching as the biosynthesis scholar walked back to the center of the room. There was not a sound in the conference hall. "At the end of this process, we have just over ninety thousand unique candidates acceptable for the project. Now it is up to you to decide what to do with them." She sat down with a flourish and stared at Anya.

A murmur began in the hall and built in intensity. Heart beating madly, Anya stood and waited for the room to quiet. It did so, slowly and reluctantly. She suspected she was not the only one who wanted to run through Siskali's forest to burn off her excitement.

Anya stepped to the center of the room and looked around. She spoke with quiet intensity. "We have a species called Chin that we owe a debt. We can only repay that debt to ninety thousand individuals. Our job is to figure out how to give them back to their planet. Let's get to work."

The planning meeting turned into a two-day conference with the various specialties breaking into sub-groups, holding smaller meetings, and then offering proposals to the conference as a whole. Arguments developed among the design teams. One faction wanted to slightly enhance the Chin species, modifying the original creatures to allow them to adapt more easily to Race technology and bumping up several intelligence factors at the same time. Another faction, just as vocal, suggested a radical change to extend the Chin lifespan significantly, making them physically tougher. That group assured Anya that the success rate could be as high as fifteen percent for the first generation. In their minds, it was no problem to cull eighty-five percent of all Chin they restored. Future Chin generations would thank them, they said.

Anya put her foot down. "No, no, no! Our Chin will be restored *exactly* as we found them! They had a million years to adapt to this planet before we came, and they thrived here. They could last a million years more after we are gone. Change them now, and if we do it wrong, we won't have time to fix it before our Race dies out. My babies will have every chance we can give them."

The final question was where to begin physical repatriation. The Race had spent thousands of years living in communities that numbered millions, so the Repatriation Group's first suggestion was to build a factory to turn out the ninety thousand Chin, build a town around the factory, and let them all live there.

Once again Nebbe came to the rescue. As usual, she used few words. "The Chin is a different sort of creature. All our data suggests they do well in small herds, possibly gathered into greater communities of fifteen hundred to five thousand individuals. No large towns until the Chin decide to build them."

Taem and Vorne listened to Nebbe intently. They wiggled their ears at each other and nodded. This was the information their work group needed. Then they gathered the members of the Repatriation work group and went back to their workroom.

The heads of Resources Board and Planetary Concerns had been sitting on one side of the room next to Nebbe during the conference. Now they stood up. Anya had watched them for the two-day conference with a great deal of anxiety. The two most powerful people on the planet had observed every finding presented and said nothing. Sometimes they exchanged glances back and forth with Nebbe, frequently making notes on their pads. The fact that they were Nebbe's spouses in no way made Anya feel more comfortable. They were as scary as Nebbe.

The head of Planetary Concerns was only slightly younger than Nebbe and slightly taller. She rippled her ears in a question to Nebbe. *"Shall I go first?"* Their husband, the head of Resources, encouraged her with a shoulder twitch and a grin. Nebbe nodded primly.

She spoke plainly, rapidly, and directly to Anya. "Planetary Concerns recognizes that you intend to start a new species on this planet before the Race is done with it. We originally thought that was a bad idea."

Anya sat straighter, alarmed to her core. While the head of Planetary Concerns stood, Sotheel and Brim came up beside her. Now each took one of Anya's hands. Sotheel made shushing noises and rippled a *"wait, wait"* tempo into Anya's palm.

The older woman frowned at the three. "For a long time, I believed this project was misguided. The fact that it was entirely funded by amateur dilettantes and staffed by volunteers did *nothing* to reassure me. Sharing our resources with another species in the waning years of our Race seemed like a bad idea. Today, I will admit I was wrong."

Anya let out a breath she had not realized she was holding. People around the room were doing the same.

"Planetary Concerns formally endorses The Chin Restoration Project. At this time, I am empowered to offer your group the entire western continent as a preserve for the Chin species. We will begin evacuating every inhabited Race City on this continent as soon as you tell us to." She sat down abruptly.

The room began to murmur again until people noticed the head of Resources was also standing with his arms held up. He was smiling as the room quieted. "I also have something to say. The Chin Restoration Project is henceforth declared an official project of the Resources Board and is fully funded until the project's completion or until the Race runs out of resources. And since projections tell us that our factories will continue functioning for centuries after all of us are gone, I think you will have enough resources to achieve your goal." He bowed, rippled one ear, and sat down with his mates.

"Congratulations, Anya," Brim murmured. He and Sotheel pretended they did not notice how tightly Anya gripped their hands. She couldn't find anything to say.

♦♦✦♦♦

The conference ended on that note, but the attendees cleared out slowly and reluctantly. It turned out that *all* of the dignitaries and most of the technical people wanted to see the site of Siskali's cabin and wanted to know how they could help the Chin project. Anya, Brim, and Sotheel spent the rest of the day walking various groups through the woods to visit the site and talk about the accomplishments of the project so far. Anya was so overwhelmed she never noticed that Taem and Vorne were conspicuously absent.

The next morning found Anya sitting at her desk, watching the sun slowly coming up over the rim of the mountains. The light slipped between the trees outside her window to paint golden shafts of brilliance on the ground in front of her cabin. She was in a positive, contemplative mood. When the door opened behind her, she twitched an ear but didn't turn around.

Taem walked through the door, followed by Vorne. They looked at each other and then walked around Anya's desk and stared out the window with her. Finally, Vorne snapped the flesh of his palms and said to Taem, "Good view from here."

Taem replied, "Yes. I can see it."

Anya cocked an ear. "What are you talking about?"

"We have Nebbe's approval," said Vorne. "Now all we need is yours."

Anya was confused for a moment and then grinned. She remembered that the brothers had disappeared the day before with their work group and evidently with Nebbe too. They had information to share and were showing off because they wanted to get a rise out of their former comrade and now boss. She let a ripple go down one arm and said, "Very well, I give my approval. Now what have I just agreed to?"

Taem gestured to his brother. Vorne twitched an ear and said, "After going over the orbital data again with Nebbe, we have identified six ideal locations for our first Chin communities. Nebbe has given us the specs for what a starter village needs, including the design of a birthing center for her work, a school, a community center, and appropriate cabins."

Now Taem chimed in. "Locations where they can reinvent sustainable agriculture was a must too."

Vorne grinned. "Outside your window, the other end of this valley is our first choice. Now that you have approved it, I will re-task our engineering groups to start learning how to build again. We will phase in each village as quickly as Nebbe gives us permission."

⬥⬥✦⬥⬥

The first experimental village went up that year. It was located on the far end of the valley everyone in the project had taken to calling Siskali's woods. No one remembered its official designation, and no one called it City 224. Instead, it was named The City. Race names were slowly but surely losing their relevance.

Five hundred cabins, based on the design of Siskali's longhouse, were scattered around the valley. The only modification was the ceilings were higher, making them barely tall enough for a member of the Race to enter. The hospital and meeting lodge were at the center of the village, and both were much taller since Race biosynthesists would interact with the Chin there.

The village designers consulted records to ensure the woods had plants the Chin would eat and the valley had land the Chin would find suitable to garden and farm. An area for light industry was set aside, although it would be years before any Chin community would need to create its own industry.

Anya was on hand the morning the first Chin baby was born, crowning months of worry on her part about the technical process. She was gowned and nervously watching several technicians as they monitored the first batch of babies in the birthing room. Then she waited while they decided who was ready to be born first.

To Anya, Nebbe's placid assurances that she knew everything about the genetics of the Chin by now was little comfort. Anya believed Nebbe's explanation that reconstituting a Chin genetic pattern to make a Chin baby was very basic bioengineering. She claimed making one baby to even ninety thousand was doable. Still, Anya was worried.

Nebbie walked into the room in clean garb that matched the technicians and walked over to Anya. "Why does it look like you have not slept?" Her tone was gruff, which was normal for her.

"I'm fine, really."

Nebbe twitched an ear, the fine white hairs of her pelt made her appear authoritative. She grinned. "I know you are determined to hold the first baby born to this species and that you have dedicated yourself to help raise it. I have already told you the hard part of parenting comes after the birth. Anya, Prime of Quixotic Gestures, come meet your first child."

Anya followed Nebbe to where the technician was waiting. The tech and Nebbe triggered the end of the automated birthing process, gently picking the infant up and handing it to Anya. Anya's voice was an awed whisper. "Welcome home, little one."

The baby started to cry, and Nebbe took it back. Ever practical, she said, "If you drop it, you will *never* live it down. This is how you hold a baby."

19

MANY YEARS OF PROGRESS

Anya picked out the path with patient eyes and excellent memory. *Morning comes slowly this time of year.* Dawn would greet the valley soon, and she hoped to be down the path and into the glade before any of her charges were up and stirring. As always, she stopped on the hillside and listened with her whole being while night tiptoed toward day. While her hearing was the match of any Chin, she didn't move as gracefully as she once had. She had to be sure the crunch of snow did not give her away. The children always delighted in catching her before she got to the glade, if they could.

Her breath turned frosty. Fog, thick on the ground, clung to trees and shrubs and coated her ears. The fresh scents of winter invigorated her spirit. She made it all the way to the plaque before she heard her first squeak. A tiny, gruff voice emerged from a fog-shrouded blanket behind the plaque.

"Anya Friend, will you ever come late? Or will you be early all my life?"

A pair of cholate brown eyes regarded her from the depths of the small blanket. Grey fur encased the eyes, and the owner's snout was wrinkled with age and mirth. A small basket sat next to the blanket, and now Anya perceived a hint of fresh baked goods wafting from it. She knew a bottle of spring water and cups would be in the basket too.

She settled next to her old friend. "There was a time when you were a child, Songkali, that you would not lie in wait for me like a wily thara stalking the watering hole."

"There was a time when my grandmother would feed all of us little ones honeyed cakes in the evening and then see if we could wake up early enough from the huge dinner to track you across the valley and down the hill before you could get to the glade. She was always here first, and it took me years to figure out how she did it." Another joyful squeak, "I am now my grandmother and you are predictable, so here I am! Children will be along presently, I am sure."

They watched companionably as the sky lightened and cold lifted slightly from the glade. Soon Anya heard the first distant squeak and then many more, interspersed with humorous barks and the occasional Race word thrown in. The first child to enter the glade streaked directly to the pillar holding the plaque and placed his little hand upon it, only then lifting his eyes to see Anya. He glared defiantly. She twitched her ears while Songkali laughed.

"Good morning, child," said Anya.

"Good morning, All Grandmothers' Grandmother." He looked around the glade. I have caught you, have I not?"

Anya agreed. "I have not yet touched the plaque, but I am afraid another caught me first." Songkali chittered and squeaked.

The little one said with great dignity, "I have caught you both—adults may not catch Anya All Grandmothers' Grandmother, but it is well known that children can catch any grandmother. And I have done so!"

Songkali shook the snow from her blanket and rose to stand beside the triumphant child. Her dignity gave stature to her diminutive height. "Anya of the Tall People, may I present Belkin, my most troublesome of grandsons."

Anya nodded gravely. "Hello, Belkin. How does one earn the title of 'troublesome grandchild' these days?"

"Obviously by being smarter than all the grandmothers who try to catch me and make me do chores," Belkin said solemnly.

He had failed to see Songkali scoop up a handful of snow while he was talking with Anya. Now she dropped it on his head. His squawk echoed through the glade. Songkali chittered and said, "You have now been officially caught by the grandmothers, little one. Go to Village Hall, and ring the bell. Announce to all that Anya Tall Person's official visit to our community has begun." Sonkali's eyes twinkled. "She can be found at my house for any who wish to visit her."

♦♦✦♦♦

All morning long, adults from nearby enclaves and more distant communities arrived in the glade. The line entering Songkali's cabin stretched down the mountain. Many cups of tea later, many small plates of nuts and berries later, and many tiny portions of bread and honey cakes later, Songkali ushered the last of the many Chin visitors out the door.

Anya sighed and stretched. She had held so many babies she lost count, praised so many mothers and fathers her voice was hoarse, and laughed and smiled so much she was bleary-eyed. Her contentment was deep as oceans and limitless as the heart itself. She was so tired that she literally could not move.

Songkali settled beside her, placing a final cup of tea before Anya. With a tired wave of her hand, she asked, "What do you think? How are we doing?"

Anya rolled a sleepy eye toward Songkali and twitched her chin thoughtfully. She took her time answering the village elder. "All through the land, Chin are thriving. On this trip, I crisscrossed the continent and visited—what is it?—thirty communities. Harvests are good in most places, births are on par with past years, and elders are healthy. As a whole, our people are doing well."

Anya gave a sigh composed of equal parts contentment and exhaustion. "Chin reliance on Race manufacturing is minimal at this point. If my people were gone today, you would be fine. And my old friend, Sotheel, called me during this trip. The Joint Academies of Higher Education are a smashing success, she says. There are a number of Chin who possess the intelligence and ability to reach prime scholars in this generation. You will have no trouble understanding and keeping any Race technology that you desire. I am sure, however, you will go on and invent many technologies for yourself."

Songkali chirped a laugh and then spoke quietly. "As the regional representative of the Chin Association, I thank you.

However, Anya Tall Person, I now ask as your friend—we see so few Tall People these days. How are *you* doing?"

Anya blinked. "I have lived with your people many years. I have truly made this area my home. In your great-grandmother's day, I would hold every child when it was born. I held the first generation of babies. It was wonderful." Her gaze was light-years in the past.

"Later, there were lots of babies, and I was able to touch and visit with most of them. This generation I have only been able to meet a few. This is wonderful too. This was my mission. I will be eight hundred years old tomorrow, and I have accomplished more than I ever imagined. So, I'm doing well."

Songkali sighed companionably, staring into her cup of tea. She had known Anya all her life and knew the Tall People were slowly disappearing from Abundance. She realized she had seen a driven Anya and a sad Anya but never a happy Anya before. This was a first. Even though she understood that Anya Tall Person was said to be eight hundred years old and she would outlive Songkali by many years, Songkali hoped some of that happiness would stay with Anya.

Anya rose and made ready to leave. "I am staying here in my cabin tonight, and it is back to work for me tomorrow. I don't have another trip scheduled for a few days. Thank you for your hospitality, my old friend."

Songkali chittered and said, "I shall see you again soon, Anya. There is always a pot of tea waiting for you on my hearth."

••✦••

The next morning the sunrise caught Anya on a high ridge above the valley. It was the morning of her eight hundredth year. She had begun her run from her cabin door in the frosty pre-dawn moments that she so loved about Siskali's valley, and she had made it to the top of the ridge in very good time.

Now she was standing on the ridge, breathing deeply from the exertion, watching the morning come into being. She looked down over the valley, and her shadow plunged down the mountain as the sun brightened behind her. The village spread out before her, and tilled fields could be seen in the distance. *Almost three hundred years of progress. This is not a long time to rebuild a species,* she thought. *There is more to do, and we can do much if we try.* She sighed happily and started down the path.

Anya's path back to the village took her by the memorial plaque that had started it all. As was her habit, she intended to touch it and listen to it as she passed. She was mildly surprised to find a small Chin waiting for her. The proudly titled "troublesome child" Belkin appeared to have been there some time.

He got to his feet and reached up the post as far as he could. "Allow me, All Grandmothers' Grandmother," he said gravely and triggered the plaque.

The two of them watched companionably as Siskali's long-ago recorded image formed in the morning air. Together, they watched her bark and squeak. When the recording's voice switched to the Race language, Belkin looked between her and Anya alertly.

"Welcome to Siskali's house," the image repeated. "All you children who have made this sign for me and visit so often—welcome!" Siskali's squeaking laughter filled the glade. "Did you understand me when I just talked to you in Chin? If I'm not home, you may find me somewhere in the park. Please come looking, but don't cheat. Find me with your eyes and ears only, if you can." The recording ended, and Siskali faded away.

Belkin stared at Anya expectedly. "Yes, Belkin," she said quietly. "You have a question for me?"

"My grandmother says Siskali is our great ancestress. Did you know her? Did you get to play with her, All Grandmothers' Grandmother?"

Anya spoke gently. "No, she lived a long time ago—many years before even I was born."

Belkin appeared to consider this. "But Siskali got to play with many Tall children, so she says. I have never met a Tall child. May I go see your Tall children, Grandmother? Do I have to travel far to meet them? Songkali says I am almost old enough to travel the world if a grandmother comes along. I'm sure she would come with me. I would like to play with Tall children."

Anya considered her reply. Every Chin child eventually asked about Race children. Anya never knew what to say. She usually just said that they were far away. *Very far away, impossibly far, young Chin. I can't take you there, but I love you for wanting to go.*

When she sat on the ground and leaned against the plaque, Belkin sat beside her and placed his hand in Anya's, saying nothing and showing a wisdom far beyond his years. Eventually, he spoke, "I did not mean to make you sad, Grandmother."

Anya sighed. "You could never make me sad, Belkin. You are one of the great joys of my life. You and every child like you are the best things in my life."

Belkin cocked his head. "Tell me a story, All Grandmothers' Grandmother."

Anya hesitated. "About what, little one?"

"Tell me about Tall children—what they are like. Why can't I meet them? Why are they all so far away?"

"That will take some telling, and I don't know how much you will understand." Anya suddenly stood up and dusted off her knees. "What if I told you that many years ago, your grandmother asked me that very same question? And I told her that someday I would give her a better answer than *far away.* Let's go find Songkali because today is that day."

If Songkali was surprised when Belkin burst through her front door and into her kitchen, she hid it well. She immediately placed a bowl of nuts on the table for the child and continued clearing the table of her breakfast dishes. She acknowledged he had Anya in tow with a raised eyebrow and a chuckle.

"I was about to have some tea. Would you like some fruit with your tea, Anya?"

Anya twitched an ear appreciatively. Songkali was very good at grandmothering everyone. It did not matter that Anya was older than the Chin by many objective years—in this kitchen, she was perceived as the young one, definitely closer to Belkin in that regard. She sat and gratefully accepted the fruit and tea.

Even sitting at his grandmother's table with his mouth full of nuts, Belkin was not going to wait for the oldsters to finish going through the niceties of adult greetings before talking about the important stuff. That was *boring.* "Grandmother," he began, "is it true you wanted to play with the Tall children when you were a child? Would you still like to? They might be far away, but would you like to go right now and visit them? Will you take me with you?"

All during this amazing feat of chewing and talking, Songkali gazed fondly at Belkin, well aware that her eager grandchild never did anything at normal speed. When she had parsed through his cheerful information dump, she squeaked a laugh and turned to Anya. "Anya Tall Person, you seem to have been very busy this morning, telling tales, encouraging my Belkin to go on a quest across the galaxy, and somehow getting me invited to go. Perhaps *you* can explain what is going on?"

Anya lifted her cup of tea and sipped delicately. She sent an amused twitch across both shoulders before setting down the cup. "Belkin waylaid me at the plaque this morning and asked me the very question you asked me at his age about where all the Race's Tall children are. I told him I made you a promise to tell you that answer first, and he dragged me immediately here. If you have time this morning, I am ready to tell you the tale."

"I wonder if I need to put on another pot of tea?" Songkali's squeaks of laughter bounced around the kitchen.

Anya settled into her Tall Person-sized chair and gazed at the kitchen hearth fire while Songkali bustled about the room. Anya called out over the clatter her hostess was making. "A few months ago, I got a visit from two Tall People I never met before. One was from a planet called Forest, and the other from a planet they recently renamed Hukin."

Songkali came to a stop, and her whiskers twitched. "Tall People are still moving through the stars? That's wonderful."

Anya nodded thoughtfully, not noticing Songkali's insightful comment. "The visit was pretty wonderful, actually. They had some amazing things to tell me. Out in the stars are some planets—very much like this one. On one of them, my people are helping a race called the Yektektek reclaim their planet, just like we are doing here."

Anya sipped the last of her tea, knowing another pot was coming, and she'd better have an empty cup ready. "On the planet Hukin, my people have successfully restarted the dominant species and think the Hukin are going to be a great success." Anya twitched an ear and did not say, *the Hukin are so violent a species that I was told the Race decided to start them on one conti-*

nent and evacuate the whole planet as fast as possible. We are giving them their planet back, which is only right, but we are leaving them no gifts of knowledge to make it easier for them to reach the stars.

Songkali brought over the pot of tea and a cup for herself, placing them on the table.

Belkin piped up, "She talks a lot, Grandmother. Perhaps you should bring more fruit and honey cakes too."

The two adults locked eyes and grinned. The elderly Chin reached over and tweaked the child's nose then bustled back to the kitchen for a bowl of fruit and nuts. Belkin rubbed his nose and waited alertly for Anya to resume.

Once all of the amenities were finished, Songkali sat back down at her own kitchen table and also waited quietly for Anya to begin again. Suddenly, the speech that Anya had been waiting to give for so many years stuck in her throat. She wished she could leap up and pace while she talked, but the kitchen was so small she knew it would be a bad idea. Instead, she relaxed all her muscles and waited for her heart to slow.

She began. "As the Chin have prospered and spread all over this continent, you have run into many Tall Person villages that we no longer live in. During the last hundred years, we have dug up many of these villages and allowed the land to go back to forest or pasture or whatever kind of land your people needed in those places." Anya stopped talking and her gaze became very distant. Belkin started to talk, but a tiny squeak from his grandmother quieted him. Anya never noticed.

After a moment, she continued. "Chin have always known us and have always seen Tall People around as we've helped you grow and prosper and cover the land. The occasional Chin has wondered why there are so many empty Tall Person villages and asked us why we no longer live there. We always deflected these questions because we thought in the early days that letting Chin know the truth might obscure our mission, which was to give you a thriving civilization."

Songkali reached across the table and delicately refilled Anya's tea. When she spoke, it was quietly, not letting any squeaks enter her speech. "Anya, my friend, all my life I have seen you be strong and positive but not happy. In fact, there is a sadness so deep inside you that no Chin has ever understood it."

Belkin said, "I don't understand, All Grandmothers' Grandmother. Why should you be sad? And what does that have to do with where the Tall children are?"

Anya let a helpless twitch cross down her arm. "I can't take you to meet our Tall children, Belkin, because the Race can no longer have children. We lost that ability a long time ago."

"No!" Belkin was very positive. "Tall People can do anything. Of course you can have children. Why don't you try?"

Anya grappled for the right words to find what would make sense to a ten-year-old Chin. "It's hard to explain what happened. But now I will try to tell you the story. Once in our travels through the stars, my people ran into a godling—or at least a very powerful being. We angered this being so much that it cursed our Race. That was a little over eight hundred years ago. Because of the curse, I am the last Tall Person child to be born on this planet."

Songkali squeaked very sadly, and Anya realized she had already suspected this answer. Belkin's eyes widened, and he said, "I want to know everything, All Grandmothers' Grandmother! Why did the godling get mad at the Race? Did this happen here on our planet or somewhere else? Where is the godling now? What are you going to do to break the curse?" He stopped suddenly and turned to Songkali. "Grandmother, this is at least a full lunch story with dessert, right?"

Anya and Songkali locked eyes and nodded to each other. It was indeed going to be a full lunch story.

♦♦✦♦♦

It was late afternoon before Anya stopped talking. The wonders of a planet ten light-years away, the strange and wonderful people on it, and the godling who looked like the natives but had the name of a Chin—all had riveted Belkin. Songkali's whiskers had twitched several times while Anya talked, but she said nothing. Her eyes were horror-filled. However, when Anya described how her people had overtaken natives on other planets, how the godling had thrown an impenetrable barrier around the planet, and how the many Tall People on the planet had been cut off from the Tall Person civilization, that made her emit several indignant squeaks.

Finally, Songkali spoke: "Friend Anya, there is so much to know from this story. And you say the godling who called himself 'Wind from the North' claimed to be a friend of all Chin, and he knew us long ago?"

"That's what I was told," Anya said. "I never looked at the records myself. So many of our scholars spent all the centuries of their lives trying to break the barrier or to cure the Race of our infertility. I could never bring myself to look at any of the recordings. I simply chose to make babies the only way I could."

Songkali got a faraway look in her eyes. Her attention came back to the room abruptly, and her whiskers twitched with decisiveness. She spoke formally: "Anya of the Tall People, I Songkali of the Chin, administrator of the first district, ask that you make all records of Sansea, 'Traveler and Wind from the North,' available to me and all Chin for review and understanding. We need to know about this." Then she squeaked a laugh. "But not before morning. It is, of course, almost dinnertime."

SONGKALI'S PLAN

The days passed quickly. In the press of running the Chin Restoration, Project Anya forgot about her conversation with Belkin and Songkali. One hundred years earlier, Sotheel, who had been with Anya at the beginning and arguably had more to do with the existence of the Chin Restoration Project than anyone else in the world, had moved on to a position with Resources Board. This move left Anya with more responsibility and more work than she ever knew existed. Sotheel never called, and Anya had no idea that she checked in on her frequently, monitoring Anya's progress from a distance.

Brim was now head of Planetary Concerns and was now responsible for the wellbeing of a whole planet. However, he stopped by once or twice a year and visited for a few hours. Anya always felt warmed by his visits, though they were brief.

Taem and Vorne had remained with the project. Despite growing older, Taem still seemed boyish and possibly a bit immature because he always wanted Anya to sit in on their planning meetings and give her approval of their next city removal project. Vorne continued to back up his brother. Every time Anya explained that they could interpret Chin population growth projections and figure out which part of the continent needed their expertise better than she could, Vorne nodded but never stopped inviting her. She always went, whether she felt she needed to or not.

On this particular morning, Taem and Vorne had booked an entire hour of her time and showed up at her office early to boot. She scowled at them, a look she had unconsciously adopted from Nebbe. She was always dismayed that her scowls never seemed to carry the same level of fear the old biosynthesis scholar once had on her. Taem simply snapped the palms of his hands affectionately and bowed. Vorne gestured her to the door of the conference room with an ear twitch. Anya sighed and followed them out of her office.

In the conference room, Taem already had a full wall topological projection of the western continent running with regional population figures, material resources, and food production schedules scrolling down both sides. He seemed uncommonly pleased with himself. *"Look,"* he pantomimed.

"At what?" Anya spread her hands and twitched back.

Vorne sighed. "Taem wants you to know we are better than on track with projections and are down to the last dozen abandoned urban sites on this continent. Every last Race member not involved with the project has voluntarily relocated to one of our remaining cities, somewhere else in the world."

Anya stared at the wall. Wilderness and reclaimed farmland zones were haloed in green and took up most of the screen. Ongoing projects were highlighted in blue. Projections of food production versus population growth showed that with current farming methods and technology used by the Chin, this continent alone could support twice the expected population till the end of the century. All of the data showed that the Chin were reaching total independence of Race technology. When there were no more Race on this planet, there would be Chin. Anya felt sad, happy, and proud at the same time.

She was framing a compliment to the brothers when she heard a squeak behind her. Vorne, who was looking toward the conference room door said, "Hello, little one. What brings you here today?"

Belkin stood in the doorway, staring around the room. His grandmother Songkali could be seen walking up the hallway, shaking her head resignedly. Anya grinned. Belkin could do that to her. The day had just gotten better, she decided.

Belkin walked up to the wall projection and looked it over carefully. Whiskers twitching, he asked, "Does this show where your spaceships are?"

Vorne looked at Taem then Taem looked at Belkin and rippled a shoulder, indicating that the conversation had just gotten interesting. He quickly reached across the table and clicked on a recorder. Puzzlement rippled across Anya's face, and she looked at Songkali.

"Good morning to you, too, Anya," Songkali squeaked cheerfully.

Anya sat on the floor, bringing her head close to level with Belkin. "It is nice to see you, Belkin. This is actually a projection showing how wonderfully your people are doing in the world. It shows things like Chin population growth and food and resource production of your people. I'm sorry, but it doesn't show any spaceships. We aren't building them anymore. It has been a long time since the Race needed to build new spaceships."

Songkali started to say, "Belkin has an idea." At the same time, Belkin nodded vigorously and said, "We need a spaceship. I need to go to Small Home and visit the godling. Grandmother and I are going to tell him he has to drop the barrier and release the Tall People colony he is holding captive."

Songkali's squeaks bounced around the room, and Anya looked dizzy. She shifted her gaze to the elderly Chin and stared unbelievingly. Songkali became more sober, though she continued to grin. She said very formally, "As Chin administrator of District One and as the appointed representative of the Chin working group reviewing the data on Small Home that you gave us a few months ago, I request your assistance in transporting a Chin delegation to the planet Small Home."

"Oh," Anya said faintly. She tried again, sounding uncertain, "Small Home is very far away. No Chin as ever been to space, I think." *Mercy, I'm glad I'm sitting down. What do I do now?*

No one noticed Taem when he picked up a communicator and walked to the back of the room. He keyed in Sotheel's call code and murmured, "Anya wants a spaceship."

Sotheel was obviously inspecting a factory somewhere or at least walking through one. The sounds of heavy machinery could be heard rumbling in the background. She didn't even look surprised, just exasperated in a very Sotheel way. "Why? What crazy thing does Anya want to do now?"

Taem twitched an amused ear and sent a compressed transmission of the conversation he had just recorded. Then he put the communicator on speaker function and walked back to the table. Now Sotheel could listen in real time to the new scheme brewing.

Songkali strode over to the conference table and pulled out chairs for herself and Belkin. She walked over to where Anya was sitting and, with great dignity offered one small hand to Anya, helping her to her feet. Then she grabbed Belkin's hand with much less formality and dragged him over to the table, sitting him firmly in one of the seats.

"That is a separate topic, of course," Songkali murmured. "All Chin have noticed for a long time that fewer ships are coming to call at our planet. And you never seem to invite any Chin along when you go somewhere off planet. Our study group has been wondering why our friends don't want us traveling with you."

"It's not that we don't want you to go places with us," Anya began, somewhat contritely. "But we have been waiting for more of your people to make it through our schools and reach scholar status before giving you this information. Some of your people now have applied engineering and theoretical engineering abilities that match our own. We have plans to explain the process of shipbuilding and space navigating to your current generation of scholars."

Anya had her hands unconsciously clenched on the table. Songkali put her small hands on Anya's bigger ones and spoke words of comfort to her oldest friend. "And the truth is that Tall People are no longer going very much between the stars because you are dying out, and you did not want to burden your friends with this knowledge."

Anya nodded miserably.

"I don't think we want to wait until we know how to build ships of our own to make this trip." Songkali's whiskers twitched with mirth. "*Instead*, we would like to borrow one of your ships and make the journey now."

"AND we want you to come with us, All Grandmothers' Grandmother!" shouted Belkin.

Anya looked around the room at Songkali and Belkin then at Vorne and Taem. She still seemed slightly bewildered. She twitched a shoulder at Taem. *"Do we have any ships?"*

"I'm already on it," he twitched back.

A SINGLE STEP

Sotheel finished her factory inspection in a leisurely fashion, giving Anya plenty of time to figure out that she needed to call her for a ship. As the head of Planetary Resources, Sotheel had theoretical control over every Race item on the planet. The fact that Resources Board didn't have any ships that were interstellar capable would never occur to Anya. *Still, Anya's whims have had some pretty profound effects on all of us*, Sotheel thought. *She is not always wrong. Maybe I will call Brim.*

Brim, as head of Planetary Concerns, was the interface with the other planets and what was left of the once wide-ranging interstellar Race civilization. Planetary Concerns was headquartered in the largest Race city still functioning on the planet, but that was four hours ahead of Sotheel; and since she was just finishing her workday, she called Brim with glee, knowing she was about to wake him up.

Brim was indeed in bed, but his call program had a list of people who were always allowed through, no matter the time of day. Sotheel was on that list, along with Anya and all the people who had been on the original preservation team. Anya didn't know this, and in all the years that had passed, she had never called him. Sotheel was another matter.

Brim authorized the audio-only function. "I know you know what time it is, Sotheel. Why are you calling?"

"Hello, Brim. When was the last time you did something exciting?" Sotheel used her administrator function to switch on Brim's video, and now he could see her smiling face.

Brim grimaced in annoyance. *All of us grow older, but only some of us grow up.* "When you were on my preservation team and you used to keep me up till dawn talking in riddles, at least I could order you to go out and do some work. I can't interrupt your sleep anymore; yet, you still have me at your mercy. Is that fair?"

"As fair as life ever is, old friend." She gestured grandly and twitched an ear in mirth. "I am actually calling about our friend, Anya. She has a favor to ask you."

"She could always call me herself." Brim watched Sotheel's expressive ears and realized she was bursting to tell him something. He grew curious. "What does Anya want now?"

"Nothing big . . . only a multipurpose ship to take her and some Chin to another star."

"Only, hmm?"

Sotheel preened herself in the video monitor, obviously highly pleased she had made Brim speechless. Uncharacteristically, she waited for him to regain his composure. When she had his complete attention again, she said, "I don't know if she is having one of those strange flashes of brilliance that we've had to live with all these years or if her brain continues to turn to mush."

"Anya runs the largest project still remaining on this planet, Sotheel—far larger than The Preservation Project, which has taken second place to her vision for the Chin for at least a century now. I doubt her brain has turned to mush."

Sotheel held up a hand, indicating Brim to wait before she said into the air, "Yes. Taem, put her on."

Suddenly, Anya's sun-drenched image appeared next to Sotheel's. Strong sunlight was obviously pouring into her office window, reminding Brim that it was no later than mid-day on the western continent.

"Oh, hello, Brim." Anya looked pleased but surprised. "I didn't know you were on the line with Sotheel too."

"Our friend Sotheel was kind enough to include me in this conference call," Brim said dryly.

Anya looked at Sotheel and Brim doubtfully. "But I didn't know I was going to call until just now."

Sotheel ran a ripple down her arm and gestured grandly. "I always have your back, little sister." Brim got a look on his face that was half disbelief and half horrified amusement. He made a sound as if he needed to cough up a hairball. Brim was sure if Sotheel *ever* exhibited any sisterly tendencies, all the stars in the sky would go nova.

Anya smiled uncertainly at Sotheel and looked back and forth at both of them. "I've got a big favor to ask. It may take a bit more resources than my budget will allow."

"Whatever it is I'm sure we can work it out," Sotheel purred. Brim's ears twitched violently one time, and then he settled down to listen.

"Well," Anya began and then stopped. "It might sound strange, but I received a request from a delegation of my Chin elders—and I would like to help them, if I can." The last phrase came out in a rush.

Sotheel nodded and twitched an ear helpfully. Brim tried to stare at her and Anya simultaneously. *Anya still calls them 'my Chin.' They all call her 'Grandmother,' so I guess that tracks.*

Anya went on. "Songkali is the administrator for the First District, and she has requested that I acquire a spaceship so a delegation of Chin can journey to Small Home and try to get a meeting with the godling holding our colony and the Caeling people prisoner."

"Why does she want to do that?" Sotheel asked brusquely.

"She has a theory that the godling has been waiting for a Chin to show up and ask it to release our people. I know it sounds crazy, but she claims to have studied our data on the godling's behavior, and this is what she thinks it wants."

Sotheel looked fascinated. "I need to talk to your Chin." She turned to Brim. "In the meantime, how do we find a ship going to Small Home?"

Brim shrugged. "That may take a bit of arranging. Except for the small contingent of Exploration Corps science vessels still monitoring the anomaly, nobody ever goes there. There is no point. What is left of X Corps rotates vessels and crews on an irregular schedule. I have no idea when the next one will come here."

Sotheel signed off with Anya after promising to visit her the next day. She kept Brim on the line, though. "I think this could be important. What can we do?"

Brim thought about it. As head of Planetary Concerns, he was also a sitting member of the Council of Intermingled Planetary Affairs, a body composed of the administrators from every planet of the Race civilization—or what was left of it. He needed to do some research.

"I will check on projected ship arrivals. The council has been very interested in the progress of the Chin—and has been waiting until the Chin are ready—to invite them to take over the administration of Abundance and join the council. I dare say everyone has finally admitted that the Chin are going to be *the* civilization when we are gone."

"Well, that should have been obvious from the beginning," Sotheel snorted. "What did the council think we were doing here on Abundance? Just wasting our time? Using up resources? Why doesn't anybody pay attention to the important things?"

Brim was staring off into the distance and not really listening. Sotheel could rant on about the most absurd things. He sighed. *I am not going to get any sleep tonight. Sotheel keeps doing that to me.* Then he felt a rising excitement. *Once, a long time ago, Sotheel badgered our team into staying up all night to prove an assumption of Anya's . . . and look where we are today.*

When Sotheel finally paused, he got out. "Find out what you can, Sotheel. I need to apprise the council and plan our next moves. Someone on the council undoubtedly knows what condition X Corps is in currently." *Hardly any ships are moving between the worlds these days*, he thought. *Mostly node-operated drones maintain contact and information flow, holding civilization together. But I'll send out the request immediately. It might take a while, but I'm sure I can get a ship from somewhere.*

A CHIN COMES TO SMALL HOME

Multipurpose Ship 331-B slipped out of non-space and came to rest a few light-minutes from the anomaly. The zone of fractured space-time seemed unchanged. Ship 331-B knew this region of space well. In the early days of the crisis, it had spent nearly four hundred years of its life stationed near the planet Small Home. Its job had been to observe and probe, assisting the technicians and scholars of X Corps in their attempts to understand and penetrate the obstacle the Race persisted in calling the anomaly.

After many years of fruitless efforts, the ship had gone on to other assignments and served the Race well. It was now quite old for an exploration vessel and should have been retired; but the Race no longer built new ships, so it kept going. Many of its parts were scavenged from even older ships, so it had added the "B" designation to its number to honor the ships that no longer flew.

In the few heartbeats before 331-B reported the ship's arrival to the captain, it once again experienced the awe it always felt when confronted with the zone of fractured space-time. Nowhere else in the galaxy was there a sight quite like it. At one time, this sky had been full of ships—hundreds of them—all working to bring down the barrier that the alien had put around Small Home. Now there was but one picket ship on station, guarding the anomaly.

Ship 331-B sent it a hail and a compressed data-stream explanation of its current mission. A few minutes later, it got a welcome reply and a compressed situation status in return. The ship's captain had worked with 331-B for many years and knew without being told what the ship was doing. He waited patiently for it to report.

"We have arrived at Small Home, Captain. The guard ship sends a greeting and reports the status of the anomaly has not changed."

"Thank you. Please determine the current location of the communications module and set a course to take us there. Also, please ask our guests to join me in the conference room—it is time to show our guests the anomaly."

Ship 331-B sent the query to the picket ship and got the coordinates. It began to make its way around the curve of the anomaly, heading for the communication module the alien had so thoughtfully embedded in the fractured space-time but then refused to turn on for the last eight centuries. Using its own sensors, 331-B determined the picket ship was correct—nothing about the anomaly had changed. Per the captain's request, it also sent invitations to all guests to assemble in the conference room.

When Anya and Sotheel walked into the conference room, the captain greeted them with a smile and a flick of his ears. The Chin delegation was right behind them. Songkali walked into the room with five other district administrators from the breadth of the western continent, all somewhat elderly Chin. To them, he gave a deep bow and offered all chairs designed for a Chin. When Belkin ran into the room with a shout, the captain's smile deepened. He held out a paw that was batted playfully. The captain still seemed bemused by his Chin guests, especially Belkin, even though they had all been on his ship for days. The Chin species was an amazing novelty to him, despite the fact that he had been around the galaxy countless times in his many years in X Corps.

When everyone was seated, the captain turned on the main viewer in the conference room. No one spoke for long minutes. The captain felt no need to fill the room with his voice. Instead, he waited to see the visitors' reactions.

Songkali thought the anomaly looked beautiful but cold. Belkin didn't pay much attention to the anomaly itself but got out of his seat and walked back and forth along the wall, looking around the sky for more spaceships. The ship obligingly expanded the view anywhere Belkin pointed. Anya seemed pensive. Sotheel glared at the anomaly, appearing annoyed, which the captain had been given to understand was her normal personality.

Finally, the captain spoke. "The sight you are seeing is a real-time view of the anomaly. The phenomenon stabilized 804 years ago and has essentially not changed in that time. We are on course to the communications module and will arrive in thirty hours." His voice took on a somber note, "Our picket ship reports the module is apparently still functioning, and there is both heat and atmosphere in the module. Other than that, I have no information for you at this time." The adults around the table acknowledged the news with nods or ear twitches, each according to their ways.

Songkali chittered quietly to Belkin, and he stopped pacing.

"I heard you, Grandmother," he replied. Then he looked at the captain and said politely, "Thirty hours means there is time for another nice dinner, isn't there?" The captain's laughter filled the room.

The time passed swiftly. The captain played host, indeed providing several good meals. He also gave his guests the run of the ship, and Belkin spent many hours on the bridge.

The following morning, Belkin got around to asking about the captain's home. The captain obliged by pulling up views of his world. "This is Forest as it was nine hundred years ago—when I was born. My people have been on Forest for ten thousand years! It is the first planet we adopted when we started journeying to places away from our home world. That was almost at the beginning of civilization."

Belkin dutifully looked at the pictures. He knew what a wood was because he had grown up playing in one. To him, woods were small shady patches of trees and shrubbery that were too small to get lost in due to being surrounded by fields and bordered by villages. He had vaguely heard that forests were much bigger. "Why did you name your planet Forest? Why don't I see any forests in these pictures?"

The captain grinned and let a pleased twitch roll down his arm, ending with a tweak on Belkin's nose. "An astute student you are! At one time the whole planet was carpeted in trees—trees that were bigger than anything you have ever seen. The smaller ones were wider than a building and a thousand feet high, and the larger ones reached the size of small mountains. But it's true you won't find a single forest in this picture. Nine hundred years ago, we didn't realize the value of what we had, even though we named the planet after them."

The captain twitched both ears, and the ship dutifully changed the view. Now Belkin watched as image after image slid across the wall. Cities started disappearing in the pictures, and open spaces appeared. Small growths began in those spaces. Some ground-level views showed small trees. Later pictures showed the trees were bigger but not yet gargantuan.

The captain went into lecture mode. "We have your people to thank for the return of forests to Forest." He waited for Belkin's inquisitive look.

"Three hundred years ago, the Race living on Abundance remembered that a species called Chin once lived there. They realized there was a chance to pass along civilization. We noticed—everyone noticed! People on Forest remembered that we had once had a native species too. They were called the Yektektek. They were arboreal, which means they only lived in trees. Our problem was that we destroyed the trees, so we have been planting trees for three hundred years."

Belkin's eyes got very round. "Can I meet one? Can I go to your home? Are there any Yektek-tek on the ship?"

The captain looked momentarily sad. "It may be hard to meet Yek for a while. It takes a thousand years for the trees we are planting today to be big enough to sustain the Yektektek. We force-grew a patch of trees on a portion of the best continent, and a small colony of Yek is living in them. They are thriving, I am told, but we are protecting them carefully."

"A thousand years?" Belkin appeared to struggle with the concept of that much time passing. "You are going to be very busy for the next thousand years, I guess."

The captain grinned at him. "Well, not me personally. I won't live that long." He continued with his thought: "Actually, the reason your elders had trouble finding a ship to take you to Small Home is because we Foresters requisitioned most of the ships still in existence. Our civilization doesn't have a thousand years left to watch over this project . . . so millions of our people are on ships right now, getting older slowly as they travel at a little less than light speed making a big circuit around the nearby stars. Every hundred years or so, a few ships will slow and return to Forest. There will be a Race presence watching over Forest for the next thousand years or as long as the Yektektek need us."

Belkin nodded thoughtfully. His nose twitched. "It's a good plan," he decided.

◆◆✦◆◆

The picket ship met them at the communications module, and the crewperson on duty picked them up in a shuttle. She ferried the group over quietly but cheerfully. Any change in routine was good as far as she was concerned. She docked with the module and became a tour guide, pointing out the octagonal shape of the module and how the module flowed seamlessly into the strange distortion zone that was the anomaly.

She raised her hand at the hatch and said, "There are weightless conditions inside. Therefore, most of you will be floating. There is room for about a dozen people and handholds for them but only one chair. Has anyone here ever been in microgravity?"

Seeing no hands raised, she positioned herself in the hatchway and assisted them in one by one. When she came to Belkin, she reached down; but he launched himself past her with a whoop and zoomed into the module, grabbing handholds as he went.

When everyone was inside, they noticed only one console and one chair. The technician-turned-tour guide had been introduced to Anya and was very impressed with her accomplishment in bringing back the Chin. She respectfully ushered Anya into the chair and indicted the console.

"I sit in this chair once a day—every day—and try to turn on the equipment. Do you see the shiny spot on the console? That is the contact you touch. It didn't used to be shiny, but we all have sat in the chair and touched the contact many times over the years. The comm equipment has never turned on for us after the alien turned it off that first year. There is no indication that it will ever function again."

Anya sat very still and let the moment build. She had never intended to come here, had never wanted to leave Abundance, and had never wanted to be impressive to anyone. She was here because her dear friend Songkali and the rest of the Chin thought they could rescue the trapped colony on Small Home, though she didn't see how. She reached out and palmed the contact.

A moment went by and then another. Nothing happened. Anya pressed the contact again.

"Don't worry about it," the technician murmured sadly.

Sotheel had a very good view of the proceedings, floating near the top of the module. Belkin was with her. She nudged him quietly and twitched an ear. He nodded. "All Grandmothers' Grandmother?"

"Yes, Belkin?"

"Would you let my grandmother sit in the chair, please?"

Songkali had never been in microgravity before, and the weightlessness bothered her greatly. Anya had to guide her into the seat. When she was firmly planted, Songkali said, "Now hand me my grandson."

Belkin swam over unassisted as if he'd lived in space for years. Songkali gently pulled him down onto her lap, and together they pressed the contact. The words "Sending" began to scroll across the screen. The technician gave a startled grunt. Sotheel's grin and full body twitch lit up the room.

FAMILY REUNION

Race City One did not actually look shabby or seem tired, but as Amethyst floated down the boulevard, the city felt older these days. Perhaps without people, the city lacked a certain vibrancy. Automatic systems kept the city functioning perfectly as always; but as the node entity made its rounds that morning, it felt that perhaps the city was a little lonely.

The entity stopped at an intersection and purely out of habit turned toward the harbor. It flowed down the street to one of the quays, listening to the waves rolling across the harbor. The air was crisp and cool, and the morning fog lingered. It would be brilliantly sunny later, according to one of the automated weather systems that Amethyst listened to every morning.

Over the years, the population of the city had declined. More than one million Race had been on the planet when the anomaly formed, but only about one-tenth of that number still remained due to no births happening. Of those, only a few thousand still made their homes in the city. As more of the Race despaired the barrier in space ever coming down, the desire to leave urban environments grew stronger. Vega, Wren, and their father helped build bridges between the Race and Caeling cultures, and with the guidance of the Rememberer's Guild, people accepted invitations to live in enclaves in the native villages.

Many had adopted Caeling customs, taking the opportunity to go thoroughly native. The Race had brought technology with them; and everywhere they went, they offered it to the Caelings. Mostly, the Caelings hadn't found much value in Race technology, but they graciously offered their woodworking and farming skills back. Generally speaking, the two races had gotten along well.

Amethyst spent most of its time in the city, possibly out of a faint sense of loyalty to the generations of scholars that had come before it. Some of its best corporeal friends had lived in this city. It could access or meld its consciousness with the many semi-autonomous systems around the planet, so it didn't ever have to go anywhere. However, walking around the city brought it a measure of joy, so it made the trek every day.

When it was done listening to the harbor waves, Amethyst followed its usual habit and turned inward toward the science building. The breeze picked up. Except for the birds chattering in the trees, the city remained otherwise silent.

Amethyst followed the same route to the fourth-floor lounge. It had used the room approximately 292,000 times in the last eight hundred years. It timed its arrival to coincide with the burn off of the morning cloud cover, so the sky cleared enough to let in direct sunlight through the huge observation windows.

Amethyst entered the gloriously sunlit lounge. It still enjoyed seeing the morning sunlight hit the table. The luminous purple highlights the alien had imbued the table-turned-sculpture with still matched the node entity's stressed space matrix perfectly. Amethyst always hoped the alien had meant the glowing table as a promise, but a promise of what it didn't know. Even though it wasn't designed to forget data, enough time has passed that the node entity had stopped reviewing or being optimistic about any implied promises.

It floated over to the window. This is where it had sat on that day with Var—old, irascible Var—and watched a native charlatan turn a table into a wonder. This is where it always came to appreciate the table. After a moment, shared only with the silent room and a few dust motes dancing in a beam of sunlight, the node approached the table.

Coming around the side, Amethyst saw the comm screen was live—that had not happened in eight hundred years! Amethyst stopped in the closest approximation to surprise that a node entity could experience. The screen read, "Receiving message. Respond?" Amethyst moved into line with the screen and hit the "Accept" button.

The image that formed on the computer's screen was even more unexpected. Two aliens—one bigger than the other—stared out of the screen at the node entity. The planetary data bank looked at the image, and that device assured Amethyst of two items of information simultaneously: one was that the creatures on the screen were identical to those once known as Chin from home planet Abundance; and the second was the Chin species was extinct, so these could not be Chin. Amethyst took what would have been an extra heartbeat to absorb the rest of the data bank's stored knowledge on the subject and then decided on a course of action. It carefully selected words in Northern Hemisphere Modern Chin, a language not spoken—as far as it knew—in over three thousand years.

"Hello. Will I be able to communicate with you in this language?"

The larger figure cocked its head to the side, appearing to listen intently. When the figure repeated the word "Hello?" in an odd but recognizable accent, the node entity diagnosed the speaker as an older female Chin. *Ah, my data seems to be out of date. I see two Chin; therefore, they are not extinct. Excellent! I suspect that means the smaller one is a child.*

Belkin burst out excitedly, "Grandmother, that's a node entity! I've seen one at school! How 'bout that—they have them here too!" Since the child had shouted this out in Race, Amethyst concluded that language would be no problem.

"Welcome, travelers, to our home. I am called Amethyst. May your feet be light, and your path continue for many leagues."

The two Chin looked at each other and seemed puzzled. Perhaps the Caeling greeting Amethyst had used for centuries didn't translate as well into Race as it had always assumed. Communicating with a Chin might be harder than it thought.

Just then a Race individual appeared in the picture alongside the two Chin. It spoke rapidly. "Scholar Entity Amethyst, I greet you. I am Sotheel, Planetary Resources Administrator for Planet Abundance. Is there a Small Home planetary administrator available to talk to?"

The node entity could not blink, and it had no fur to ripple. Yet, its purple matrix sparkled, and it projected a wry tone that indicated amusement. "There are no planetary administrators in the sense you mean, Administrator Sotheel. Race are not in charge of this planet—Caeling are. They do have numerous social organizations that help broker the flow of goods and services, and they have some to help mediate disputes."

"I know what local jurisdictions are," Sotheel shot back. "They are quite common among some species, and lately I've been helping the Chin reinvent them." This elicited a look of disbelief from both Songkali and Belkin. "With no planetary boards, I guess we are stuck with you then," she grumbled.

Amethyst was delighted. She very much reminded him of his old friend Var, and he knew many stimulating conversations would be possible with her. "To what do I owe the pleasure of this visit, Administer Sotheel?" His tone and his matrix sparkle made it clear he was tweaking Sotheel's nose.

She understood immediately and realized she was talking to a master of the conversational form. She twitched one ear in amusement at herself. "Actually," she said dryly, "we are not here to visit you at all. These people are here to visit someone else." She sent a ripple grandly down her arm toward Belkin and Songkali who were sitting in the chair, and then she drifted out of the range of the pickup.

Even though Amethyst was now aware that the smaller Chin had seen a node entity before this encounter, it realized the young Chin might not be able to read the subtleties of node matrices. It addressed them. "Greetings, individuals from Abundance. Welcome to Small Home. How may I assist you?"

Belkin took a big breath and then looked up at his grandmother. She gave him a nod and a squeeze. "Hello, node entity," he said. "We have come to visit Sansea. May we see him, please?"

Amethyst was unsurprised. The communicator had turned on for the first time in eight hundred years because a Chin—who was here to visit Sansea—was sitting in that chair. All of this had a certain type of logic to it. The node entity nodded soberly and said, "I will try."

The picture froze, and static began to break up his image. The shuttle technician popped her head into the module and said, "Hey, do you know that your comm unit is relaying a huge volume of data to the ship right now?"

"What does the data appear to be?" asked Anya.

The technician listened to the ship for a second and grinned. "It's a regular planetary upload . . . just eight hundred years' worth of uploads. This is going to take a while."

••✦••

Amethyst queried the planetary net first. The climatory sensor net was the biggest web of interconnected Race hardware on the planet, comprised of thousands of sensors in near-space orbit, stationary ground installations, and even oceans. Every instant of the day, the net tracked weather, built climate models, assessed vegetation patterns, and predicted future Race needs. Its secondary function was to help with navigation and monitor individual Race tracking locators, allowing any Race member to request any type of material assistance instantly.

For eight hundred years, it had also scanned for any hints to the whereabouts of the alien Sansea, presumably still masquerading as a Caeling. It had never reported a sighting. The sensor net updated its daily report for Amethyst now and confirmed still no sightings. The node ordered it to go to continuous scan—the highest priority—until told otherwise.

"Do the easy first," Var had said numerous times when terrorizing students and being especially querulous. "Then when it doesn't work, do the harder task." Amethyst remembered the old prime scholar ending with "And when that doesn't work either, use your brain and do the right task."

Amethyst had done the easy task. He had started eight hundred years of planetary uploads to the communications module, and hopefully that information would get to the Race ships beyond the anomaly. If the node entity was right, the constant transmission would keep the comm units linked and switched on. Querying the sensor net was not really a hard task, and it didn't take much original thinking either.

Next, it said to the net, "Identify the location of every Race member still alive who attended the Sansea demonstration that day and/or attended the meal afterward, especially Wren and Vega." Time to think smart. He set about making comm calls to every individual on the list. There were only seven, including Wren and Vega. Simultaneously, he released a short message to every Race individual on the planet, asking them to contact any Caeling they knew and asking Caelings to assistance in contacting Sansea.

Then he had an afterthought. He added a repeating message to the planetary upload stream on the assumption that it was going out through the anomaly: "Sansea, you have visitors. Please contact us immediately." If the alien was not on Small Home and if he was beyond the anomaly, perhaps he was paying attention to the current events with some part of his consciousness. Amethyst hoped so. Node entities could hope after all.

LONG-DISTANCE CALL

When the call came into Vega's communicator, she had just finished knocking ice off the outside shutters of her little house prior to opening them to the cold winter morning. After a period of wandering, she and Wren eventually settled in the mountain village where they had met Sansea many years before. While Wren traveled the world most of the time, Vega did not. She stayed put and wound up moving onto the property next to Mali after all. She and Mali became friends for a lifetime.

Vega had the opportunity to watch as the Caeling grew quickly into a young woman and eventually became Amali, the wise woman who was a power in the small mountain village. She watched and helped Amali raise a family of her own. Amali tried to call her Avega, but Vega resisted being cast as a wise woman—she wanted to be an auntie instead. Vega was officially named Taswia by Mali's children, which didn't exactly mean "auntie" but translated more to mean "a settled person and a part of our extended family who isn't going anywhere." Many generations of Mali's family had now called her that, so Vega felt truly part of the community.

She stamped the snow off her feet and walked into the house. She laid the wood in the hearth but did not start a fire yet. She was running water into the sink when she heard the communicator go off. As she walked to the device, she wondered what part of the world Wren was calling from because it was awfully early for her sleepyhead brother to be up if he was in any nearby time zone.

The image that formed in front of her was so unexpected that she twitched both ears and sniffed in surprise. She had not gotten a call from another Race individual for a long time. She had certainly not talked to one of the few node entities on the planet for hundreds of years. Still, she knew this one. She spoke formally, "Greetings, honored scholar Amethyst. May your feet be light, and your path continue for many leagues."

The node entity's stressed space matrix sparkled cheerfully. "Thank you. I can describe the lensing effects of solar coronal gravitational fields with a degree of precision even I find boring, but I have never been able to master the various Caeling greetings. This one, however, I try to use myself, and I thank you for your graciousness.

"But I must get right to the point. The communicator through the anomaly is working again, there is an individual of the extinct species of Chin sitting in the chair of the communications module, and it is asking to visit Sansea."

Vega stared at the node entity stunned. She started to say something, stopped, and looked around her house. She was now over nine hundred years old, which was beginning to be elderly for a member of the Race, and this had been her home for almost longer than she could recall. She remembered studying the ancient texts about the Chin of her home planet in her youth. She had mourned their passing all her life. "There is no Chin species anymore." She said crossly, but there was hope in the way she cocked her head.

"Hence, my statement. When I said I was looking at a member of an *extinct* species, I was not kidding. I assure you the two individuals I saw were Chin. I cannot be fooled by any media about what I am seeing."

A storm of emotions held her riveted to the spot, staring at the node entity in the communicator. Vainly, she looked up. If she were standing under the night sky, she would be able to see the anomaly by its effects on the starscape—but not through her roof, not even from her window, and not in the daytime. Finally, she found her voice. "Is the anomaly gone?"

"No."

"Then how are they going to get through it to visit Sansea?"

"I imagine Sansea has thought of that," the node entity said gently.

Vega took a deep breath and let it out slowly. *A Chin has come to visit Sansea—I can't even grapple with how profound that is. Oh, wonderful! Wonderful! But I have no idea where the alien is—he might not even be on Small Home. Does Amethyst think Sansea planned for this? How did Wren get ahold of him the last time visitors came?*

"I climbed a *very* tall tree!" The words came out as a shout.

Amethyst stayed quiet. Most of the organic beings it had known would occasionally spout gibberish. The trick was to give them time to notice they had done so, and then ask for clarification. In this case, it sounded as if Vega had quoted something. Eventually, the node entity made an interrogative sparkle.

Vega started by snapping the flesh of both palms and wrinkled her nose, laughing at herself. "Something Wren said. He wanted it down in the record that he'd climbed a very tall tree when he called Sansea back from wherever he was that first time all those years ago. Wren insisted I write it down exactly that way."

"A tall tree is in order then," Amethyst said dryly.

With thoughts of lighting the morning fire and of eating breakfast forgotten, Vega nodded vigorously. "I will make the call."

⬩⬩✦⬩⬩

Wren walked down from the island village under a brilliant sun. He reached white sand and looked up and down the shore for his beached skiff. Spotting the skiff, he noticed how far from the water it was. He realized he must have landed at high tide when he dragged it up on the beach three days before. He walked up to his skiff and regarded it with an experienced eye.

He considered the wisdom of asking one of the local youths to assist him in relaunching it, but he was still very strong for his age and no destination required him to hurry. He simply settled down to wait, laughing at himself. After all, high tide would return eventually, and he didn't want anyone suspecting he was becoming a lackwit in his old age.

Wren moved through the world more slowly these days but still had a sure stride. In the early years, his feet had taken him to many interesting places in the company of Sansea. He had met and played his pipes for numerous village children, and he had inquired with the elders about miracles particular villages needed. Wren would offer a miracle sometimes from his meager knowledge of planetary lore and sometimes from the Race's technological bag of tricks.

Those were good years; but eventually, Sansea had begged off the excursions, pleading important work elsewhere. Wren thought he seemed more tired, faded, and worn in ways unexpected from a god—it was almost as if Sansea were running out of vitality right in front of him. When Sansea took his leave, he wished Wren good health and joyous travels as if he didn't expect to be coming back any time soon. Then he shook Wren's hands, stepped back, and faded out in front of Wren.

In memory of these excursions, Wren formed the Society of Travelers, with himself as the first permanent member. He had now walked around the world several times, spreading knowledge and tricks of living and starting chapters of the society on every continent. He almost couldn't walk anywhere anymore without bumping into another traveler.

Even though Wren made little use of Race technology in his current life, the skiff contained several items that every Race member would need. A part of his mostly disassembled flight rack contained a suite of sensing and communication modules. He used the communicator to talk with Vega regularly. When the device chirped now, he got up from the sand and reached into the skiff.

"Greetings, big sister. Your timing is superb. I am waiting for the tide to come in and have plenty of time to talk." Wren's voice was warm with a self-deprecating chuckle.

Vega wore the perplexed look on her face that Wren always delighted to see. *Why is Wren waiting for the tide to come in? Where in the world is he? No, don't ask.* "Greetings, Wren. Where are you?" *Oh no, I actually asked that!*

"I am about forty yards further up the beach than I wanted to be, but the view is spectacular. Do you want to fly over to the islands and help me drag my boat down to the water's edge?"

"No, little brother. I do not want to fly down to a beach somewhere and help you put a silly boat in the water." The exasperation in Vega's voice was automatic, and the instant she heard it come out of her mouth she knew Wren had done it to her again. She didn't even have to see Wren grinning. She trumped him, however, by her next words. "Are there any large trees nearby that you can climb?"

Wren automatically looked around the area. The nearest trees were far up the beach. *Why does my addlebrained sister want me to climb a tree?* Then he stared hard at the communicator. Vega was many things but faint in the head was not one of them, and she never joked.

When Vega was sure she had Wren's attention again, she said gently, "There are aliens beyond the barrier. They have come asking to visit with Sansea."

Wren appeared uncomprehending.

"*Aliens*, Wren. Live *Chin* from our home planet are sitting in a ship beyond the barrier. Chin haven't existed for thousands of years . . . but they are here, Wren. I need to talk to Sansea."

Wren looked a little worried, which surprised Vega. He was slightly hesitant in his reply.

"It's nice to know the little aliens that you were so sad about not meeting when we were growing up are now at the barrier. You may get to meet them, but . . ." He let the last word draw out. "Sansea wasn't looking so good the last time I talked to him."

Vega watched Wren's ears go down sadly, which alarmed her more than his words. "What are you talking about, Wren? What could possibly happen to Sansea? He's immortal."

"Immortal or not, he looked awful the last time I saw him. He even faded out in the middle of our conversation. He may not be able to come back from wherever he went."

"Try, Wren. Please try. It's really important." The desperation in her voice surprised both of them.

Wren nodded. "Of course." He twitched his ears up in a vague attempt at humor. "*Anything for you, sister dear.*"

When Vega signed off, Wren sat watching the beach for a time. Climbing a tree had a certain appeal, at least symbolically. He sighed. *I haven't climbed a tree in hundreds of years. And last time I didn't employ a tree either—a whisper in the wind was all it took. I don't think that will work this time.*

The sand was warm, and the breeze was gentle. Waves marching to the beach made quiet shushing sounds. Wren leaned against the side of the skiff and shut his eyes. He tried to remember how Sansea had looked the last time they spoke, evoking every detail of voice and mannerism in his mind. *Yes, that's his voice and that is what he looks like. Now imagine him walking. Hear him singing, tell him a joke, hear his laughter . . . .*

♦♦✦♦♦

Vague, formless shapes moved through a starscape anchored by gravitational set points. Standing waves created connections between the implicate and explicate. Time and duration were continually created and destroyed by shifting tension points between various dimensional reality sets. Tracking the information flow from all the variables consumed energy scavenged mostly from holes in the fabric of reality.

The essence known as Sansea was spread through a volume of space and time that far exceeded what Sansea had ever tried. The task he set required contact below the quantum level with regions measured in thousands of cubic light-years. There was no way to influence and keep track of the volume of reality he had dedicated himself to, but he tried; and in the trying, he had mostly lost himself.

A small awareness of a tiny place in the cosmos that he was interested in began to impinge on his senses. Almost an annoying prickle, buzz, or taste sifted slowly into his awareness. The smell of earthiness became more insistent. Sansea's consciousness began to reassemble.

♦♦✦♦♦

When a hand formed and grasped the gunnel of the little boat, Wren was jolted from his dreamy state of contemplation. He had been trying to cast his consciousness into the universe to reach Sansea, knowing that no such action as casting one's consciousness was possible. Yet, as Sansea had stated again and again, "Information is the pillar of reality. It cannot be destroyed and is not bound by time."

Wren had spent the afternoon calling and calling, imagining Sansea standing in front of him, real and solid. Now there was a hand then a misty form behind it, and suddenly Sansea stood before Wren. Sansea looked around and without hesitation asked, "Why is your boat so far from the water?"

"I could use a hand," Wren replied cheerfully.

MEETING OF FRIENDS

Wren noticed that Sansea seemed to take a great deal of pleasure in lifting his half of the boat and carrying it across the beach to the wet sand. His black spots gleamed brightly as he and Wren carefully set the craft just beyond the surge but well inside the spray zone. They carefully positioned the boat prow out for easy launch.

When they were done, Sansea stepped back and stretched mightily. "Where are we going?"

Wren twitched an ear in humor. "Welcome back, Sansea. My, you have been away a long time. You are looking good. So nice to see you. How have your travels been? Fruitful, I trust?"

Sansea smiled in genuine pleasure, his pattern of spots flashing a gay tempo. "Yes, Wren, I have missed you too. You may be the most irreverent being on this side of the galaxy. I couldn't hope for a better welcome home." He looked around the beach. "We are getting into the boat, I trust."

Wren snapped the flesh of his palms and bowed in Caeling fashion. Together, they pushed the boat into the water. When a retreating wave picked up the boat, they climbed in.

The water between the island and mainland was choppy this time of year. Wren spent much of his attention keeping the boat on course. Sansea spent most of his time looking around the area, as if seeing everything for the first time. It became obvious to Sansea after a while that their destination was a particular harbor. Slowly, Race City One grew larger on the mainland.

Sansea sighed. "Why are we going to the city, Wren?"

Wren called back over the choppy seas, "I assumed you knew. Don't you know everything that goes on, especially on this planet?"

Sansea grinned at Wren. "You know I prefer to live in the moment just like the beings around me live. I do have ways of knowing things if I have to, but that's rarely the best way to live, don't you think?"

Wren grunted. "I think I will call up my sister and let her explain it to you. You have never been able to push her around with your brilliance."

"I deserve that." Sansea came over and squeezed Wren's shoulder. He wandered back to the front of the boat. "Make the call."

As Wren made the call to his sister, Sansea spent his time looking ahead of him, studying the mainland and Race City One. As more of the city came into view, Sansea noted that it seemed smaller than it had been the last time he saw it. It became obvious that parts of the city had not been in use for a long time. Sansea intuited that at some point many of the Race had made the choice to live elsewhere. He was curious as to where they had gone. *Why would the creatures who called themselves the Race and who loved urban environments abandon a city? The answers might be very illuminating.*

As they neared the harbor and the cross-chop got stronger, Wren ended his phone call. Sansea came back to give Wren a hand steering the boat.

"Vega is getting ready to fly down from her home right now and is going to meet us in the city. Do you remember the node entity Amethyst? It is one of our remaining senior scholars. Amethyst wants to meet with you too."

"Since I am obviously going to the city anyway, I will happily meet with Amethyst. I remember the node well." Sansea flashed his spots, smiling again. "Where does your sister live these days?"

"About a five-minute walk from where you first met her. She bought the land next to Amali's parents and has been part of their extended family forever. She is an umpty-great aunt and a pillar of the community."

"That is wonderful to hear." Sansea found himself unaccountably filled with strong emotions of satisfaction tinged with a touch of sadness. Little Mali and big Vega had been an obvious choice for lifelong friends. He was glad they'd recognized this and acted on it. He and Wren were peculiarly also perfect for friendship. Sansea had to face it—having a friend had not happened very often in a life measured in eons.

Their craft crossed the interface, and the harbor was suddenly calm. It didn't take long to tie up at a pier. Wren jumped out of the boat and looked around. "I have been asked to bring you to the science building where you gave us your demonstration . . . but I haven't been to the city in a long time, and I'm not sure where it is."

"In that case, nothing has changed from the first time you showed me the city. I guess we are just going to have to wander around looking for it." Sansea grinned again, flashing his spots once more at Wren. Wren rippled both arms back in glee and bowed. They both looked at the several streets.

Wren picked one and started walking. Possibly his memory was better than he thought—or hundreds of years of practice in the Society of Travelers had paid off—because he had picked the right street. Soon they were in front of the low four-story building with the wonderful wraparound windows.

Amethyst floated out the front door in time to see Wren gesturing at the building and talking to Sansea. For some reason, Wren was giving himself a congratulatory ear twitch and palm snap. The node entity sparkled its matrix, and Sansea nodded back, brightening his spots in a complex pattern. Wren, totally unconcerned, turned and gave Amethyst a brilliant smile. "Look who I found on a deserted beach," he called out.

"It was my understanding you were going to employ a tall tree," the node entity countered. "However, deserted beaches are acceptable."

Amethyst addressed the alien. "Welcome, Sansea. Please come in."

They followed the node entity into the building and made their way to the fourth floor. The conference room was bright and airy. The glossy brown wood conference table with its lovely violet hues and melded-in communicator remained where it had been placed all those years ago.

Wren immediately went and sat in the chair. The communicator turned on, and a small unfamiliar face stared at him from the communications module embedded in the anomaly. Wren twitched an ear in amusement and called out behind him. "Sansea, I believe this call is for you."

♦♦✦♦♦

Belkin's excited squeaks hit maximum volume and bounced around the octagonal space of the communications module. His grandmother came rushing in from the picket ship attached to the module, saying, "Not so loud, child. Please use town voice, not woods voice."

Belkin immediately grabbed Songkali's hand and pulled her into the chair in front of the comm unit. "Look, Grandmother!"

Songkali looked into the monitor and saw a Race individual smiling back at her. Over his shoulder was a type of person she had never seen before. Presumably, that individual with black spots across portions of its body was one of the natives of Small Home.

"Hello," she said politely. "My name is Songkali, and this is Belkin. We and our companions have come to visit Sansea. May we talk with him please?"

The native brightened some of its spots. "Pleased to meet you, Songkali. I am Sansea."

Belkin whispered, "Told you." He squeezed his grandmother's hand and said, "Are you really the teacher? You don't look anything like I expected."

Sansea nodded gravely. "I have been called teacher."

"When you travel, what direction do you come from?"

"I have been a traveler many times, little one. And sometimes I come from the north. You must be Belkin."

Belkin nodded grandly. "Good to talk with you, Traveler. Please wait a minute—I have to get someone." Belkin launched himself out of the chair and spun in space so his hands and feet were pointed down like the pro he had become and shot through the doorway into the picket ship. The gravity field of the ship took hold, and he hit the deck running. "All Grandmothers' Grandmother! He answered! He answered!"

Anya and Sotheel were already heading to the module, having been alerted to the incoming transmission. Belkin met them in the corridor, grabbed their hands, and pulled them along faster. Songkali waited for everyone to assemble, and then she spoke rather formally.

"Sansea of the Many Journeys, I have read many stories about you, and I have always wanted to meet you. In the stories, you are always the traveler, always the teacher. However, *we* have traveled to see you on a manner of importance. Will you let us come down to the planet?"

"Are you sure you can't just tell me what's on your mind right now? I am listening."

Songkali's whiskers quivered with mirth. "I have noticed that children and adults of any age listen better in person."

Wren, standing behind Sansea snapped his palms loudly and chuckled. Sansea rolled his eyes at the sound and didn't bother to glance over at the irrepressible Wren. He knew what Wren's vote was. He pondered for a moment.

"Very well. I see four of you. There is a small craft attached to the module on my side of the barrier. There is plenty of room for four. Please have your engineering specialists check to confirm it is flightworthy. When you are ready, you may come down to the planet."

The bulkhead behind the comm unit had always been blank. Now there was a door there. Belkin squeaked in delight and, before anyone could stop him, launched himself to the door, looking for a way to open it. The door had a standard design latch, and he was cranking it open when Anya caught up with him. Gently, she scooped him up.

"There are people who have waited their whole lives to find this door, Belkin. Let's let them open it first."

The tech had been waiting discreetly in the doorway of the picket ship while the conversation with Sansea had been going on. Gratefully, she came in and began studying the door. She touched her communicator and murmured into it. Soon the module filled with crew people carrying all manner of equipment.

Songkali turned her attention back to the screen where Sansea waited patiently. "We thank you for your gracious invitation, teacher. We look forward to seeing you soon." She signed off and rubbed her whiskers contemplatively.

She and the Chin study group had extensively gone over the X Corps reports from Anya's people. Those reports had concluded that this alien was a bit of an entertainer and a showoff. She was beginning to see what they meant. *But we have a door and an invitation*, she thought as she put her chin in her hand and squeaked quietly, satisfied with the progress so far.

Sitting quietly in the conference room, listening to Sansea talk, Amethyst waited. He watched the alien sit back in his seat and stare at the dark communicator screen. The node entity had the feeling that Sansea had been a little surprised at how the conversation turned out. The node, however, was quite pleased by the way Songkali had presented her case and was looking forward to meeting her.

Amethyst hesitated a moment, then broke into Sansea's contemplation. "Sansea, while you were talking with Songkali, I received a message from Vega saying she was on her way. Apparently, it will take a while because her plans have changed, and she is walking."

Wren muttered mournfully, "I know that walk—it's so much easier to fly."

Sansea's spots brightened, and he grinned. Turning back to Amethyst, he wrinkled his nose. Amethyst matched his grin for a sparkle.

26

WE ALL STAND TOGETHER

Vega bustled around her cottage, pulling together travel clothes and checking out her elderly flight rack. She had kept it functional with periodic maintenance through the years, though she hardly ever used it. She almost never went anywhere these days; her life was in this village and with these people. She packed hurriedly.

With her usual morning routine upended, she tried to think of anything she'd forgotten. *Sansea is back! He's finally back! Wren actually did it. And now the boys are on a little boat crossing the ocean, heading for the city. I have to tell Amali about this—she will be so surprised. Then I am really going to go down to the city. Mercy, I haven't been there in forever. After Sansea changed everything, there was never any reason to go back.*

Vega came to a complete stop and stared hard into the distance. She shook herself gently. *Why did I think of Mali just now? She has been gone for so many years. I meant to say that I have to tell my friend Mearri. Was she Amali's great to the fourth granddaughter or the fifth?*

She sighed. *Oh dear, I have no idea how long I'll be away. I have to tell the school to cancel my classes, and the elders will want to know Sansea is back too. Maybe, if I just ask Mearri, she will tell everyone for me.* She hurried out the door.

Mearri's home was next door as far as mountain village distances go. The five minutes it took Vega to run to Mearri's house shouldn't have winded Vega, but it had been years since she had run at full Race speed. She banged on Mearri's door, knowing she was wearing a manic grin.

"Oh hello, Auntie!" Mearri pulled the door open quickly and came out onto her porch. She looked around Vega. "What have you been chasing, Aunt Vega? Or what is chasing you? You look like you have run all the way down from the mountaintop."

Vega rippled a grin across her face, then wrinkled her nose in Caeling fashion. Being twitted by her fourth to the great-grand-niece was a pleasant bit of silliness. Vega let her breathing slow. Then she said, "I must leave for the city, Mearri. I just got the most amazing news from my brother, Wren. Sansea of the Many Journeys is back. He and my brother are going to the city, and I must meet them there. Would you apologize to the schoolmaster for me? I will have to cancel the rememberer's training—I mean, the history classes I am teaching—for the next little while. I have no idea how long I will need to be gone."

Mearri's eyes got huge. "Aunt Vega, you never go to the Sky People city, and I can't remember the last time you left the mountain. Are you sure you have to go?"

"Yes, I have to go. My people from the outside have been able to establish contact through the anomaly, and they are asking for a meeting with Sansea. Now the traveler is back, and I have to talk to him."

"Then may I go with you?"

For the second time that morning, Vega came to a complete stop. She stared at her niece. *Mearri never leaves the mountain—she is the ultimate homebody.* Vega felt deeply touched by the offer as she remembered Amali slouched and sad, moving away as Vega left the first time she visited. After a moment of thought, she said, "I think my flight rack will still carry two people. I would be honored if you came to the city with me."

Mearri flashed her spots and declared, "I see that this is momentous news for you. I will pack and let the schoolmaster know we are leaving. I shall join you at your home shortly. Please walk home, Auntie. You've done enough running for one day."

Vega bowed and wrinkled her nose at her niece. Then she was off Mearri's porch in a flash. Using her long legs and not quite running, she returned to her cottage to continue her preparations.

Fortunately, she had no crops to tend to this time of year, and like most of the villagers, she had never owned any individual livestock. Being a part owner in the communal herds meant the wealth and responsibility was spread to others too. All of the village livestock was safely penned in the meadow before the caves by day, and then the animals wintered in the caves at the base of the mountain at night.

Vega set about closing down the cottage and packed for her trip. She retrieved one cherished item from a box and stared at it. It was a scrap of cloth from the blanket that Amali had given her long, long ago with the request that Vega take it on all of her adventures. Vega always did so. She placed it carefully in her pack and was surprised to find that her eyes were moist.

When she heard footsteps on her porch and a knock at her door, she had determined her flight rack would safely carry two and she had finished her packing so was ready to go. When she opened the door, she was surprised to find a small crowd of villagers standing on her porch behind Mearri.

"Hello, Mearri." Vega peered past her at the crowd, visibly puzzled. "Hello, Headmaster Atrum. Hello, everyone. I don't have a lot of time to talk right now. May I help you?"

Headmaster Atrum had a kind look, and age had given him many more grey spots than black. He wrinkled his nose at Vega. "Amearri tells us you are leaving us."

Vega blinked. "Why yes, I have to go to the city. That is why I asked Mearri to let you know I won't be able to teach my classes for a while."

She looked at what seemed to be half the village standing on her doorstep. She spotted Marki, the herd mistress, standing in the back of the crowd. Vega waved and said, "Mistress Marki, I am glad to see you. I know my hooting isn't very effective at keeping our cattle near the caves, but will you kindly find someone to take my shifts for a few days while I am gone?"

Mistress Marki had almost as many gray spots as the headmaster, but she never let age slow her down. She replied with a merry hoot that stopped just short of hypersonic. Vega twitched an ear in appreciation.

"So," Headmaster Atrum caught Vega's attention again. "You are going to the city. Amearri tells me that Tantea of the Many Journeys is back, and you are going to meet with him."

Vega rippled an arm in agreement. "Yes, he has come back and is with my brother right now."

"Our lore tells us that you first met the teacher here in our village when he was our guest. Because of this, you and your brother have been trapped on our world for many years." Atrum looked angry.

Vega felt touched by his words. "Headmaster, it is true that I first met Sansea here many years ago. But I don't feel trapped here—this is my home."

"Yes, this is your home—for now and for many generations to come, if you wish. But it is possible that you may want some justice from Tantea because he stopped you from going back to the stars, and so you had to make your home with us. We are angry on your behalf and have always been so. We know this happened from the letters Amali wrote to her children and then to her grandchildren and, hence, to all of us. Tantea abused our hospitality by doing this to you."

Vega felt helpless for a moment, not knowing what to say. The events she had triggered into play so many years ago by her conversations with a traveler who turned out to be a godling were not the responsibility of the good people of this village—not in Amali's time and not now. Suddenly, Vega felt very loved.

"Atrum, I am so privileged to be a part of your lives. You are truly my family. Here is where I belong, and here I intend to stay."

"Good." Atrum nodded curtly, turned to the crowd, and let out a long low hoot. Everyone on the porch joined in, each in their own register. When they were done, Atrum turned back and said, "With your permission, we have a request. We would all like to accompany you to the city. We wish to meet this Tantea and remind him that his rudeness has not been forgotten."

Vega stared at him for a moment. *My flight rack will hardly carry one these days. How do I get all these people to the city?* Then she wrinkled her nose in laughter. "You are all welcome to accompany me, my family. I see we will be walking. I will have to repack. And call my friend Amethyst. We leave as soon as everyone can make ready."

••✦••

The tech who opened the mysterious new door that appeared in the bulkhead of the communications module found a corridor. That passageway led her to a small ship attached to the other side of the module, which she had never seen before. She stopped and breathed softly when she realized she was *inside* the anomaly.

The little ship was of a type common a thousand years ago, and it had to have been that old. It was eminently space-worthy, however, to no one's surprise. The power plant and environmental technicians swarmed over the small cargo vessel, giving it a complete checkout. When they were satisfied, they gave their blessings.

The tech who had first showed Sotheel and Anya around the communications module wound up spending her every waking moment in the little ship or in the corridor leading into the ship. She poked and measured, put on an environment suit, went outside on both sides of the anomaly, and measured again. Every time she walked from the module into the little ship, she would stand in the new hatch, touching the doorframe. Belkin was often with her, and he would solemnly touch the frame too.

The captain came over from Multipurpose Ship 331-B and walked through the communications module into the cargo ship. He looked out the viewscreens and personally saw the inside of the Small Home system for the first time. The star that Small Home circled sat cheerful and bright, a mere five and a half light-hours away. Small Home itself was visible in the lower corner of the viewscreen. The captain watched for a long while in silence. He did not hear Belkin approach and was surprised when a small hand grasped his own. He looked down at the Chin child.

"Do you know anyone down there, Captain?"

"No." The captain sighed. "It's a big universe, Belkin. My home is a long way from here. Forest on the far side of Race space. I had just become an adult and had not yet left Forest when the anomaly formed. This is the first time I've ever seen Small Home. It looks lovely. I envy you for going there."

The captain pulled a small package from his pocket and squatted down beside Belkin. Then the captain gravely handed it to him. Belkin turned it over, found the clasp, and started to open it. He stopped and looked up at the captain quizzically. "What is it?"

"In this package is a leaf from a world tree. I can't introduce you to a Yektektek, but I visited my home a few years back and went—call it, on a pilgrimage—to the fledgling world Forest and met a young tree. I picked up this leaf and have carried it ever since. I think it's time you had it."

Belkin nodded in an adult fashion. "I will keep it safe."

"I know you will." The captain stood and ostentatiously dusted off his pants as if he'd been kneeling in a forest. Belkin squeaked with glee, and the captain flicked an ear.

••✦••

All too soon, everything was ready for the trip. Songkali sat slumped in her seat on the cargo vessel, looking exhausted. She had spent the previous twelve hours rehashing goals and plans with the other Chin elders, all of whom were disappointed to be not going with her. She promised to try to get them space on the next shuttle to Small Home, if there ever was another shuttle to Small Home. She carried greetings and overtures of friendship for the Caeling people as if they were a real delegation from the Chin to a new race.

The elders also wanted her to give Sansea a piece of their minds about his highhanded treatment of their friends the Tall People. Songkali solemnly promised to deliver their lectures and only declined to "tweak the godling's nose," as one of the elders demanded, if he did not appear to be listening to their wise council.

Sotheel sat in the command seat, ears still twitching in annoyance. The cargo craft was fully automated, which was good because none of the passengers had ever piloted a spacecraft. Sotheel had taken an abbreviated command training session from the picket crew—under protest—which theoretically gave her the skills to perform an emergency landing in the event of catastrophic AI failure. *Theory be damned*, she thought.

Anya and Belkin sat side by side, staring out the viewscreens and quivering with excitement. Belkin whispered, "If I forget to ever say it again, thank you, All Grandmothers' Grandmother, for listening to me and my grandmother. This is so much fun."

Anya nodded to him and rippled a pleased shrug down her arm. *Life is an adventure when seen through the eyes of the young. Thank you, Belkin.*

The ship decoupled and dropped slowly away from the communications module. It began to pick up speed. Sotheel put the retreating module on a viewscreen. In a moment, the octagonal module shrunk and then became so tiny that it was lost to view, leaving only the swirling light-smeared underside of the anomaly in the viewscreens. They were on their way.

♦♦✦♦♦

Amethyst paused in its morning walk through the city, giving all the appearance of listening to something intently. Sansea, walking beside it, stopped and stared at the node entity quizzically.

"You know the ship is on its way, do you not?" Amethyst said.

"How would I know that?" Sansea was grinning.

Amethyst's matrix sparkled. "I suspect you also know that the city has maintained the ship landing pads for over eight hundred years, waiting for another ship from the outside to land. Its systems are quite happy this morning."

Sansea brightened a few of his spots and said reflectively, "You have too high an opinion of me, Senior Scholar Amethyst. I never claimed to know everything."

Amethyst sparkled again, which was his version of a grin. He made a call, speaking out loud so Sansea could hear him. "Wren, please find your way to the landing area and greet our new arrivals. Accommodations have been prepared for them in the Transient building. If they want to see the city first, that is fine too. When they are ready, please bring them to the meeting room."

Wren's merry voice flooded out of the audio. "Righto—find the landing pad, find Transient Housing, find you. Sounds easy enough. When does Vega arrive?"

"She is due any time now." Amethyst signed off and spoke meditatively to Sansea. "Wren always finds his way eventually. I am sure he won't get our guests too lost in the city."

Sansea brightened his spots in agreement. Then he grinned. "Perhaps a walk to the harbor, old friend, before we head back?"

They turned toward the harbor and walked in companionable silence. When they got there, the harbor was awash in sunlight and a stiff breeze rippled the waters. Sansea could smell and taste the salt-ladened air. The day had a vibrant quality that he realized he had sorely missed. The shorebirds set up a glorious racket as they walked out onto the quay. Amethyst made a good companion, though it was quiet, so there was no telling how the node entity experienced the harbor.

Presently, they looked up to see the shuttle lance across the sky and begin its turn and descent toward the city landing pads. They tracked it until it was lost to sight behind the taller buildings. Then they each returned to contemplating the bay, lost in their own private thoughts.

The first sight of the city from space was a small dark patch on the horizon next to a tiny circular cutout on a long, unbroken stretch of coastline. The mountains inland, marching parallel to the coast, seemed gentle from high up. The view from the shuttle was breathtaking as the vista unfolded for the two Chin looking out the viewscreens.

Neither Songkali nor Belkin had ever landed on a planet before and did not quite know what to expect. The small auxiliary, which had picked them up from Abundance so that they could make connections with interstellar-capable Multipurpose Ship 331-B, showed them no images of the planet they were leaving. They didn't know to ask, and no one thought to offer such a view.

Belkin had been riveted to the forward viewscreen for all the hours during the approach. He now squeaked excitedly every few moments as the view of the primary continent got larger and more distinct. Songkali had watched for a while and then closed her eyes and tried to nap.

When the bay next to the city became visible and the buildings of Race City One were discernable, Belkin shouted, "Grandmother, wake up! Wake up! We are here!"

Songkali opened her eyes and followed Belkin's pointing finger. She leaned over and rubbed his head, watching the ground get closer. "They do have a lovely planet, don't they?"

Sotheel had been to space many times so watching a planet get larger was no big deal for the planetary administrator. However, this was the first time she had been the theoretical pilot. Her eyes were closed too, but she had not been napping. She had been listening to one semi-autonomous system after another report on the ship's status. She knew range, bearing, and projected landing time. Also, she knew the city had assigned them a specific landing pad. She was glad that the thousand-year-old craft worked so well that she had nothing to do except listen.

The landing was as smooth as Sotheel expected. Belkin was first to unbuckle his seatbelt, but Songkali barked a single word, causing him to stay in his seat. It was Anya who went to the hatch and cycled it open. A male of the Race stood on the walk outside the door.

With a big smile, the fellow said, "Hi, I am Wren." Then he said very formally, "Greetings, travelers from afar. May your feet be light, and your path continue for many leagues."

Anya snapped her palms and repeated his greeting back to him. "Now what does that mean?" she asked.

Wren wiggled his ears and grinned. "You have received your first lesson in Caeling culture. It means 'Nice you see you' and 'I hope you are well.' There are many other things you will learn about the people of Small Home. This is one of them." Now Wren made a big production of wrinkling his nose, which made Anya stare and Songkali squeak with mirth.

He bowed. "It is wonderful to see a fellow member of the Race from outside the barrier and new companions as well. I'm sure you have many stories to tell. My sister, Vega, will be very interested in meeting you all once she gets off the mountain. Now, if you are ready for a tour of the city, please come with me."

Anya stared again at Wren, trying to fathom his cryptic remarks about mountains and sisters. Then she turned back to the pilot compartment and reached out a hand to Songkali. "I believe the honor of being first to step on this planet belongs to you."

Songkali lifted herself out of the chair and barked a mirthful laugh. Belkin was right behind her as she approached the door. Small Home awaited.

27

HOMECOMING

When Sansea walked through the door of the meeting room the next morning, he noted that the interior had changed dramatically. The beautiful purple-hued table, shining gently with its own light, and its attached chair were still in their accustomed place at the front. However, every other piece of furniture, designed with the comfort of the Race in mind, had been removed. Where forty or more tall chairs had once adorned the room, now settees and low couches were scattered in their place.

An elderly Chin sat on one of the settees watching a smaller version of herself race around the room. Seeing the two Chin brought a smile to Sansea's face. He also noticed Wren appeared delighted to be sitting with and talking to the older Chin. Two tall Race members were there too. One sat on a settee staring at the purple table. The other Race member had come with the group and was sitting at the table. She was punching at the communicator console and muttering angrily while in the only Race chair in the room.

When Sansea moved deeper into the room, he saw Vega and a couple of Caelings from Vega's village talking with Amethyst. Amethyst sat near the wraparound window with its magnificent view of the harbor. This had been the node entity's customary perch every day for over eight hundred years, and it had automatically assumed the position when it opened the meeting room that morning.

When Amethyst saw the group enter, it excused itself from the conversation with Vega and the Caelings, and it moved toward Sansea, prepared to make introductions. However, Belkin got to Sansea first. "Hello, Teacher. Won't you come sit with me and my grandmother?"

Sansea found his hand grasped and pulled to the settee where Songkali waited with her whiskers twitching in amusement. Anya stood by the couch. Belkin said, very formally, "This is my grandmother, and *this* is my grandmother's grandmother."

Sansea bowed and flashed his spots. "Very pleased to meet you."

Wren also got off the couch, knelt, and whispered to Belkin. "Even grandmothers have names."

Belkin snorted. "Songkali is my grandmother. Everyone knows that Anya is 'All Grandmothers' Grandmother.'"

Sansea sat down on the settee and gave Belkin a wide smile. "Thank you for the introduction, Belkin."

Songkali squeaked a very high-pitched syllable in Chin, and Belkin nodded abruptly and sat down. One didn't have to speak Chin to know what it meant when a grandmother made that sound. Sansea suppressed an even bigger grin. She might have been the smallest adult in the room, but when she barked, she got the immediate attention of everyone. Even Sotheel stopped punching at the communicator on the beautiful purple-wood table and gave the Chin her complete attention.

"Perhaps you know why we are here, Teacher." Songkali's voice was forceful and calm.

Sansea looked at her steadily. "You came a long way to see me. It would be rude of me to assume I know why you did. Would you like to tell me?"

Songkali squeaked quietly again. She had a stern look in her eye. "You are called 'Teacher' by many people— I know of at least two races who say this. That means you think you have lessons to teach." She shrugged and looked around the room. "Perhaps that is so, but several hundred years ago, you stopped being a teacher. Instead, you gave yourself the job of protector. You decided to step in and change the dynamic of a whole species, and you placed an impenetrable barrier around this world so that no one could get in or out. That was a unilateral act. You didn't ask anyone what they wanted—you chose for them. That was wrong."

Sansea nodded slowly. "It could certainly look that way."

Songkali's eyes narrowed. She replied, "It was wrong then and still wrong now. It is time to remove the barrier and let the Race trapped here go home, if they want. It is time to let the Caelings have visitors and have the ability to leave their planet, if they want. I ask this on behalf of the Chin and the Race who are our friends."

Anya hugged Songkali and twitched an ear at Sansea. Sansea let his spots go dull. His shoulders slumped. He had a faraway look. He spoke very quietly. "What is the definition of a 'miracle'? When is a miracle over?" His gaze swept the room. "Help me," he said simply.

Amethyst and Vega came over to stand beside Sansea. Amethyst spoke. "Vega asked for the Caeling to be safe. Are the Caeling safe?"

Sansea looked at him sharply. "That is not quite what she asked. She knew the Race that built you would overrun the Caeling and cause their extinction as they have three other intelligent species. She wanted that not to happen."

Anya and Vega looked at each other, looked at Belkin and Songkali, and nodded together. Vega said softly, "I am so proud of the Race right now. Thank you, Anya, for finding a way to bring back the Chin."

In a strong ringing voice, Vega said, "I have my wish, Sansea. I have talked much with Anya and Songkali and Belkin." Here, she stopped and sent a shy grin Belkin's way. "I believe the Race has changed, and Caelings have no need to fear my people. Thank you for this miracle. It is over."

"But what do the Caelings want?" Sansea challenged.

Vega wrinkled her nose and laughed out loud. "It is long since you walked the world indeed, Sansea, to ask me that question. For hundreds of years now, my friends adopted family in my village, and every other Caeling I meet asks me when the traveler is coming back. They want to know when you are going to stop squabbling with my people, by which they mean the Race. They ask when you will open the starways."

Sansea looked at the several Caelings in the room and saw them nodding. He shrugged. "I am squabbling, am I? Very well, the barrier will come down."

Songkali squeaked to get Sansea's attention. "You are not done, Teacher."

Sansea nodded slowly. "Go on. But before you ask for anything more—know this. The Race will always be a threat."

Now Songkali rose to stand beside Anya and Vega. "I am Chin. I love Anya. I also love Sotheel and Vega, whom I've only known for a short time. I believe the Race is friend to me and mine."

Sansea frowned. "State your request."

"Very well. I, as a representative of all Chin, ask you to restore the fertility of the Race."

Sansea looked around the room. His pattern of black spots became duller. He sighed. "I do not see a Hukin here, nor a Yektektek. They were also wiped out, root and branch, by the very people you are pleading to help. What do you suppose their vote would be?"

Belkin, who had been extraordinarily quiet, snorted and said, "I know the answer to one of those, Teacher."

Sansea knelt and addressed the smallest person in the room. "Tell me."

Belkin swelled his chest importantly. "Someday, I am going to Forest to meet the Yektektek. The captain of Ship 331-B has invited me to his home to see them, and I am going." Belkin pulled a small package out of his pocket and proudly showed it to Sansea. "In this package is a leaf from a World Tree. I have been made the guardian of this leaf by my friend, the captain. All Race and all Chin are now friends to the Yektektek, and we will guard their safety."

Sansea appeared quietly impressed by Belkin's eloquence. "You have declared yourself and your people protectors of the Yektektek?"

Belkin gave a huge nod.

Sotheel had been quietly seething in her seat by the purple table. She stood. "I can speak for the Hukin, though you know exactly what I am going to say, Teacher."

Sansea turned to Sotheel and brightened his spots in a complex pattern. "I listen," he said simply.

"Shortly after we began trying to learn how to restore the Chin to their planet, representatives of the Race living on Hukin came to us and observed our efforts. They went back to Hukin and used the same techniques to find Hukin remains and recreate the Hukin people. They were wildly successful."

Sotheel marched over to Seasea and spoke directly to him. "They created the true ancestral version of the Hukin and built a vibrant and successful breeding population. And do you know what they found? Hukin are vicious, argumentative, and combative by nature. And they don't like us."

Sotheel twitched her shoulders and snapped the flesh of her palms for emphasis. "Every effort to teach the Hukin any form of civilization ended in failure. In the end, when a sufficiently large enough breeding population of Hukin was created to ensure successful recovery of the species, the Race destroyed any trace of our ever being there, fixed any ecological problems we knew had occurred, and moved entirely off the planet.

Sotheel concluded. "The Hukin, even though they currently don't know we exist, vote for extinction of our kind."

Sansea nodded and looked sad. He seemed startled when Vega took his hand. She said, "I remember the first time I brought you to this city. You looked around and were surprised to only see Race faces. You asked us where all the other races of our federation—our family—were. At that time, my people didn't know how to do that. But look around you. What do you see now?"

Sansea looked around the room and was plainly skeptical. "I see a diverse assemblage of individuals of four races, if I count Node Entity—the esteemed Amethyst—a separate species. Alright, I stipulate you are plainly getting along at the moment."

Sansea's eyes narrowed, and he wrinkled his mussel but not in amusement. "Songkali claims to speak for all of Chin. Who can speak for all of the Race?"

Sotheel laughed, drawing everyone's eyes. "Songkali was right about you, Teacher. She came to me before we started our journey, and we talked. She said she had read everything the Race compiled about 'the alien,' which was all of our scholars' conclusions. The records said you only asked us one question."

Bowing, Sotheel continued. "You have just asked that question. Again. My answer is I am empowered to speak for the Race in all matters pertaining to our treatment of other species—so says the Council of Intermingled Planetary Affairs, which encompasses all of the remaining Race in existence . . . except, of course, for the Small Home colony on this world. They were out of touch and unable to give the council their input."

Sansea brightened his spots again to indicate he was listening and sat down on the settee next to Belkin.

"Here is the policy Council has implemented: An agreement has been made with the Chin, giving Chin free access and travel to any planet currently occupied by the Race. Education and transfer of knowledge and technology will continue as long as any of the Race are still alive to assist the Chin. Emigration by Chin to all planets in our federation is allowed and encouraged.

"The Race and Chin have developed a partnership whereby we have become one society, allowing civilization to continue after the Race has died out. The Chin have offered to look after the Yektek after we are gone and apparently are intending to offer the Caeling people membership in our federation." Sotheel cocked an ear at Songkali when she said that. Songkali gave a contented chirp in return.

Sotheel continued, "I speak for the Race. Ask your questions."

"Has the Race changed?" Sansea asked this bluntly.

Sotheel took a breath. "Yes. No—it doesn't matter. The Race has its blind spots. We have been careless. We failed to see that the 'other' is also 'us.' We will make different mistakes but never that one again."

Sansea stared at her, expressionless in a way none had seen from him before. The silence stretched out.

He sighed and turned to Songkali, but he really spoke to the room. "Think of what you ask. I am the traveler. When I leave, I may find myself on the other side of the galaxy. I might not be back for tens of thousands of years. That is plenty of time for the Race to repopulate and destroy you all—again. You really wish to risk that?"

The small mountain Caeling woman who had been Vega's constant companion, stood, flashed her spots in a bright pattern, and spoke for the first time. "I am Amearri, descendant of Amali. Vega is my aunt. I speak for my village, and I believe I speak for all Caeling in this matter. We don't see Sky People when we look at the Race—they are just people. They are our friends and neighbors. Tantea, as the Chin have spoken, we speak now. Restore our friends."

Sansea listened carefully. He was certain that the room was unanimous in their desire. All of his spots went dull, and his shoulders slumped. He sighed before he spoke quietly. "Very well. I grant your request."

There was a moment of silence, and then the room erupted. The hubbub went on for a long time.

"I grant your request, but I have a favor to ask. I . . ." Sansea looked unusually pensive. He started again, "This is not a requirement of any of you, but there is an obligation that I have had for a very long time. This is important to me, and if you will help me, I will deeply appreciate it.

"I have a friend who lives alone but shouldn't. This friend has lost all family to the ravages of time . . . and other reasons." Sansea stopped again, not one of his spots was bright. In a very soft and uncertain voice, he said, "May my friend come here to live with you?"

"You have family?" asked Songkali.

"Someone to play with?" asked Belkin.

"Community, of course," stated Amethyst.

They all nodded. A murmur of "Yes" went around the room.

Sansea closed his eyes, and the room watched him fade. In a moment, he was gone.

Once again Sansea stood on a rocky point, looking down into a familiar wood. He followed the well-worn path between tall trees, through dappled shadows, and past a stream and thicket to a meadow not far from a cabin. He stopped under the shade of a broad thick tree. He didn't have long to wait.

Siskali came out of her cabin door and onto the front porch. She settled onto her bench cushion to let the morning sun warm her fur. Slowly, she swiveled her head, and her gray muzzle twitched once and then again. Her blind eyes looked due north, and she let out a happy squeak. "Traveler, you have come again.

I can smell that your journey has been a long one. Has it also been fruitful?"

Sansea laughed a full and rich sound. He realized it was the first time he had laughed in over a thousand years. "Bless you, Grandmother. I have indeed had a long journey. And I think it may end very well."

Siskali padded the bench beside her. "Tell me all about it."

Sansea sat and began to speak. He spoke of people and time and space. He spoke of triumphs and sorrows. He spoke until the shadows were long across the meadow, and the warmth of the day faded.

Siskali sat and listened and took it all in. Finally, Sansea stopped. Then he waited.

The silence built, and the last remaining Chin of her era seemed in no hurry to break it. Then she sighed and squeaked very loudly, startling into flight some birds that had landed in the meadow while Sansea was talking.

"You are the traveler, and no one—not even I—can judge you. However, you keep calling me 'Grandmother,' so I will accept the position of grandmother to you. And I tell you, I am very proud of you, Grandson." She leaned over and licked both of Sansea's cheeks. Sansea began to cry.

After his tears passed, Sansea said, "Thank you, Grandmother. That means the world to me. My heart is lighter now." Sansea took a breath. "I have one more path to follow—back to people who care about me. I know this has been your home for a long time, but you are not needed here any longer. There is family waiting for you at the next place I am going. Will you come?"

Siskali nodded serenely. "I will come."

"I have to warn you that I wear a different form in the place we are going, so you might not recognize it by voice, scent, or touch."

She squeaked louder again. "As if there were ever a grandmother in the universe that could not recognize her own grandson. I see I will always have something to teach you, Teacher."

Sansea took her hands and murmured, "This may be harder than it looks. When I usually travel, I follow the path of information and build my physical presence when I arrive. We are going back a slightly different way so you can come. Fortunately, you have lots of relatives where we are going, making it much easier for me to zero in on our destination."

Siskali gripped his hands tightly. "To journey with the traveler is a dream come true. I am ready to go wherever you take me."

"I think I am taking you home. And in a strange way, I might be going home too."

There was a shimmer and a pause, and the world seemed to sigh. A moment later, the meadow was empty.

THE END

ALSO BY THE AUTHOR

DESPERATE ENDEAVOR

Thirty-five years after the only interstellar war Humanity has ever fought, one man has wondered his entire adult life why the hell that war happened. . . . Mikail's job is to ensure the safety of Humanity's secrets. But the AranthChi's long-term conspiracy is beginning to unravel . . . Humanity is in more danger than ever before . . . and time is running out.

ABOUT THE AUTHOR

G. W. Olson (Glen Olson) is a fiction and nonfiction author. His two previous books are the science-fiction novel *Desperate Endeavor* and the nonfiction book *Fifty Years of Polyamory in America.* He grew up in the San Fernando Valley, a suburb of Los Angeles, California. He would have had an absolutely normal childhood except for one fact: His best friend's father worked in Cold War aerospace and owned a mimeograph machine, allowing Glen and friends to put out a neighborhood newspaper—which they shamelessly did! This encouraged Glen's lifelong love of writing. Along with this, Glen was a paramedic for the Los Angeles City Fire Department for over thirty years, where he had several roles, including disaster preparedness educator, inspector, and captain. Writing training manuals by day, he dove into his fiction by night. Today he is a full-time writer.

www.ingramcontent.com/pod-product-compliance
Lightning Source LLC
LaVergne TN
LVHW090935080826
845145LV00003B/752

* 9 7 8 1 9 6 6 3 6 9 3 8 7 *